I0776951

The
Long
Cold
Winter

a 509 Crime Story

by Colin Conway

The Long Cold Winter

Copyright © 2019, 2023 Colin Conway

Original Cover Design by Zach McCain
Updated Cover Design by Rob Williams

First Edition – 2019, Second Edition – 2023

ISBN: 978-1-961030-05-3

Original Ink Press, an imprint of High Speed Creative, LLC
1521 N. Argonne Road, #C-205
Spokane Valley, WA 99212

Visit the author's website at www.colinconway.com

What is the 509?

Separated by the Cascade Range, Washington State is divided into two distinctly different climates and cultures.

The western side of the Cascades is home to Seattle, its 34 inches of annual rainfall, and the incredibly weird and smelly Gum Wall. Most of the state's wealth and political power are concentrated in and around this enormous city. The residents of this area know the prosperity that has come from being the home of Microsoft, Amazon, Boeing, and Starbucks.

To the east of the Cascade Mountains lies nearly two-thirds of the entire state, a lot of which is used for agriculture. Washington State leads the nation in producing apples, it is the second-largest potato grower, and it's the fourth for providing wheat.

This eastern part of the state can enjoy more than 170 days of sunshine each year, which is important when there are more than 200 lakes nearby. However, the beautiful summers are offset by harsh winters, with average snowfall reaching 47 inches and the average high hovering around 37°.

While five telephone area codes provide service to the westside, only 509 covers everything east of the Cascades, a staggering twenty-one counties.

Of these, Spokane County is the largest with an estimated population of 506,000.

For those who have
lost someone too soon.

It's gonna be a long cold winter… without your love.

Tom Keifer/Cinderella
"Long Cold Winter" (1988)

The
Long
Cold
Winter

MONDAY
NOVEMBER 27th

1

Snow fell as I drove along Government Way. It was the first snowfall of winter, and it was already sticking. The forecast was for several inches to accumulate by day's end. The consensus of the local weather forecasters was that a tough season was approaching.

That was also my prediction, and it had nothing to do with how the impending La Nina impacted weather patterns.

The Monday morning traffic, even on a secondary arterial, crawled due to the snow. It was my first day back at work, but I didn't feel ready. Sooner or later, I would have to return. I realized that. It's who I was. In my head, I knew I'd been gone long enough. In my heart, though, it felt like I'd only been gone a minute.

The tires slipped as I turned off Government Way and into the parking lot. I slowly drove to where my wife was waiting.

I climbed out of the car and looked up into the gray sky, snowflakes landing on my face. I took a moment to compose myself. Shoving my hands into my pants pockets, I walked over to her.

"I'm late," I said. "The weather." It was a lame excuse. She would know better.

I bent down and wiped the snow from the flat marble headstone, revealing only her name. *Roberta "Bobbie" Ann Nash.* I didn't care to see the date of her death. I knew that too well.

"Today's my first day back," I whispered.

She didn't answer. She never does. I'm not crazy.

I stood and shoved my hands back into my pockets but left my coat open. The cold worked its way inside and nipped at the lightly covered areas of my body. I didn't pull the long coat closed, though. I wanted to feel something other than the hurt inside.

I told Bobbie about my morning. How I managed to burn over-easy eggs yet forced myself to gut them down. The black coffee I was now putting creamer into. She always drank it with flavored creamer, and I had always taken it straight. Now, I can't stand the idea of it without some sort of flavor in it. Opening the refrigerator and seeing a creamer inside reminds me of her. I described my outfit for the first day back—black suit and a light blue shirt. I explained to her about my trouble focusing on the newspaper, no matter how hard I tried.

Then I told her about the song I woke up with inside my head.

The morning music was a recurring event since her passing. Today's song was "Gimme Shelter" by the Rolling Stones. It doesn't take a psychology degree to figure out what my subconscious was telling me. Or maybe it was all random musical gibberish since yesterday's morning serenade was Judas Priest's "The Green Manalishi (with The Two Prong Crown)," a song I hadn't listened to in a decade. Bobbie hated Judas Priest, so I rarely listened to it when she was within earshot.

For a moment, I had the idea that Bobbie was trying to send me messages. I quickly dismissed that notion.

Thanksgiving had recently come and gone. I spent the weekend alone in our house, answering calls and texts from friends and family. Most of the conversations were one-sided and played out the same way. They talked, and I muttered affirmations that I was fine and would take care and wouldn't do anything to hurt myself. I don't know why people assume I would do something like that.

I never told them about those thoughts, so how would they know?

When I ran out of things to say, I watched the snowfall accumulate on her headstone.

"I miss you," I said, hoping for an answer. None came.

As I said, I'm not crazy.

When the snow eventually covered her name, I fought to control the tears.

2

I found a parking spot in the lot reserved for officers and detectives. The falling snow provided a strange muffle to the police department, the neighboring jail, and the county courthouse. Unlike the fuel supplied by a hot summer day, a dark wintery morning mutes the activity outside. The police department and its neighbors can seem almost peaceful. Even the jail, the blocky cement behemoth full of criminals and malcontents, takes on a nearly benevolent image when framed in falling snow.

The walk toward the department was quiet. Others were hurrying to their respective buildings or out to their cars, but no one was taking their time in the cold and snow—except me. If I could have found an excuse, I would have lingered outside a little while longer.

My hair was wet from the melting snow, and my face was still cold from visiting Bobbie. The only way to avoid going inside meant turning around and going home. Going home meant quitting, and quitting wasn't an option.

At least, it wasn't today.

***

Inside the Public Safety Building, warmth immediately enveloped me.

I stood just inside the lobby for a moment and smelled the building. It had a distinct aroma, one that certain structures develop through time, especially when its people are committed to the service of humanity through dedication, perspiration, and years of varied foodstuffs eaten in every nook and cranny of office space. The heavy application of Pine-Sol added to the building's unique bouquet.

When I arrived at my cubicle, there was a single manila file on my desk. Besides the phone, it was the only thing in sight. Everything else had been cleared and put away by someone while I was on leave. Probably the section's receptionist, maybe my partner. Regardless, the desk was clear except for the folder.

Bobbie's picture was pinned to the rear wall of my cubicle. She was lying on our hardwood floor, her chin resting on the backs of her hands. It was a playful picture taken earlier in the year. I'd taken it while lying on the floor directly opposite her. The day we made it had no special meaning. It was a random Sunday spent lounging around the house, listening to music, reading books, and drinking coffee. I unpinned the picture and put it inside the top desk drawer.

I took off my long coat and hung it on the coat hanger at the edge of my cubicle. The melting snow was already dripping from it onto the carpet.

A glance around the detectives' office showed a number at their desks already. Quinn Delaney and Marci Burkett were huddled together over something on Burkett's desk. Andrew Parker and Jessie Johnson were both at their cubicles working on their computers. No one looked my way. The next desk over, my partner's, was empty.

I slid the file across the desk closer to me. Its blue label read *Williams, Jennifer M.—Homicide—05/10/1987.*

It was a cold case.

Jennifer Williams, I thought. The name seemed familiar, but my mind was clouded. The harder I tried to clear my thoughts, to focus on the task at hand, the louder

I heard "Gimme Shelter" wailing in my head. Mick Jagger's opening line, about a storm threatening his life if he didn't find shelter, reached a crescendo.

I curled the file folder in my hands, closed my eyes, and swore.

I sat that way for several moments until I couldn't take the song anymore. When I opened my eyes, I stood quickly, shoving my chair back, and headed toward the captain's office.

Captain Gary Ackerman was on the phone when I peeked past his open door. He waved me in and pointed to a leather chair. I sat and glanced around his office. It was clean and organized. Department awards and city recognitions were prominently displayed on the walls. He continued his phone call, mostly by mumbling various uh-huhs and nos while listening to the person on the other line.

Ackerman had long been a climber in the department, and everyone knew he had his eye on a chief's chair someday, whether it be in Spokane or elsewhere. He'd been promoted to captain the previous year, replacing another captain who retired. Before that, Ackerman was a lieutenant in the Special Investigations Unit, so stepping up to run the entire Investigations division was a big deal for him. He bucked the system by not wearing a uniform. The current chief wanted all command staff in uniform, but Ackerman continually showed up in a dapper suit and tie. He argued he needed to look like his team to lead his team, which sounded good, but no detective dressed as nicely as he did. Ackerman dressed this way even when he led SIU, and all those guys were in jeans and T-shirts. The chief finally relented because Ackerman looked sharp. The rule was modified for command staff to be in uniforms or suits, so Ackerman once again got his way. His silver hair was expertly cut, and he had an air of power beyond his rank. There were rumors he had undisclosed business dealings outside the department, but those conflicts of interest had never materialized.

Finally, Ackerman said into the phone, "That all sounds doable. Write it up and send it to me. I'll get it in front of the chief and see what he says."

When he hung up, I tapped the folder in my hand and said, "What's this?"

"Thanks for coming back, Dallas. We could really use the help."

I nodded, acknowledging his thanks, but held up the file.

"While you were gone," Ackerman said, "Lieutenant Brand re-assigned your cases. I asked him to have something waiting for you when you got back. With nothing in your pipeline, something out of the cooler seemed the best way to ease you back in."

"You and I both know these are a waste of time," I said. "I can take my cases back if they still need working."

Ackerman shook his head. "The others have them now. You'll get a new case soon enough since you're first up on the rotation. Besides, cold cases are good for public relations. Dust the file off, review it, and see if anything shakes loose. If it does, track it down. If it doesn't, then file it away. Don't bust your pick on it, but write a report just to show you spent some time with it. That way, the department will get the credit for working it."

I stared at the file, knowing it was a fool's errand.

"Dallas," Ackerman said.

I lifted my eyes to him.

"It'll be okay. It's like riding a bike."

There was a part of me that wanted to yell, *no shit. I know how to do this.* But there was also a piece of me that felt out of my element—like I had forgotten how to do my job.

"Did you know I had a son?"

"No," I said. "I didn't."

His voice softened. "He was a beautiful boy. Eight years old. Just learning how to throw a football." The captain turned around and grabbed a framed photograph from the credenza behind his desk. When he faced me, his cheeks had flushed, and his eyes were distant. "Eric was killed by a teenager speeding through our neighborhood. My son was riding his bike, and the other kid never saw him. One kid being stupid while another kid was being a kid."

Ackerman handed me the picture. It was taken at a Seattle Mariners game. The boy wore a Mariners baseball hat, eyeglasses that looked too large for his small face, and a Scooby-Doo T-shirt.

"I was a detective when that happened. I took almost two months off." His eyes were wet as he spoke, and he didn't make eye contact with me. Instead, he looked slightly off my shoulder. "When I came back, it was difficult. It felt like fumbling in the dark for some time. Then I found my way. I found my purpose again."

I handed back the photo.

"I'm not saying the job is your purpose, Dallas. Only you can determine that. What I'm saying, though, is you'll get where you need to be by showing up. It doesn't have to be any more complicated than that."

I stood and left Ackerman studying the picture in his hands.

***

A few days before Thanksgiving, Captain Ackerman had visited me at home. I was renovating the master bathroom in my house. It was a project Bobbie had repeatedly asked me to do since we'd bought the place eighteen months prior.

I ripped out the fixtures and replaced them with a new tub, shower enclosure, toilet, sink, and vanity. I was in the process of laying the tile Bobbie had picked out.

"What prompted this?" he asked.

"I never got around to it," I said. "I promised her I'd do it when I had more time."

He examined my tile work, judging it with a satisfied grunt.

"I never made it a priority. It seemed like I always had more important things to do. I don't know why, but it feels meaningful now."

"How are you feeling?" he asked, his eyes carefully examining a tile cut.

"Fine."

"About ready to come back?" he asked, still without looking at me, his fingers running along the tiles.

"No."

"They need you," he said, finally turning to me. "I need you. The team is short-handed since Glenn's ACL surgery. That leaves Parker and Johnson and Delaney and Burkett. You and Glenn are the senior investigators on the team. It won't be a stretch for you to work alone until he gets back. I wouldn't worry about sending you out solo."

"Can't you call up a couple of other guys? Maybe from Property Crimes?"

Ackerman shook his head. "Major Crimes is the big league, Dallas. You know that. We don't pull up a new detective and assign him homicide cases. And I can't pull from other teams, because that would throw *their* units out of whack—everyone's understaffed. You know the current state of things. The department is lean, the officers are unhappy about it, and the city still has criminals that need to be caught. We either play with the cards we've been dealt, or we quit. And there aren't a lot of quitters in this department."

What he was saying was true, but it didn't make it easier to accept. I didn't want to leave my house. The world outside no longer held anything for me.

Ackerman put his hand on my shoulder. "Listen. If you want to stay here, that's up to you. We'll survive, and I'll figure out how to make the rotation work, but we could use your help whenever you're ready."

He left after that, and I went back to tiling.

I called him later in the day and said I would be in after the Thanksgiving weekend.

It came faster than I expected.

****

After the visit to Ackerman's office, I went back to my cubicle.

Detectives Andrew Parker and Jessie Johnson were milling around the Major Crimes bullpen. When they saw me approach, they nodded in my direction and walked away. They were a couple of younger hotheads who wouldn't know how to deal with their feelings, let alone mine. Glenn and I had had our share of run-ins with them since they'd been pulled up to the team to replace a couple of senior detectives.

Parker and Johnson didn't like us, and we didn't like them. Over the years, we'd become the old dogs of the team. The young pups smelled blood and wanted to assert their dominance. In a world fueled by testosterone, seniority only means something when you can back it up with the ability to stand your ground. You're in trouble once the wolves—whether they are on the street or within the department—sense your weakness.

The rest of the early morning was spent shaking hands and pretending I wanted to be there. Nobody asked how I was doing. Either they could see the truth on my face, or they didn't want to hear an answer to their question. Either way was fine. I wanted to be left alone.

By mid-morning, I finally opened the cold case file and read it. The investigating detective was Alan Tannenhill, a cop who had retired before I ever made it to the department. His reputation today is neither sterling nor poor. It just is. Probably the same as mine will be after I decide to leave the department. History has a way of lumping most of us into an adequate category. Only a few will stand out as genuinely great or incredibly bad.

The body of Jennifer Marie Williams was found at the intersection of Pine and Riverside on the morning of May 10, 1987.

She was seventeen years old and attended Ferris High School. No significant physical evidence was found at the scene. An autopsy revealed bruising around her throat, consistent with choking. It also mentioned bruising around her left eye.

Her parents stated Jennifer was out earlier in the day with her boyfriend, Johnny McCoy. The investigating detective interviewed McCoy and found he had left Jennifer and joined his friends camping in northern Idaho, about an hour away. Two friends both confirmed McCoy joined them later for the camping trip. The three friends then returned to the city late Sunday night, well after Jennifer's body had been found.

She had been seen by her parents after her meeting with McCoy when she returned home. Jennifer went back out later that day. Her parents didn't know which friends she was seeing; they never asked, and Jennifer never said. McCoy also didn't know who she was seeing. Jennifer Williams left her parents' house at approximately 4 p.m. and never returned home.

McCoy's parents also stated he had gone camping with his friends. Neither Jennifer's parents nor the investigating detective could ever explain the gap in her whereabouts prior to her death. They chalked it up to Jennifer telling stories to go do something she didn't want either party to know about.

There were photographs of the body that I flipped through slowly. The pictures had the tint of time. There was bruising around her eye that showed she had been assaulted before being strangled.

I froze when I saw a picture the parents had given the investigating detective.

Jennifer Williams wore acid wash jeans with a red bandana tied around her thigh. She had on a black T-shirt featuring the rock band Poison, cut just below her breasts to reveal a skinny waist. Her hair was teased up in the style familiar with the late '80s. Behind her was the old Ferris High School and a parking lot full of cars from that era. She brightly smiled as she stood with her hands on her cocked hips, obviously enjoying the moment the photo was taken.

It wasn't the fashion or that she was an attractive young girl that gave me pause.

What stopped me was the fact that I remembered seeing Jennifer only a few days before her death.

3

I was sixteen years old in 1987, and along with the entire teenaged population of Spokane, I cruised Riverside almost every Friday and Saturday night.

Cruising ended in the mid-'90s when a handful of overactive do-gooders waged war against the activity. They said it was harming downtown businesses and the nightlife of Spokane. They argued that some teenagers drank alcohol while they cruised, which, of course, they did. I occasionally did as well. We were teenagers, for God's sake.

These do-gooders worked with the police department to push cruising out of downtown. Business owners were happy as the kids moved on. Unfortunately, the city and the do-gooders didn't thoroughly think about the problem. Once the kids were pushed out, they had to find somewhere new to go.

They moved their activities north to Division Street, a state highway, where the slow downtown cruise turned into racing and kids hanging out in parking lots spread out across a larger geographic area. It was the classic bureaucratic backfire and a nightmare for the cops.

However, in 1987, teenagers still gathered in downtown Spokane on Friday and Saturday nights and slowly drove in bumper-to-bumper traffic along Riverside Boulevard. When they passed Monroe Street, they'd turn around in front of the Masonic Temple. On the opposite end, when they passed Division Street, they'd make a U-turn on Riverside, which dead-ended in an industrial area. The speeds never got higher than a couple of miles per hour due to the thick traffic.

The Riverside and Pine area is now dubbed Martin Luther King Boulevard, and the Masonic Temple has long since been sold and remodeled for office use.

But on that May night, my friend Barry McKenzie and I cruised with Barry's older brother, Randy, and his friend, Curtis. The four of us were in Randy's 1975 Plymouth Duster and had stopped at Dick's Hamburgers at the corner of 3rd and Division. Dick's was the hub of activity when cruisers took a break for Whammy burgers and milkshakes.

The four of us attended Rogers High School together but, in the melting pot of cruising, we could meet anyone from any high school. We'd meet new friends every weekend. There were even times we met new girls, which was mostly the point. Cruising downtown was *the* social network of that time. There was no such thing as Facebook, Snapchat, or Instagram. Getting in a car and physically going downtown meant something.

That night, Randy and Curtis met up with a guy they knew, a tall blond kid whose name I couldn't remember. My memory of the kid was that he was handsome and talked a lot. He pointed to Jennifer Williams across Dick's parking lot and said she was his girlfriend. Jennifer was talking to some other girls and wasn't paying any attention to her supposed boyfriend. She never even looked our way. I remember thinking Jennifer was cute and stole several glances at her.

Randy's friend enjoyed showing us the new stereo system he had installed in his Datsun B210 more than talking with his girlfriend. We didn't care too much, though. The stereo system was awesome, and the good-looking kid had all sorts of cassettes with the latest headbanging hits.

The four of us hung out at Dick's for a while before we went back to cruising. A few days later, the news reported that Jennifer Williams had been murdered.

That story was a big deal since she was our age and we had just seen her. I read the paper and watched the news to find out the latest developments in the case.

The television news crews stated the police were interviewing the boyfriend, who claimed his innocence and had an alibi. I don't remember how we heard the name of the boyfriend, but it wasn't the kid we met at Dick's Hamburgers. We chalked it up to teenage bragging about a girl he never actually knew. We had all done that at some point while we were young, so it didn't seem completely abnormal.

However, as a detective, I would have liked to talk with someone claiming that.

And there was no kid in the file matching the guy in my memory.

*** *

I finished the file but decided to flip through it again. There had been some random, worthless notes made in various places that didn't match the handwriting of Alan Tannenhill, the original lead detective.

Had someone else looked at this file? If that was true, why wasn't it noted somewhere?

The more I thought about the case, the more it bothered me.

Finally, I grabbed the folder and walked back to Captain Ackerman's office. He was bent over some paperwork, pen in hand. I knocked on the door, causing him to look up.

"Nash?"

"Why now?" I asked, lifting the file.

"What?"

"Jennifer Williams. Why now?"

"I don't understand the question."

"The case is more than thirty years old. We haven't looked into it since then. So why now?"

Ackerman put his pen down and leaned back. "It was assigned before."

"There's no log sheet in here. How many times was it assigned?"

"Just once."

"Who?"

"Devlin."

My shoulders slumped. Henry Devlin was the poster child for a union rabble-rouser and malcontent. He made his way up to Major Crimes by doing exemplary work, then coasted the last couple of years until retirement. When he left the department, he had become a pariah due to his outspokenness and confrontational attitude about anything and everything. Cases he picked up in the rotation were worked with unbelievable focus. He worked those like a dog with a bone. Other cases, though—such as the ones that landed on his desk pre-solved due to patrol officer involvement—Devlin appeared to believe weren't worthy of his time, and he would work them less than diligently. It was well known that Devlin hated cold cases and would give them even less time if they landed on his desk. His teammates believed Devlin felt it beneath him to work on someone else's failures. Why he was allowed to stay in Major Crimes with an attitude like that is a question former administrators would never be forced to answer.

"Why was it assigned to him? I wasn't even a detective, and I knew his reputation."

Ackerman shrugged. "I wasn't in charge then. My guess is they wanted to show it was put into the rotation. For the bean counters, that's as important as if it was actually worked."

I stared at the file in my hand.

"Shit," I said.

***

I picked up the telephone and called an old friend.

"Hello?"

"Hey, man, it's me."

"Dallas?" He drew the word out, pronouncing each syllable carefully, as if saying my name recklessly could have a bad result.

I hadn't talked with Barry McKenzie in a couple of years. Not since I had to give him the bad news his daughter had been murdered and we had the suspects in custody. She'd been running around with a known gang member and got caught in some crossfire. I picked up that case and, along with a chaplain, delivered the news to my high school friend.

Telling him about his daughter pushed what little relationship we'd had after school into the nonexistent.

"What's going on?" Barry asked.

"Just a question about when we were kids. Got time for a cup of coffee?"

Barry sighed with relief. "Yeah. Definitely. Now?"

***

We met downtown at Indaba Coffee on Howard Street—a hipster coffee joint tucked back from the corner of Main Street. The coffees were expensive and ridiculously named, the baristas overly serious about beans and roasting, but the actual product made it easy to understand why people got excited for craft products such as these.

Barry looked happier than the last time I saw him. His eyes were brighter, and he looked as if he'd lost some weight. His blue suit fit nicely, and his blue and yellow paisley tie looked sharp against his crisp, white shirt.

"You look good," I said. "Things going well?"

"They are," he answered. "Iris and I are getting ready to go to Hawaii after Christmas. We're really looking forward to it. I've been working out with a personal trainer, trying to eat right. It's hard at this time of the year, but I'm making a go of it. How about you?"

"I'm good," I said. I should have told him about Bobbie, but I avoided it. It was easier to keep it bottled up rather than bring it to the surface every time someone bumped into my reality. "I'll be happy when the holidays are over."

He sipped his coffee, waiting for me to bring up the reason for our meeting. We were seated at the back of the coffee shop. Younger, hipper patrons occupied several other tables. They glanced at us repeatedly. Their disdain for us invading their not-so-secret hide-out wasn't masked. We looked out of place among the myriad of beards and oversized beanie caps.

"Do you remember cruising Riverside?"

Barry's face lit up. "Oh my god, those are my favorite memories of high school. Remember that time we took my dad's station wagon?"

I smiled. "Not smart for so many reasons."

"He was so mad when he found that beer can in the back seat. He never once believed I just picked it up to throw it away."

"He was a smart man. He knew what we were up to."

Barry nodded and sipped his coffee. "The ol' man," he said wistfully.

"Do you remember that girl who attended Ferris High? The one that was murdered?"

He squinted in a moment of concentration. "Yeah, I think so. The one we saw at Dick's, right?"

"That's the one."

"I remember she was murdered. That's about it. Why?"

"Her name was Jennifer Williams. I've been assigned her case."

Barry furrowed his brow. "Her case? I thought they found who did it."

"No, never," I said. "The case went cold and was filed. It was recently pulled and landed on my desk."

"Is that why we're here?"

I nodded. "I wanted to pick your brain and see if you could remember anything about the night we saw her."

Barry frowned. "I'm sorry, Dallas. I really loved those time. They're some of my favorites, but they're all kind of a blur now. Maybe not even that. They're more like a hodge-podge of images. Does that make sense? I start telling Iris a story about something back in high school— or worse, grade school—and I lose track of the details and end up in a completely different story. I'm never quite sure if I remember things accurately. I get the gist of my own history if you know what I mean. It's the finer points of it I wish I could remember clearly. Age has been cruel to my memory."

"How about the kid's name? The one who said he was Jennifer's boyfriend. Any chance you might remember that?"

His smile was one of resignation. "I don't. Sorry. But he wasn't her boyfriend, right? We figured that out, as I remember. Weren't the cops, I mean, the police after someone else?"

"*Cops* is fine. And yeah, they were looking at someone else. But there's no mention of a possible other boyfriend in the original report. Would Randy remember the kid's name?"

"Maybe. Call him. I'm sure he'd love to talk with you. That's a guy who remembers the past like it was yesterday. 'Glory Days,' you know? That Bruce Springsteen song from when we were in high school? That's Randy. He relives those days every time we talk."

Barry read me Randy's phone number from his phone, and I jotted it into my notebook.

We sipped our coffees for a bit and made small talk.

"You know, we should probably get together now and then for no other reason than just to say hi. It's been a few years. Maybe more."

I smiled at my old friend. "I'd like that."

"I don't have many friends," Barry said. "I don't know what happens when we age, but friends seem harder to make now. When you're young, you have a ton of them, and you think you'll be with them forever. Then we grow older, start moving in different directions, making grown-up decisions, and then one day you find yourself alone with your wife. Your new so-called friends are all strangers you don't really want to spend time with. You'd rather be alone."

"I know what you mean."

Barry tapped the table with his finger. "Then I will take the responsibility for calling you and setting up something. We'll get together with our wives and do something nice before the holiday."

"I'd like that more than anything," I said, my voice already starting to catch. "But I need to tell you something."

4

Bobbie died in a one-car collision on November 3, returning home from her friend Carmen's house in Newman Lake, just east of Spokane Valley. The route from the lake is a winding road with trees lining the asphalt. There are rarely shoulders, leaving little room from steep embankments or other cars, which often cross the center line as they race in whichever direction they're headed, oblivious to their danger or that of others.

I'd driven that road with her several times to visit her friend. In the summer, it was a nice drive to spend time at the small lake. It was something we'd look forward to doing. She'd occasionally visit Carmen to have dinner and share a movie. Sometimes she'd have a glass of wine, but she didn't have any that night. Unfortunately, it didn't matter.

On her way home, Bobbie clipped a deer that must have jumped from the trees. The collision report stated she had tried to avoid it by swerving and lost control of her Jeep Compass. Her car left the road, hit a tree, and rolled down an embankment.

The airbags deployed. The roof was crushed. The Jeep finally stopped rolling when it wrapped itself around a tree at the base of the embankment.

When a passerby found the scene and alerted 911, she was already dead. The Sheriff's Department responded immediately, as did the Newman Lake Fire Department.

The deer had a broken leg and was lying on the side of the road. A responding Sheriff's deputy euthanized the animal.

Chaplain Gabriel Greene came to my house with Captain Ackerman to notify me of Bobbie's death. They knocked on the door shortly before midnight. I'd gone to bed, thinking that Bobbie was staying late at Carmen's house. When I saw them, I immediately knew something terrible had happened.

Her body was gone by the time I arrived at the scene of the collision. The chaplain and the captain had given me a ride there. No one said a word during the thirty-minute trip. Her Jeep was still down the embankment as the county's traffic team was reconstructing the collision. They had already cut the car open to get her out. I stared for a while at the crushed vehicle and the ragged hole where the driver's door had been. The chaplain and the captain stood behind me, giving me space to work out my emotions.

It *felt* wrong.

She was dead, but she wasn't there. I couldn't see her and get the proof. People were telling me my wife was gone, that she was never coming home again. I had to believe what they were telling me, but I didn't want to accept it. Instead, I wanted to yell at them to take me home. This was some elaborate hoax. A cruel joke played at my expense.

I walked over and saw the deer. A sizeable chunk of its skull was missing from the euthanizing shot. Something caught in my chest, and I fought it. I struggled with it for several moments until Chaplain Greene put his hand on my shoulder. The sobs started then, and I stood there, crying over the dead deer.

When I gained my composure, we walked back to the chaplain's car. They drove me home, and the chaplain stayed with me until I fell asleep on my couch.

The medical examiner performed an autopsy, but I never read it. I knew what happened to a body during that process and didn't want the image of my wife on a stainless-steel table in my head. She was dead and gone. That's all that mattered.

We had a memorial for Bobbie at Greenwood Cemetery on the north side. My brother, Dean, and his wife, Arlene, helped me plan and schedule the ceremony. They helped me keep everything together. I wanted the memorial small, but a lot of my friends from the department came. Bobbie's family and friends were there. Her mother was an absolute wreck. She melted into the arms of her boyfriend, who did his best to hold her together.

Afterward, the group moved back to my house for a get-together Dean and Arlene planned. Somehow, it turned into a massive potluck. Maybe there's a natural urge to eat after someone's passing, to remind us we're all still alive. All I knew was there were people and containers of food everywhere. The conversations were about nothing until I came by, and then it became soft condolences. It was too much. I escaped into a bedroom, looking for some silence.

Dean found me soon enough, hugged me, and told me everything would be okay with enough time. Over the next hour, he quietly ushered everyone out.

I thought he might come by and tell me goodbye. He probably heard me crying and thought it best to leave me alone.

I'm glad he did.

***

Bobbie didn't deserve to die the way she did, and I'd like to think I didn't deserve to lose her. Life doesn't care about who deserves what, though. It just takes.

We were high school sweethearts. We first met in our freshman year, but she didn't agree to go out with me until we were seniors. She always thought I was too dorky until then. It wasn't until I gained some weight and made the football team that I finally caught her eye. Before then, I was just a skinny guy who wrestled.

We got married in our second year of college. I had never loved another girl before her and never once thought about another woman after being with her. She was everything to me. I was lucky to meet her when I was a kid.

We tried to have children for many years, but it never happened for us. It was the universe's plan, Bobbie said, and we stopped worrying. We got to focus our love on each other and had a great time together. Every year we picked one new place we traveled to and experienced. By the time we were both forty-five, we had visited every continent in the world, including Antarctica. Traveling together was our passion.

I spent almost every day with her for more than thirty years.

Now, I was forced to learn how to walk alone again.

It was something I would be forever angry about.

5

That night, I thought about boxing up some of Bobbie's clothes, but I put the task off for another day.

Instead, I went to my music collection. Between Bobbie and me, we had collected more than a thousand CDs and had them arranged alphabetically. She had teased me about my fastidiousness regarding the arrangement. Still, I repeatedly explained with a collection as large as ours, the music needed to be carefully put away, or we would never find what we were looking for. Even though she saw the logic in my argument, it wouldn't stop her from teasing me again or occasionally putting a disc out of order on purpose.

We had a great sound system set up in the living room where we would spend nights listening to music. Whenever we were home, there was always music going. That's how we lived. Since her death, no music was heard in the house.

My eyes scanned the titles as I thought about "Gimme Shelter," the song I awoke to in my head that morning. I pulled *Hot Rocks 1964–1971*, the double album of greatest hits from the Rolling Stones. "Gimme Shelter" was the fifth song on the second disc.

I put the album back and pulled Judas Priest's *Hell Bent for Leather*. "The Green Manalishi (with The Two Prong Crown)" was the seventh song. It was the song I'd awoken to yesterday morning.

With my middle finger, I flicked the album once before putting it away.

Just like all the nights since she'd been gone, I had no desire to hear any music. The house would once again remain silent.

6

The next morning, I reread the Williams file before calling Alan Tannenhill, the lead detective who handled the case. He took my call, said he was home, and invited me to meet with him.

Snow continued to fall, albeit lighter than the day before, and the temperature was now hovering around 30 degrees. The roads were slick, and I heard several officers out with collisions over the patrol radio.

As I drove, the lyrics to the *Cheers* theme song played in my head. I'd awoken to that stupid ditty in the morning and couldn't seem to escape it. I didn't want to go where everyone knew my name—quite the opposite. The more I thought about the lyrics, the more anxious I became. I thought about turning on the radio to try and clear my head with another song, but for some reason, I held back from doing so.

Maybe the theme song was supposed to mean something. Perhaps I was supposed to think about it, even if it made me angry. Just thinking about that caused further agitation. The songs weren't messages. They were mental detritus. Putting a value on them would only cause me stress.

Tannenhill lived in the Suncrest area, a nice neighborhood in northern Spokane County. His home was a late 1960s rancher with blue paint and white trim.

I parked in front and walked carefully on the snow-covered sidewalk toward the front of the house. My dress shoes had rubber soles, but they did little to prevent me from slipping on ice. When I got to the door, it opened before I could ring the bell. A woman in her mid-seventies stood in the doorway. She wore navy blue slacks and a light-colored sweater with a thick, rolled-over neck wrap. She looked over my shoulder at my unmarked patrol car. "Al's in his office," she said and stepped back so I could enter. The look on her face told me she'd had police visitors before and didn't appreciate the interruptions to her retired life.

The house was incredibly warm, the temperature easily 75 degrees.

She took my coat and escorted me without any pleasantries to the far end of the house. I entered a room with a large stuffed chair and an oak desk covered in papers. On the wall hung various awards, newspaper articles, and photos from a career in law enforcement. A toilet flushed in a nearby restroom and, a moment later, a gentleman in his early eighties limped into the room, a cane in his left hand. He wore dark blue jeans, a scarlet *Wazzu* sweatshirt, and brown slippers. On his right hip, in a holster, was a revolver.

He smiled at me and stuck out his right hand. "You must be Nash."

"Yes, sir."

"Call me Al, kid." His voice was strong, and his eyes bright.

Al's wife brought coffee as we made small talk about the department and how it had changed over the last thirty years since he'd left. Al pointed out his various commendations on the walls, along with the pictures he'd taken with dignitaries through the years. He enjoyed reliving his days in the department and telling me how things were better and more honest than they were now. I would have argued with him, but I couldn't. My heart wasn't in it for various reasons, only one of which was he was probably right.

Al took the final swig of his coffee and said, "Ok, kid, what have you got?"

I handed him the Jennifer Williams file. He flipped it open and read through the report. When he was done, he closed the folder but held on to it.

"Do you remember the case?" I asked.

"Mostly, yeah," he said. "It was one of the last cases I worked before retiring."

"You didn't like anyone for it?"

"Not really. Everyone had an alibi, and those alibis checked out."

"What do you remember about the crime scene?"

Al tapped the folder. "Just what the report says."

"Nothing stood out?"

Al smiled. "You're still young, and this stuff is fresh in your memory. Let me tell you something you may not believe. After a time, a lot of it will fade. Only the really bad ones stand out, which is a relief when you spend your days and nights being a citizen, worried about your garden and grandkids, trying to focus on the remaining goodness in your life."

"I see," I said, trying to keep the disappointment out of my voice.

Al tapped the folder again. "A girl was strangled and left in an alley. She wasn't sexually assaulted. No DNA. We didn't have any cases before or after that matched a pattern. No family or friends stood out. The boyfriend was with friends the night she was murdered."

"Was there talk about another boyfriend?"

Al handed the file back to me. "It's not in the file, so I've got to say no. I would have made a note in there and tracked it down before closing the file."

I opened the folder and looked through it, trying to think of other questions to ask.

"Why ask about another boyfriend?"

I glanced up from the file. "When I was in high school, I met a kid who said he was Jennifer's boyfriend. He's not the boyfriend listed in the file."

Al lifted an eyebrow. "You knew the girl?"

"I saw her one time but never talked with her. It was down at Dick's while we were cruising Riverside. That was a few nights before she was murdered."

Al shrugged. "I never heard of another boyfriend. I wish I had, but it doesn't change anything now. She's still dead, and her case isn't my problem anymore. It's yours. I wish you luck, kid."

***

After the talk with Tannenhill, I detoured to visit Bobbie. The roads were slick as the snow continued to fall.

I pulled into the Greenwood Memorial Cemetery and parked. Before leaving the car, I put my stocking cap and gloves on. At her headstone, I knelt to wipe the snow from the marble, exposing her name.

I then stood to watch the snowfall. Snowflakes drifted down and slowly obscured her name. When the letters completely vanished under the whiteness, I turned and walked back to my car.

***

Again at the department, I called the phone number in my notebook for Randy McKenzie, Barry's brother.

The phone rang several times before it was answered. The voice was only vaguely familiar, but the jocular nature jibed completely with memory.

"Yo yo yo, this is Randall. Leave your info, and I'll call you back. Or I won't. Who knows?"

When the phone beeped, I left a brief message and hung up.

***

"I was hoping to see you today."

"Good morning, Father," I said and shook his extended hand.

Chaplain Gabriel Greene put his free hand on my shoulder. He caught me in the hallway, returning from the restroom.

"How are you this morning, Dallas?"

"Fine."

Gabe was now in his late sixties and moving slower as age continued to creep upon him. Rumors floated around the department he would soon retire from the position of lead chaplain, a position he'd only recently assumed. He led a team of men and women who provided care and support within the department for officers, their families, and the community. While it must be a personally rewarding job, it appeared stressful. Gabe's face looked as if he had aged twice as many years as the dozen he'd served with the department.

Regardless, his care for the men and women in the department had never been higher.

"Getting back into a routine?" Gabe asked, his eyes searching mine. "That can be important after a tragedy."

I shrugged.

"Are you talking with someone, Dallas? Friends? Family? I'm available if you'd like to talk with me. I hope you know that."

"I appreciated you leading the service," I said, trying to change the subject.

He pulled his hand from my shoulder, understanding that I wasn't going to be reached that morning. "If you need anything, you know where to find me."

"You bet."

He watched me for a moment, wanting to say something further but knowing better than to push. He patted my shoulder before he turned and walked away.

7

At home that night, I sat on the floor in front of Bobbie's closet. Her clothes were scattered around. Empty boxes sat on both sides of me. I'd been considering packing her clothes for a week now but hadn't made any progress. I was committed to filling at least one box, but I couldn't decide what to keep and what to donate.

Why would I keep any of her clothes, anyway? It was a stupid idea.

I glanced at the bottom of the closet. How did a woman have so many shoes? Or, for that matter, why did she have so many pairs of jeans? I grabbed a shirt from the floor next to me. We'd bought it while visiting Houston.

Maybe I should keep it.

Why would I think that? I couldn't wear it.

That's weird. Get rid of it.

I felt its soft silky texture with my fingers, the same way I did when she wore it for the first time. I foolishly held it to my nose, hoping to catch her scent. It smelled like all her clothes did now—like they had been washed some time ago and had been hanging in a closet for months.

I looked at the shirt once more, trying to recall how she smelled and confusing it with the smell of musty clothes.

My cell phone vibrated, breaking me from my thoughts. The caller ID showed it was the department. I carefully laid the shirt on my lap.

"Nash," I said when I answered.

"Detective, this is Annie in radio. You're needed on the scene of a homicide."

Annie gave me the address, and I wrote it on the edge of an empty box. "I'll be there as quick as I can."

I stood and stared at the pile of unboxed clothes.

There would always be time to pack them later, I decided, thankful for the interruption.

***

The snow was falling again as I pulled to the side of the road. Several patrol cars were already on scene, along with an unmarked supervisor's car. Their emergency lights flicked back and forth, and their directional spotlights were focused on a vacant lot.

The forensic unit was already on scene, standing by for my arrival.

The crime scene was taped off at the corner of Nevada Street and Lincoln Road, a vacant lot comprising several acres. Apartment complexes surrounded the open dirt field. Why this corner hadn't been developed while the surrounding areas had was a mystery only a real estate developer would understand.

Two lines of yellow caution tape formed an area around the body—an outer and an inner perimeter. No one was in either perimeter at the time. The first perimeter of tape was about one hundred feet in from the corner.

I got out of my car and approached Caleb Mitchell, a first-year lieutenant, still getting familiar with the responsibility of leadership. He wore the black jumpsuit most officers chose in the winter months. A black beanie cap was pulled down tightly on his head. "Dallas," he said as we shook hands, "Good to see you."

"What have you got?"

Caleb turned to face the crime scene. "A body. Appears to be male. Not sure how long he's been there, but his body is covered with at least three inches of snow."

"Longer than today then."

"Yeah."

"Who found the body?"

"Some kids crossing the field. They live in the apartments over there," he said, pointing at the buildings to the south. "We got their statements and sent them home."

"Have you ID'd the body?"

"Not yet. Nobody disturbed it. It was clear it had been there for some time. Forensics took some overall photos, but that's all we've done. We called for a detective immediately."

"Let's take a look."

"You don't have a partner on this?" Caleb asked.

"The team is short-handed. I'll handle this alone. If you're good with it, I'll have you witness."

He nodded, understanding what would be expected of him.

Caleb shadowed me as we walked toward the body. The snow had covered the corpse and even the freshest tracks from the boys who had discovered the victim. The footprints from the initial officers were filling in with the new snow.

"This is a mess," I muttered.

"We taped it off immediately," Caleb said, his words quick and clipped. "Nobody screwed with the body. We did everything by the book."

I put my hand on his shoulder and forced a smile. "Your guys did great. I meant the weather is screwing us. It's nothing personal."

His face relaxed, and he smiled.

"Can you get a canopy out here, Caleb? Let's get photos of the body's condition with the snow before we start touching. We're in no hurry."

I walked back to my car and turned on the heat. I reached for the radio but stopped. I'd had enough songs playing in my head lately from my subconscious. I wasn't going to add more fuel to the fire. I leaned my seat back and closed my eyes.

The theme song to *Cheers* started in my head again.

***

An hour later, I was awakened by a knock on the window. Caleb stood outside and pointed at the canopy that had been erected over the body. I turned off the engine and climbed out.

"Photos have been taken. We're ready to roll."

"Let's figure out who he is," I said.

I opened the trunk and grabbed an extra pair of latex gloves. I also grabbed a new handheld broom with vinyl bristles. The brush was wrapped in plastic.

We walked across the field toward the canopy. Forensics had brought in portable lights and set them up to illuminate the area surrounding the body. Power cords ran beyond the outer perimeter to generators that hummed loudly in the night.

Geri Utley stood near the body and watched us as we approached. Part of the forensic team, Geri was wrapped in a puffy blue coat, and her blond hair peeked out from underneath a blue beanie cap. A large camera hung around her neck.

Usually, Geri would offer me some playful banter, but tonight she nodded once and then averted her eyes—

another person unable to deal with Bobbie's death. I nodded back, not bothering to lessen her uneasiness.

My breath was visible in the cold as snowflakes continued to fall outside the canopy. I removed my leather gloves and stuffed them in the pockets of my coat. I pulled the latex gloves onto my hands. "Damn, it's cold."

"Twenty-two degrees per The Weather Channel," Caleb said.

I shook my head and pulled the brush from its plastic. I crouched and slowly, methodically, brushed the snow from the body, like an archaeologist removing dirt from an artifact. Geri photographed my actions, documenting every investigative move I made.

"Facedown. Male," I said to Caleb. I watched with satisfaction as he jotted my observations in his notebook. I continued brushing the snow away from the body, working from the head down the back. He was wearing a red and black flannel shirt.

"No coat," I said. "Was that intentional, or did someone take it?"

When I removed the snow past the back of his jeans, I felt in his back pockets. "No wallet. Did your guys pull it when they found him?"

"No. Once they realized he was dead, they secured the scene and called me," Caleb said, jotting something into his notebook. "Think it might have been a robbery?"

"Maybe. Or maybe he doesn't carry a wallet. Or maybe it's in his front pocket. Or in his missing coat, if he had one." I finished brushing the snow from the back of the body. "Nothing else," I said and handed the brush to Caleb. I grabbed the body and carefully rolled it over. His shirt and jeans were partially frozen to the ground, as was some of the skin. As I got the body rolled over, I could see the wound in the neck and the blood down his chest that stained the white T-shirt under his flannel shirt.

"Appears to be mid-sixties," I said. "Knife wound to the neck. Right side. Doesn't appear to be any other trauma to the facial area. Some sort of trauma to his hands. Might have been in a fight." I studied the body as I moved down to the jeans and the pockets. I patted the outside of them first before sticking my fingers in them. "Nothing in the left pocket."

From the right pocket, I pulled a receipt that said NEVADA QUICK-E-MART, which was about three miles from where we were. The timestamp read November 26, 23:17. I read off the information to Caleb, and he jotted it in his notebook.

"That was from a couple of nights ago," Caleb said. "What did he get?"

"A pack of cigarettes, a six-pack of beer, and twenty dollars and change worth of gas. Paid with cash," I said.

Geri opened a paper evidence bag, and I dropped the receipt into it.

We finished checking the body and stepped back. Geri then hollered for a couple of other crime scene technicians, and they moved in. They began the process of scouring the body and the immediate site for further evidence. They would be out in the cold for hours.

As Caleb and I walked back to our cars, I suddenly stopped and looked back at the canopy. "Why were they there?"

"What?" Caleb asked.

"Why were our victim and his assailant in the middle of the field?"

"I don't know."

"Was he stabbed elsewhere and dropped there? Or did he walk to this point after getting stabbed and drop dead?"

"If that's the case, he couldn't have walked far."

"Caleb, we should look for a knife. I don't know how big or what type. We really won't know until we get the ME's report back. Would you ask the techs to grab a metal detector and sweep the ground in the area? Bag whatever they find. Who knows if it will be of use, but we've got to go through the steps. I'll head to the convenience store and follow up on the receipt."

***

The Quick-E Mart was at the corner of Bridgeport Avenue and Nevada Street. It was a beat-up gas station built sometime in the 1960s. I parked my car at the edge of the lot and checked out with dispatch. They asked if I wanted a backup officer, but I declined.

Outside, I noticed cameras pointed at the gas pumps and above the entry door.

I walked in shortly before 1 a.m. Rap music played through hidden speakers. I worked a register while I was in college. The boss would never have let me listen to music like that. The kid behind the counter was leaned over a college textbook. His eyes tracked me as soon as I walked in. When I approached the counter, he straightened and studied me with suspicion. He was thin, dark-skinned, and handsome.

I showed him my badge and introduced myself. There was a camera behind the register.

He straightened up. "Sir?"

"What's your name?" I asked.

"Marvin."

"Marvin? Really?"

He shrugged and smiled. "What can I say? My dad liked *The Dirty Dozen*. He could have named me after Telly Savalas. I'm glad he didn't."

"I hear you. Marvin, I'd like to see your camera footage."

"I can't do that," he said with a headshake.

"What do you mean?"

His eyes widened. "No disrespect, Officer. I just mean you'll have to call the owner. I don't have access to the system."

"Can you get him on the phone?"

He looked at the Keystone Light clock hanging near the restroom. "Man, it's late. He'll be upset if we call him at his hour."

"Blame it on me. He'll understand."

Marvin blinked a couple of times and then asked, "You're not leaving until I call him, right?"

"That's correct."

He sighed and turned to the phone. "I'll call him," he said, punching in the number, "but he's gonna be pissed." It took a couple of minutes before Marvin handed me the phone.

"This is Detective Nash," I said.

"Hello, Detective, this is Duke Haney." His voice was groggy from sleep, but he wasn't as angry as Marvin had predicted. "What can I do for you?"

"Duke, I apologize for waking you. I need to see your camera footage from a couple of nights ago."

"Were we robbed or something, and we don't know about it?"

"No, sir. We have a homicide victim that had a receipt from your business in his possession. He may have stopped in here the night of the murder. We'd like to know if he was with anyone."

"Do you have the time of the receipt?"

"Yes, sir."

"Well, then, it should be easy. The camera footage is web-based."

"Meaning?"

"We can access it from your department if you'd like. I can come in on Thursday if that works for you."

"Can you come in tomorrow? I'd like to jump on this while it's still hot."

"Detective, I'd love to come in and see you tomorrow, but I've got a follow-up examination with my doctor for a procedure that's too embarrassing to talk about with a stranger. I hope you can understand."

"Can you come in before the procedure? Maybe after?"

Duke cleared his throat. "Listen, Detective, what I've got to go through is not only embarrassing, but it's going to leave me in a bit of an awkward position. When it's done, all I'll want to do is come home."

Pushing harder for him to come in tomorrow wouldn't get me anything but a lack of cooperation. Besides, I wouldn't get it any faster if I had to get a subpoena or search warrant.

"Thursday will work fine," I said and gave him directions to the station.

8

I was back at the department shortly after ten the next morning, stopping by the scoreboard on the way in to see the new line that was added.

John Doe—Homicide—11/28—Nash

It was written in red ink to show it was an active case and announced I was indeed back in the rotation. There were a few cases that had moved to black over the previous days. They would be removed from the board at the end of the week.

There were a few blue lines on the dry-erase whiteboard. Those were the cold cases that had been reopened. If a real lead were found, the line would be rewritten in red. If it went nowhere, it would be quietly removed when the case was refiled. Written in blue, several lines above the newest entry was,

Williams, Jennifer—Homicide—05/10/87—Nash

The scoreboard was a recent addition by the section's lieutenant, George Brand. He was an accounting type who had pissed off the chief and ended up in our world. Publicly, the department said Brand's reassignment was to clean up the inefficiencies in Major Crimes, but I think the chief thought we would wear him out. Brand had the occasional useful idea, but most of them were fastidious bullshit to keep all of us worried about administrative details instead of focusing on real police work.

After the visit to the scoreboard, I reviewed my notes from the previous night.

The song "How Soon Is Now?" by The Smiths was stuck in my head. I hadn't listened to it since high school but awoke to it playing in my head that morning. It was a favorite of Barry's. I don't even know if I ever voluntarily chose to listen to that song. Barry got into The Smiths for a bit due to some girl, and he played their music relentlessly whenever we were in his car. He even got a mohawk and wore eyeliner for about six months—the things we did back then to meet girls.

My partner, Glenn Higgins, hobbled into the office with crutches under his armpits, helping to support his weight. He wore khakis and a flannel shirt; his holstered Glock was on his hip. A thick, black brace was wrapped around his right knee. "Hey, buddy. Good to see you back in the halls of justice."

I nodded.

"Sorry I missed your first days back. They had me working with dispatch for a couple." The combined county/city dispatch operation was housed in a separate building. Years ago, it had been in the basement of the Public Safety Building. "I'm now back in CA," he added, meaning Crime Analysis.

"Seems like you're doing well," I said.

"Are you kidding me? Light duty sucks. I'm going crazy with the busywork. I'm dying for some good old-fashioned police work. I came in this morning, and the data crunchers were talking about a homicide you picked up last night. Need any help?"

"I'm fine. It's just a body in a field at this point."

"If you need anything, and I mean *anything*, let me know. I'm going coo-coo for Cocoa Puffs down there."

Glenn's new assignment, Crime Analysis, was an integral department, built around data accumulation and statistical modeling. The five-person team was staffed with civilian employees, typically accountant types, good with numbers and patterns, but their personalities didn't usually mesh well with cops. It was a classic situation of Type As and Type Bs working together. Officers recovering from injury or surgery were often assigned to Crime Analysis or some other non-field duty department.

"It can't be that bad," I said.

"Have you ever worked it?"

I shook my head.

"Those people are freaks. Don't get me wrong, they're nice and all, but they have zero sense of humor. I can't get a laugh out of them. They're down in that hole every day chewing data and enjoying it. I mean, *really* enjoying it. It's weird. They're weird."

"We need them."

"I know that," Glenn said. "But could they at least pretend to be part of the human experience? They're all one step away from androids." He shook his head. "I should be able to work my cases, even if I'm deskbound."

"That's policy." I shrugged. "Besides, how would you interview people?"

"That's what the phone is for. And you, now that you're back, I'd have backup if I needed it."

"Ask Ackerman, then."

Glenn snorted. "That climber? He won't buck policy for anything other than his wardrobe."

The old me, the guy before Bobbie's death, would have discussed the light-duty policy with him at length. I'd have listened to Glenn's arguments and maybe even played devil's advocate with him. Today, though, I didn't care. None of it mattered.

He pointed a crutch at me. "Come down and get me if I can help. I may not be able to run the mile, but I can still work a puzzle or two." He patted my shoulder. "I'm glad you're back."

I watched him limp down the hall on the crutches. We'd been partners going on five years. It was one of the longer runs the department had tolerated. Both Glenn and I operated under the radar. We were vanilla ice cream. Neither of us caused problems for the administration, and we quietly and effectively did our jobs.

Until his knee surgery and Bobbie's death sidelined us, we were an unstoppable team.

****

That afternoon, I was so deep in concentration wrapping up the initial report for the homicide, I didn't hear the approaching footsteps.

"Nice to see you're finally working again," said a voice, the sarcasm hard to miss.

I looked over my shoulder and saw Detective Andrew Parker leaning against the nearest column, an opened file in his hands. He didn't make eye contact with me, pretending to read the file instead. Parker stood barely 5'8", but he was built like a mini-Schwarzenegger. He and his partner, Jessie Johnson, were the resident gym rats.

"Morning, Andy."

"It's Andrew," he said, his eyes lifting now to contact mine.

"Sure."

"Is your boyfriend still milking his injury?"

I opened my mouth to say something, but Parker flexed, his chest muscles straining against his dress shirt. His eyes challenged me to something. Whatever he wanted, though, I had no idea.

"Did someone spike your steroids this morning?"

Parker pushed out his lips, thinking about his next cut down. "I'd say it's good to have you back, but we barely noticed you were gone. It's been nice to see what it will be like when you and Glenn finally retire."

"Why are you always such a dick, Andy?"

"It's Andrew," he said, snapping his folder closed and walking away.

I turned back to my desk to finish the report. I guess not everyone was happy I was back.

THURSDAY
NOVEMBER 30th

9

Duke Haney was a big man, over 6'6" and at least 275 pounds. He had a gray flat top and a salt-and-pepper mustache. His hands were tucked into his brown Carhartt jacket as I approached him at the front desk. A stomach built through years of beer and red meat pushed against the coat.

He had made it through the metal detectors and the hired security guards at the front of the Public Safety Building. They'd always been in place, but everything tightened up after 9/11 and showed no signs of ever going back. It was the new reality. Although, after these many years, could it really be called "new" anymore? Wasn't it just reality now? What was it like before the planes crashed into those towers? It was almost hard to remember now, except maybe when there was a reminder from the past, like watching a movie from before that moment when everything seemed so foreign and naïve.

Duke leaned against the front desk with an elbow on the counter, affably chatting up the senior volunteer who staffed the front desk.

"Mr. Haney? I'm Detective Nash."

Duke turned to me and stuck out a thick, calloused hand for me to shake. A broad smile spread across his face. "Duke, please. How ya doing?"

"Did you bring the camera footage?" I asked.

"No need. Like I said on the phone, it's web-based. Let's go to your computer, and I'll show you what I'm talking about."

He followed me back to my cubicle. When we got there, he gave me the web address and a login screen popped up.

"Before our meeting, I created a user ID and password for you. *Spokane Detective* is the username. Capital *S*. Capital *D*. A space in the middle of both worlds. *police* is the password. No capital."

I typed in the words and was greeted with a new screen with five different location choices.

"Pick the Spokane store," Duke said, tapping the monitor with a thick finger.

I clicked the Spokane icon, and a new screen opened with images for six different camera feeds. Two cameras on the gas pumps, one on the front door entry, one behind the counter, one showed a general area of the store, and one on the stockroom. All of them ran at the same time.

"That's slick," I said.

"It should be. It cost me a pretty penny, but I own five stores. This is the only one in Spokane. The others are in smaller towns like Deer Park and Colfax. This way, I can monitor all the stores from home or if I'm on vacation. Works pretty well."

"How do I find the footage I'm looking for?"

Duke pointed at the screen. "Click that button."

I clicked a button labeled *Archived Footage*, and a new screen appeared.

"Input the date and time you'd like to start your search. All camera angles will switch to that time. Once we find what you're looking for, we'll be given different options."

I checked my notebook for the time listed on the receipt in our victim's pocket and input the date and time, backing up the time to ten minutes prior. Duke and I watched various cars and customers come into view.

"How long does the archival footage remain?"

"Ten days unless marked for retention. Then it's saved forever until deleted."

Six minutes later, a white Toyota Tundra entered the view and pulled up to one of the inside pumps. The driver, a white male with gray hair combed in a businessmen's style, climbed out. He wore a bright red ski jacket with gray shoulders. He walked into the store and to the back cooler. He grabbed a six-pack of Rainer beer and headed to the cash register.

"That's our guy. Ever seen him before?"

"Not me," Duke said. "Maybe one of my guys has."

"Is there any sound?" I asked.

"No, but that would be a neat trick. That would create a storage nightmare, though. The data files for this are already huge."

After a brief exchange, the female clerk put a pack of Marlboros on top of the beer and rang up the purchase. The customer handed the clerk several bills and received some coins in exchange. He walked back out to his truck, put the beer inside, and started pumping gas.

"Too bad there's not a better angle on the truck. I wish I could get a license plate."

"This is the best I got for that pump," Duke said with a shrug. "I get plates for a couple of the other pumps. Unfortunately, I had to make a couple of sacrifices. This is one of the times the system comes up short. Most of the time, though, I love this thing."

For the next thirty minutes, Duke showed me how to save the footage we'd just watched and how to print a picture of my unidentified victim.

***

As I walked to Crime Analysis, the hook from Aerosmith's "Dream On" wound round and round in my brain, courtesy of my now expected morning ritual. Weeks prior, I had started listing the songs in a notebook I kept on my nightstand.

I liked the Aerosmith song so much that I walked to my music collection and found their *Greatest Hits* disc. While I pulled the disc from its case, I continued to sing the song to myself. I paused, the disc in my right hand, case in the left. I remembered the lyric that mentions the Lord coming tomorrow to take someone away. I put the disc back in the case and put the album back. The house remained silent.

I found Glenn seated behind a computer screen with his head in his hands. "What are you doing?" I asked as I looked at a screen full of data points laid over the city's boundary.

He looked up, his initial surprise turning to embarrassment. "Setting the line-up for my fantasy football team. What's it look like I'm doing?"

"How about some real police work?"

Glenn smiled, relief flooding his features. "What have you got?"

"Ask your team if any missing persons reports have been filed in the last day or so?"

"You can check that from your own computer, partner."

"I already did, but nothing's been entered by our department. I was hoping you could check a little deeper with neighboring agencies for recent reports. See if someone matching this description has been reported missing in the last couple of days." I handed Glenn a piece of paper with the victim's description as well as a color photo from the Quick-E-Mart's camera.

"Haven't you got prints back on this? An unidentified vic seems like a high priority for Ident, right?"

I shrugged. "They've got his prints. Forensics sent them out immediately. When I asked Ident why it was taking so long to get them back, they gave me a song and dance about AFIS being down, which has caused them to be backlogged with so many entries they're doing them by hand now." AFIS was the Automated Fingerprint Identification System and was managed by the FBI. "When's the last time you heard AFIS being down for more than an hour or two?"

Glenn screwed up his face while he thought.

"Exactly," I said, my irritation for the matter just below the surface. "They're not going to let it go down that long. Therefore, I think Ident's screwing around. They're still fighting against next year's budget. Its passive-aggressive bullshit is what it is."

"I don't think they'd do that, man. I think they'd still be professional."

"Whatever," I said. "Until those people get their act together, we need to focus on our job, which is finding this guy. Think you can help me out?"

"Sure," Glenn said, his eyes drifting to the photo I gave him. "Not much to go on, though. Mid-to-late sixties white guy. Red jacket. Not many of them in Spokane."

"Here's a photo of the victim's vehicle as well. I don't have any plate information."

"Don't want to make it too easy, right?"

"If it was easy, what would I need you for?" I said and playfully tapped him on the back of the head.

***

I stopped by the office of the on-duty patrol lieutenant. Brenda Brady was seated behind her desk, bent over some paperwork. I knocked on her door, and she looked over the top of her glasses.

"Nash. Come in."

"Lieutenant," I said, stepping into her office.

Brenda was in her early fifties with dark eyes and long gray hair tied into a bun. She had a smile that wouldn't quit and a mouth that would make a sailor blush.

She leaned back in her chair. "If you would have told me the majority of my job was going to be administrative bullshit, I would have passed on the promotion and stayed a fucking sergeant."

"It can't be all that bad."

"Wanna bet?" she said. She pushed the paperwork she'd been reviewing across the desk toward me. "Set your peepers on that."

I picked up the papers and thumbed through them. "First-aid kit reviews from other departments?"

"Yeah. City Hall wants to make sure our officers are as safe as humanly possible. One of our illustrious city council members got the bright idea on a recent ride-along to look at the first-aid kit in the trunk. It was fucking atrocious. Our guys had been raiding it for some time and not restocking it. Guess what happened after that?"

I held up the papers.

"It rolled right downhill until it landed on my fucking desk. Now, I not only have to make a recommendation on commercially available first-aid kits out there, but I've also got to create a fucking plan on how to maintain those fucking first-aid kits because some patrol officers can't keep their fucking equipment in condition-ready status."

She paused to take a deep breath, her face red.

I put the papers back on her desk and handed her the sheet of paper with my handwriting.

"What the fuck is this?" Brenda asked.

"Geez, you're fired up."

Brenda waved my paper around in a sort of apologetic fashion. "Sorry, Dallas. I'll put a regulator on my temper. Let me start again. What is this incredibly important item you've brought for me to review?"

"I'm looking for a late model, white Toyota Tundra. The homicide victim from last night was driving it prior to his death. I believe there's an Oakland Raiders sticker in the small window behind the driver's door. I can't be sure, as I saw it in reverse through the front window, but that's what I believe it is."

"You don't have a plate listed."

"No. No idea on the plate. I don't have an ID on the victim yet, either. I'm hoping we'll get something from his prints. There's been no missing person's reports filed in the last couple of days with our department, so I'm up a creek right now."

"It's paper thin, Dallas, but I'll put it out. Let's see if we can get something."

"Thanks. I appreciate it."

"You bet."

As I turned to leave, she said, "Nash."
"Yeah?"
"How's the first-aid kit in your car looking?"

<h1 style="text-align:center">10</h1>

I stood in front of the refrigerator. Both of its doors were open as it invited me to make a choice.

Unfortunately, there was nothing edible inside. There was a Domino's pizza box with one slice several days past good. *I should throw it out*, I thought and shoved the box back in.

There was also a half-eaten Jimmy John's sandwich. *That too should be tossed*, I thought and stacked it on top of the pizza box.

I found a single egg in the door that I couldn't remember buying. I shook it, not hearing anything. *Was I supposed to hear something?* I wondered. I put it back in the door, deciding I'd test my luck with it another day.

I looked in the meat drawer. It was empty. I knew there wasn't anything there before I even opened it, so why did I even bother? I'd eaten the last of the sandwich meat days ago. Or was it last week?

There weren't any beers in the fridge, either. They'd been gone for some time.

Slowly, I closed the doors and turned to the pantry. It was essentially the same story as the refrigerator, just less cold. For several minutes, I rummaged around until I settled on a can of corn.

I opened it up and smelled it. What was I expecting it to smell like? I thought about dumping the contents into a pan to heat it, but at the last moment, I reconsidered. Using a tablespoon I pulled from the dishwasher, I sampled the cold corn.

It wasn't apple pie, but it tasted fine.

"Hell with it," I muttered. It would do for dinner.

11

When I arrived at the department, there was an email from Ident waiting in my inbox. I stared at it for a moment, waiting to open it. My mind was still on Bobbie.

I'd stopped by her grave to visit her that morning. I told her about the song that I woke to. It wasn't really a song, though. It was a Coca-Cola jingle. The one about wanting to buy the entire world a Coke and teach it how to sing. It was a stupid commercial inside my subconscious.

There was no way that was a message. It was just subconscious garbage or mental gobbledygook. The goofy idea about Bobbie sending me messages was a fantasy. I was just giving myself some sort of false hope.

I saw it all the time with family members of homicide victims. They willed themselves to believe their loved ones were okay, that they would miraculously come home someday, or that they were watching over them from the great beyond. I was just doing the same thing to myself.

I couldn't allow myself to be foolish. I'd told Bobbie that this morning, that I was done hoping for something from these songs.

She didn't tell me I was wrong. I hadn't really expected her to. I'm still not crazy.

I clicked on the email from Ident. His fingerprints identified the homicide victim from the vacant lot as Hamilton Gene Martin.

I quickly called up the All Vehicles Registered (AVR) screen and entered Hamilton Martin's name. It would take several minutes to search.

I then ran Martin through NCIC, the national criminal database system, and the Department of Licensing.

He had been fingerprinted for a concealed carry permit back in 2007. The address on the card showed him on Bigelow Gulch Road, the same address the Department of Licensing showed for his driver's license.

Hamilton Martin had no traffic-related entries, whether it be speeding tickets, parking tickets, or traffic collisions.

He had no complaints as a crime victim.

Martin had been contacted multiple times and arrested twice for domestic violence-related complaints and assaults. All of these were within the last few years, with the most recent being roughly six months ago. However, no convictions ever resulted from the arrests.

The system dinged that the AVR report was ready. I flipped over to the report. Only a single vehicle was registered to Martin: a white Toyota Tundra. The first puzzle pieces were starting to fit together.

I then pulled up the last arrest report for domestic violence. It was an incident in early May. The victim was a woman, Kelly Winslow. Police responded to a downtown pub on a witness report of a man slapping a woman. When officers arrived, Martin denied hitting Winslow, and she denied he hit her. Both Martin and Winslow were intoxicated. The witness hadn't stuck around and refused to give the dispatcher a name for further contact. This left the officers to go on only what they could see, which was some slight reddening on the left side of her cheek. The state's domestic violence laws are very specific on arrest when domestic violence is suspected. There's no leeway, and officers are trained to err on the side of making an arrest. Not surprisingly, they arrested Martin against Winslow's protests.

Winslow's address was on the report, but she had refused to provide her telephone number. The address was a house near Corbin Park.

Based on the report, I could see why the case had gone nowhere after the arrest. Uncooperative victim, no witness, and weak evidence. On the scale of crimes needing prosecution, this one would have gotten pushed off some prosecutor's desk immediately.

***

I drove a few blocks north and parked on Glass, a few houses away from my destination.

The house was a small blue bungalow and sat back on the lot. The sidewalk hadn't been shoveled since the snow season started. The woman answered the door before my second knock. She was in a pink bra and black spandex boxer shorts. A baby perched on her hip, and there was an unlit cigarette in her mouth. She regarded me with obvious scorn. "He ain't here," she said.

"Who?"

"Who do you think? Benny. Your buddies picked him up a couple nights ago. Don't you cops talk with each other?"

"What's your name?"

She squinted and moved the baby in front of her, hugging it tightly. "Why?"

"I'm looking for Kelly Winslow. She's not in trouble. Are you her?"

Her face relaxed. "Nah."

"How long have you lived here?"

"Since the summer."

"Do you know where Kelly Winslow lives? This was listed as her last known address."

The woman shook her head. "Never heard of the bitch. The house was empty when I moved in."

I nodded. "Sorry for disturbing you, ma'am."

As I walked back to my car, she yelled, "When's Benny coming home?"

***

The weather warmed slightly, although that wasn't saying much. It was supposed to reach the mid-30s for a few days before a returning cold front would drop it back below freezing during daytime hours. The sky was clear, and the snow was gradually melting.

It was a little after 10 a.m. when I drove along Bigelow Gulch in northeast Spokane. It was an older portion of town, initially developed by those who wanted to escape the early urbanization of Spokane's north side. Growth had long passed this area, leaving it an island of privacy amid urban expansion.

The house was an old rancher, its brown paint peeling. The roof was free of snow, a victim of poor insulation, its shingles starting to curl at the edges. I pulled into the driveway and parked.

A patrol car pulled off the road and into the driveway. Officer Pauleen Sherman climbed out of the vehicle. She was a husky woman with an intense demeanor. She wore a black patrol jumpsuit, and her hair was tied back into a bun. As she walked toward me, she slid a baton into the O-ring on her duty belt.

"What the hell are we doing way out here?"

"The homicide from a couple of nights ago," I said. "The victim lived here. We're going to attempt contact with anyone else who resides within."

"I appreciate the opportunity for a field trip," she said, "but let's not make this into a sit and watch. Calls are stacking up in the real world."

Without asking, Sherman led the way up the porch. Her gait was confident, almost confrontational. I knocked several times on the front door, with no response from inside. I peeked through the front window and saw a couch and television, a dining table with papers on it, and a kitchen in the back of the house. I tried the front door and found it locked.

"There doesn't appear to be anyone else here," I said.

"Want to walk the perimeter?" Sherman asked.

I glanced down at my dress shoes and, for a moment, didn't want to get them any dirtier than they already were. There was another part of me that didn't want Sherman going back to the other patrol officers and telling them how I was too sissy to walk around a house because of my shoes. "Sure. Let's take a look."

We stomped around the exterior of the house. The snow was soft, and I sank deep into it—the cold bit at my ankles through my thin socks. As expected, Sherman's combat boots held up a heck of a lot better than my shoes.

In the back was an unattached garage with a partially restored '72 Pontiac in it. A stack of wood ran along the end of the house. I climbed the steps and tried the back door. It was also locked.

I looked through the side window into the kitchen. Everything was clean and put away.

"I'm not sure if he knew his neighbors, but we should talk with them," I said. "See if anyone lived with him or if they know of any family."

We returned to the front of the house and out to the street. Traffic whizzed by. Bigelow Gulch was a snaking arterial over hilly terrain that connected northeast Spokane to Spokane Valley. The houses tended to sit back off the road and were hidden by trees, undulating terrain, and ill-shaped lots.

I headed to the home on the west side while Officer Sherman walked toward the house on the east.

My shoes were now soaked through. I tromped along the road and took a splash of dirty slush across my dress slacks from a passing car. I turned back to see the vehicle that had splashed me and got blasted a second time with the dirty sludge by a passing truck. I spun and sprinted until I got to the driveway of the neighboring house. I looked back across the snowy yard and over a row of three-foot-tall hedges at Martin's house.

I walked up to a nicely maintained rancher. Two cars were parked in the driveway, a mid-'90s Ford pickup, and an early 2000s Buick.

The front door opened before I could reach the porch, and a man in his late sixties stepped out. Suspicion was on his face. "Can I help you, son?"

I showed him my badge. "Detective Nash. Spokane Police Department."

"Spokane? You realize you're in the county, son?"

I now realized why Sherman's demeanor was so poor. I'd pulled her into another jurisdiction.

"What's going on?"

I pointed to Martin's home. "Your neighbor—"

"Ham?"

"Hamilton Martin."

"Yup. That's him."

"He was found a couple of nights ago. Murdered."

The older man shook his head. "Well, son, you better come on in."

I looked down at my pants and shoes. "It's probably better if we talk outside."

"The drivers out there aren't very kind, are they? Why don't you come on the porch then? Let me grab a coat."

A moment later, he stepped out of the house wearing a large blue parka. I stepped onto the porch, and we shook hands. "I'm Tom Simms," he said.

"What can you tell me about Mr. Martin?"

"I've known Ham for almost twenty years. He was a… complicated man."

"Complicated?"

"I was trying to come up with a nice word. Don't speak ill of the dead, that sort of thing."

"Anything you can tell me would be of help."

Tom leaned against one of the porch columns and crossed his arms. "Well, after his wife died, he had some occasional problems with the law. Mostly about his girlfriend, I think."

"How did his wife die?"

"Lucinda died almost seven years ago. Cancer. It ate her up something fierce. That did a number on Ham. They'd been married a long time. Her death hurt him something bad. It changed him in ways most folks didn't like. He became isolated. When he did come in contact with people, he wouldn't talk as much as he used to."

I made notes on my pad, but I couldn't help feeling like Tom was talking about me.

"You mentioned Mr. Martin had a girlfriend," I said. "Do you know her name?"

"Kelly Winslow. Pretty gal. Not sure what she saw in Ham, but what do most of them ever see in us, anyway?"

Tom and I shared a knowing look before he continued. "She and Ham seemed to fight like cats and dogs whenever they got together, but they stuck it out. It didn't make a whole lot of sense to me. At night, when the traffic dies down, we could hear them yelling at each other next door."

"Did she live with Mr. Martin?"

"No. I think she lives out in the valley now. Don't know where or I'd tell you."

"Do you know anything else about her? Where she works?"

"Not really. She always seemed nice enough, but she drinks too much whenever I've seen them together. They both do, to tell the truth. Maybe that's why they stuck it out together. That was their glue, if you will."

"Did anyone live with him?"

"No."

"Does he have any family?"

"He never had any children. He's got a niece somewhere back East from a brother that died during Vietnam. He talked about her some."

"But no family in Spokane?"

"No. He did have a friend who used to come around a lot, a Dennis something or other—chatted with him a couple of times. Nice enough fellow. I haven't seen him for some time. If you can find him, maybe he can give you some help."

"You don't know his last name?"

"Sorry, no."

I jotted the name Dennis in my notebook, then asked, "Was Ham employed?"

"He worked for Anderson Electric. He was an electrician."

As I made notes in my notebook, Tom asked, "You need a key to Ham's house? He gave me a key for emergencies. I never had to use it before."

"Yes, that would be great. I'll let myself in once I get my warrant."

"You don't need a warrant, Detective. You can let yourself in. I'll give you permission if you need it."

"I appreciate that, but we'll need a warrant to make sure everything is official."

"Ok, have it your way. Wait here for a minute, and I'll get the key for you."

***

Before leaving the scene, I asked Officer Sherman to secure the Martin residence and left the key to the house with her. No one would be able to get in or out without her noticing.

"I asked for this not to be a sit and watch," Sherman said, not bothering to hide her irritation.

I shrugged. "Most of our job is sitting and watching."

As she walked back to her car, Sherman muttered to herself and dismissively waved me off.

12

I got to work on the search warrant for Martin's residence.

When it was done, I took the paperwork to Judge Coughlin's office for his approval. He was roughly ten years older than I, and rumor had it he was considering not running for reelection. He'd been a decent judge for law enforcement, so to see him leave would be unfortunate.

He sat behind his desk with the sleeves rolled up on his white shirt. His thick white hair had been mussed somewhere, somehow in the morning. I'd caught him in the middle of lunch, which was a Subway sandwich and a bag of potato chips. *The Spokesman-Review* was opened in front of him.

He waved me into his office when he saw me.

"What are you dragging around today, Dallas?" he said through a mouthful of food. "Please tell me it's more interesting than this article about internal bickering within the city council." His finger tapped the opened newspaper. "Why do I even read the local news section anymore? It's the same story about the same malcontents every day."

I handed him the documents and gave him a quick briefing of the Martin case. He intently listened as he chewed. When I finished speaking, he turned his attention to the warrant.

I glanced around his office while he read. There were law books everywhere, some arranged neatly on shelves and others scattered about on the floor. There were pictures of the Gonzaga campus on his wall, as well as his degree. A photo of Albert Einstein sticking his tongue out was the only non-legal thing in his office.

When he finished reading the affidavit, he pulled his glasses off. "Seems straightforward. Any suspects?"

"None."

"Truly random?"

"I can't speculate. Not enough information."

He harrumphed. "Tis the season, I guess. Murder and merriment." He signed his approval and handed the documents back to me. "If I don't see you before the holiday, Merry Christmas, Dallas." He returned his attention to his lunch and the newspaper.

***

When I arrived back at Hamilton Martin's home, Corporal Mark Tripp was in front, photographing the house. Tripp was a bulldog of an officer with a face to match. He let the camera hang from his neck and walked towards me. Officer Pauleen Sherman got out of her car and trotted over to join us.

"Hey Mark, are the exterior photographs done?" I asked.

"Yeah. I'm ready to go in when you are," Tripp said, his jowls jumping as he spoke.

"Pauleen, you've got the key," I said. "Let's make this official."

She rolled her eyes and headed toward the front of the house.

I knocked loudly on the front door three times before yelling, "Spokane Police Department! We have a search warrant!"

As expected, there was no answer.

Sherman unlocked the door. She and Tripp entered the house with their guns drawn. I stepped into the house after them, listening as the two other officers quickly moved through the various rooms. When they returned, Tripp said, "All clear. We're good to go."

I went to my car and pulled several brown paper bags. I handed one to Sherman.

"What are we looking for?" she asked.

"I don't know," I said. "We don't have a lot to go on. Just look for anything you believe might have some relevance or significance. If you find something, call it out, and we'll discuss it."

Tripp photographed each room before helping us search.

We slowly and methodically moved through the various rooms. We found nothing in the living room except a ceramic pipe and a small bag of marijuana. Since marijuana was legalized in the state of Washington in 2012 and the first retail store opened a year and a half later, there was no longer anything exciting or useful in finding something like that.

Nothing was found in the kitchen.

A Smith & Wesson .32 was in the nightstand in the master bedroom. I unloaded it and would later log it into the property room for safekeeping. Also, on the nightstand, I found a birthday card from Kelly Winslow with her return address on the envelope. I jotted it in my notebook. Her handwritten sentiment inside the card read *Happy Birthday, Ham—Kelly*. Not much sentimentality.

The second room, which looked to be set up as a guest bedroom, turned up nothing of interest.

The third room was set up as a home gym with a treadmill and a small weight set. A television hung on the wall. Again, nothing of evidentiary value was found.

We moved into the basement. Nothing there, either.

We concluded the search, secured the front door and gathered near our cars.

"That was a boring search," Tripp said.

"Maybe he was just a nice guy," Sherman said with a shrug.

"That nice guy smacked his girlfriend around," I said. "At least a couple of times."

Sherman curled her lip. "Well, thanks for ruining that."

13

That night I sat in my bedroom amidst Bobbie's clothes scattered around the floor. I had put some of them into boxes, only to pull them out again when I changed my mind about what I wanted to do with them.

Tomorrow was Saturday, and I didn't have anything to do, which would give me more time to miss her. As much as I hated being back at the job, it occupied my mind and distracted me from the hurt.

While procrastinating on what to do with the various garments, I suddenly realized the birthday sentiment Kelly Winslow had written to Hamilton Martin bothered me.

Happy Birthday, Ham—Kelly.

It was so simple, it was ridiculous. That's not what a loved one says to another, right? There was absolutely no sentiment to it, no thought given to those words.

Had she bought the card in a hurry, perhaps when she realized too late it was Ham's birthday? She'd mailed it, so there must have been some forethought to it. However, if she would go to the trouble of buying a card and sending it so it arrived before a birthday, why was so little consideration put into what she wrote?

When I became honest with myself, I knew I wasn't really bothered by Winslow's sentiment or any implication it might have toward Martin's case.

What bothered me was I'd written the same sentiment to Bobbie before. Numerous times, I had hurriedly stopped by a grocery store on the way home from work because I forgot some holiday—her birthday, our anniversary, Valentine's Day. I then sat in my car, hastily scratching I love you or some other sentiment along with my name, tucking the card into the envelope so I could race home and hand her the thoughtlessly purchased gift.

Why didn't I put more effort into buying her cards? How come I couldn't be bothered to spend more time writing down my feelings for her?

I just assumed she would know. It wasn't a mystery, right? I was her husband. We'd been together since high school. That alone had to show her she was the love of my life, right? She had to know without me telling her.

I laid my head down on a pile of her clothes and went to sleep.

14

My brother, Dean, insisted I come over for dinner with his wife, Arlene.

They were a sweet couple, but I didn't want to hang out with them.

Dean didn't give me a choice, though. He said either I could come to their house for dinner or they were coming to mine. He said Arlene was worried about me and wasn't going to let this go. I chose their home so I could escape easier. I figured it would be harder to get them to leave my house.

Dean picked up a growler of ale from Six String Brewery for us. I told him I wasn't drinking yet, which put a damper on the night.

What was it about the human condition, that when someone announces they aren't drinking, everyone else feels a little guilty about their own consumption? It seems to require everyone else not to imbibe or cut back substantially.

In the end, the three of us drank cranberry juice with dinner.

"How's work?" Arlene asked.

"Fine."

"Glad to be back?" Dean asked, while taking the tamales from the oven.

"Not really. I returned out of duty more than anything."

"Probably helps to keep your mind off things, though, right?" Arlene's question was carefully structured.

"My thoughts are never far from Bobbie."

We were silent after that while Dean finished preparing dinner. He was an excellent cook, and dinner smelled fantastic. However, like work, I was there out of duty.

The conversation intermittently started and stopped until I asked, "Do you ever wake up to music?"

"Like from the radio?" Arlene said. "I prefer just the alarm. Otherwise, I'll just lay in bed, never moving."

"No, I mean like a song you haven't heard in years pops into your head during a dream. Or maybe not even a dream. You just wake up with it playing in your brain."

Arlene shook her head.

"I have," Dean said. "If I've listened to an album a few times in one day, like if I'm working on a project and don't bother changing the CD. I've woken up with a song in my head after hearing it several times in a day. Is that what you're talking about?"

I shrugged. "In a way, sort of."

"Is that happening to you?" Arlene asked.

"Now and then. I was just making conversation more than anything."

Dean said, "Ever hear a song, and it turns into an earworm?"

"Earworm?" Arlene said with a grimace. "That sounds gross."

Dean laughed. "It's where you can't get a song out of your head once you hear it. Like 'Afternoon Delight.' That song is an earworm every time I listen to it."

They looked my direction, waiting for me to chime in. "Earworms," I said and shook my head. "Never happens."

We finished dinner in silence.

When the table was cleared, Arlene asked, "Want to play a game? Maybe start a puzzle?"

"No, thanks. Dinner was fantastic," I said, picking words I would have used in my previous life. "I'm tired and just want to head home."

They said in unison, "We understand."

We were all thankful the night had ended. Our duties to each other over.

15

I spent Sunday in bed.

I woke to a chorus of a song repeating in my brain that crushed me. Firefall's "Just Remember I Love You" looped through my mind, paralyzing me. It had been a song that played at our wedding. It was one of Bobbie's parents' favorite songs and one they often danced to during her childhood. Bobbie said she loved the song, and it held special memories for her. I always thought it was loaded with 1970s sugary sweetness, but the song grew on me after she wanted it to be ours. At our wedding, her parents led the dance to that song, and we later joined them. It was a beautiful memory, but I kept getting hung up on the lyrics.

"Just Remember I Love You."

Maybe the songs weren't mental garbage or subconscious nonsense floating through the darkness of my brain. Maybe Bobbie was trying to send me a message. Just pretending it could be something from her made me miss her more and invited the pain back inside.

I tried getting out of bed to do some chores, some basic hygiene, but I couldn't find the willpower and kept ending up back in bed. Daylight succumbed to the evening, and before I knew it, the alarm clock was beeping for me to get up and return to the office.

I was happy to have somewhere to go.

16

Rima Sepulveda was waiting for me when I entered the brightly lit room.

"You almost look comfortable, Dallas."

I wore a set of blue medical scrubs and blue footies while a blue medical beanie covered my head. Protective glasses were over my eyes. "I always feel like a dork wearing this getup."

"It's not the clothes that make you a dork. Besides, you look better than this guy," Rima said, thumbing toward the body on the table.

Rima walked over and put her hand on my upper arm. She was the new medical examiner, having taken over a few years ago. She was in her late forties, and her black hair was just now showing a sprinkling of gray. A mixture of Spanish and Arabic lineage, her skin was a light olive tone. Even though she was still relatively new to the position, she'd been a great examiner and had become a friend. "Are you doing okay?"

I shrugged. "Working on it."

"That's what they say, right? Time heals or something of that sort."

"Something like that."

She patted my arm. "Ready to get started?"

I nodded.

"Who have we got this time?"

"Hamilton Martin," I said. "He was found dead in a vacant lot. As always, I need to know what made him that way."

"Let the answers begin."

She pulled back the sheet to reveal the body of Hamilton Martin. She pressed a button on the floor with her foot to begin recording.

"Subject is Hamilton Martin, a white male—"

***

No song greeted me that morning, and it left me feeling oddly alone. I always believed dreams were the result of the brain processing and sorting information, and the subconscious attempted to understand all those bits and pieces being organized.

Due to that, I don't usually believe in dreams as messages. I also don't believe in the ability to talk from the other side or other realms or higher planes or whatever you want to call it. But Bobbie did.

She loved that stuff. She read books about it. She attended seminars with friends who were also into that philosophy. She occasionally practiced meditation and would work towards transcendentalism.

I didn't understand her preoccupation with it, nor did I ever want to discourage it. Mine is a world of individual cruelty and generational meanness. Hers was a world of hope and positivity. Her world was better. I just didn't know how to get to it.

The songs in the morning, though, were new. They had never happened to me until she died. Maybe she really was trying to communicate something to me. Was I, therefore, a hypocrite to my beliefs by thinking it might be her?

Why the theme song to *Cheers*? Maybe she wanted me to cheer up? Or was I supposed to go where everybody knows me? Would that be my family? I surely didn't want that. I loved my family, but they didn't understand me or my world.

And if it was Bobbie sending me messages, what was with "Gimme Shelter?" Was that something for me, or was she telling me she needed help?

If she was trying to help me, then why send me a message like "The Green Manalishi?" I had no idea what a manalishi was, let alone if it was even green. How could that help me?

And, heaven help me, I woke up weeks ago to The Scorpions' "The Zoo" careening around in my brain. What the hell was I supposed to do with that?

Was I cracking up?

***

"All done, Dallas."

"Huh?"

"I'm finished," Rima said. "Why don't you go outside and wait for a few? You look a little pale. I'll be out in a minute and give you a brief on it."

After changing out of the scrubs, I waited in the lobby, embarrassed. I had zoned out during the entire process.

Rima walked out and handed me a 3x5" notecard with her handwriting. "The official report should be done later today. I'll get you a copy by tomorrow, but here are the important facts. The blade went 7.4 centimeters deep, just a little under three inches deep. The knife was an inch wide, single-edged, with a serrated portion near the back. I can't dial in the exact length of that portion, but its existence is obvious from the tearing of the skin. As for the angle of attack, it came in from a downward strike, almost 45 degrees, on the right side of Martin's neck. It severed the right external and internal jugular veins and the common carotid artery."

"Are you saying the attacker was taller than the victim?"

"Possibly, but you could make that strike by coming overhanded." She mimed a big, overhand knife strike, like something from a bad slasher film.

"Seems like that would be a clumsy attack."

"You know as well as anyone fights are messy and unpredictable, Dallas. Maybe your victim was on his knees, and he got it that way. All I know is the angle was almost 45 degrees. Other than that, you need to work it out. I can't do everything for you, Detective."

Rima patted my back and walked away.

* * *

I sat in my cubicle with my computer on. I'd called up both the Hamilton Martin and Jennifer Williams reports. I wasn't interested in doing any new work or tracking down leads. I only wanted to be left alone.

I reread my reports several times that morning, correcting small spelling errors and rewriting sentences that were already fine. At various times, I refilled my coffee and went to the restroom, just to waste time.

Marci Burkett came over to check on me. "Hey," she said.

"Hey," I said, exchanging our familiar, non-touchy-feely greeting.

Marci was a ball of fury, one many of the guys had crossed, sometimes unsuspectingly, sometimes willingly. She carried a chip on her shoulder due to her size and her gender, but she was the best fighter in the detectives' office. There were some whispers that, pound-for-pound, she was the best fighter in the department. I don't know if that was possible since some UFC animals were wearing the uniform today, but who knew? What I knew through rumors and firsthand experience was she proved herself during the sanctioned training at the academy and in unofficial bouts in the gym. The department had a padded room on the second floor for practicing combat tactics. Most guys underestimated Marci, and she made them pay for it every time.

I had to partner with her once in a defensive tactics refresher course. I'll never forget how quickly apparent it was she was the better fighter. I move like a barroom brawler. She moves like a mist, disappearing and reappearing where you least expect it. I quickly checked my ego, and she spent the rest of the class helping me understand the new material the instructors were teaching. Her fighting skills may have humbled me, but I was appreciative of how much time she took to help me get better.

"Where's your partner?" she asked.

"Still in injury exile. Where's yours?"

"Court. How long before Glenn gets to come back?"

"Another month at least before they clear him for rotation. He's going crazy with the number crunchers."

"What about you? How are you doing?"

"I'm fine."

"Anything I can do?"

"Not really."

She pulled her ear while she thought. Her eyes studied me.

"Seriously, Marci. I'm fine."

"Want to hit the mat at lunch? Putting on the gloves and hitting something always makes me feel better."

"You're like the ringside version of Dr. Phil."

"Mock it if you want, but it works."

"I'm not mocking, Marci. I just don't want my ego broken along with my heart."

"I'd go easy on you, Dallas."

"You've never gone easy on anyone, Marci."

She thought about it for a moment before smiling. "Well, I would *try* to go easy on you."

***

When the end of the day finally arrived, I walked outside into the cold and headed toward my car. As the heater warmed the interior, I realized I'd accomplished nothing. I'd spent the entire day pretending to do something to look busy. I'd never done that before in my whole career.

For a moment, I felt ashamed and wanted to walk back into my office, start working immediately, and give renewed effort to the only two cases I had.

Instead, I dropped my car into gear, left the parking lot, and headed home.

I would deal with shame another time.

TUESDAY
DECEMBER 5th

17

I sat in my car and stared at the area where her grave marker lay.

It was cold out but not colder than it had been recently. Besides, I had my coat, gloves, and a hat, just like every other morning. Nothing should stop me from getting out and walking over to see her, but I couldn't face it this morning. It had happened once before, although at that time I was filled with resentment. I blamed her for her death.

Why did she have to go out to Carmen's house that night?

What was she doing that caused her not to see the deer in time?

How could she leave me alone?

It was selfish to blame her, I know, but I did it.

This morning, I don't know what caused me to sit there, but I couldn't get out of the car. I wasn't blaming her. I wasn't blaming anyone, not even God, and I had condemned him a lot over the past month.

The heater had warmed the car to an uncomfortable level, especially considering I was sitting in my coat. I thought about turning the heat down, maybe lowering a window, but I didn't. Instead, I let it get warmer.

Sweat formed on my back and under my arms, but I stayed seated, watching her marker, wondering why I was so panicked to get out and see her.

I whispered to myself, "You should get out."

Instead, I dropped the car into gear and headed toward the department.

18

When I arrived at the department in the morning, a report had been assigned to me for review. Since I wasn't called out regarding it, I already knew the level of urgency was low.

Overnight, patrol officers responded to a robbery. Officer Leya Navarro was part of the response and wrote the report.

Victor Gerardi was listed as the suspect, while Alan Kadner was the victim. Alan had accused Victor of assaulting him and later threatening him with a gun so that he would open his storage unit. Officer Navarro witnessed abrasions and cuts on Alan's face. Digital photos showed the wounds.

Alan stated he knew Victor through mutual acquaintances but denied knowing any reason for the attack or the demand to open the storage unit.

When interviewed, Victor stated Alan had taken his "stuff" and locked it away in a storage unit. Victor claimed Alan broke into Victor's car and stole his belongings. He'd been living out of his vehicle at the time.

This theft was done, Victor claimed, as retribution for him sleeping with Alan's sister—who Alan was also sleeping with.

I reread that sentence twice, to be sure. Then I shook my head in disgust. Just when I thought people couldn't get any worse.

Officer Navarro interviewed Alyce Kadner and confirmed she was indeed in a physical relationship with both her brother and Victor. Navarro made sure to indicate in her report that Alyce clarified she and Alan were only half-siblings from different fathers, so it was both "medically and socially okay." I smiled because Navarro had included that last sentence in the report in quotations.

Victor had a loaded handgun in his possession at the time of contact. He admitted using it to get his stuff back from Alan. Officer Navarro found video surveillance footage of both men at the storage units. Victor was clearly seen using the gun to direct Alan.

A background check on Victor found him to be a felon with convictions for possession of stolen property, assault, and driving under the influence. His driver's license was suspended.

Alan Kadner was wanted on a felony hit-and-run warrant. He also had an extensive background of drug possession and burglary charges.

Alyce Kadner had a misdemeanor warrant for Failure to Appear on a shoplifting charge.

Navarro, with the help of additional officers, arrested the Kadner siblings for their warrants and Incest, which was a felony in Washington State. Victor Gerardi was arrested for First Degree Robbery and Felon in Possession of a Firearm.

Due to the Robbery charge, the report required additional follow-up. All reports of this type were assigned to a detective, even when the suspects had been arrested. I stared at the report until the words blurred. It was criminal-on-criminal violence. Prosecuting and pursuing justice, in this case, wouldn't change anything.

Alan only wanted retribution for Victor having sex with Alan's sister. Victor wouldn't change his ways after this arrest. No citizens were harmed. This case was just another useless cog in a pointless machine.

Should we even care?

19

That afternoon melancholy overwhelmed me while I sat at my desk. I felt like I was drowning. I looked around the office and heard the talking of various persons, detectives, and administrators, and knew I needed to get out before someone came over to make nice.

I pushed away from my desk and got into my car.

***

The snow had returned. It was falling lightly from the gray, oppressive sky.

I headed eastbound to the academy and firing range. It was a short drive from the department and, as officers, we were afforded the luxury of firing as much ammo as we wanted. The department wanted us to train.

Sergeant Don Boone was behind his desk, hunkered behind his computer, studying something. He lifted his head when the door creaked open. Recognition was almost immediate as I stepped in.

"Nash," he said, standing and walking towards the check-in booth. "Here to shoot?"

I nodded as I completed the mandatory sign-in sheet.

"How many boxes?

"A couple."

He vanished inside for a moment and returned with two boxes of .40 ammunition and three magazines.

"No one is out there today. It gets quiet when it's cold, although more guys should practice in conditions like this."

"Yeah," I said and took the ammo.

I felt like I should talk with him more, but nothing came out. We stared at each other for a moment before Boone gave me a kindly smile.

"Good shooting," he said, and headed back toward his computer.

I laid the ammunition and magazines in one of the clearing cubicles. I removed the magazine from my Glock as well as the round from the chamber. I didn't bother doing it in the clearing barrel. No one was in the room with me, and Boone was at his desk. He couldn't see what I was doing. Therefore, I would avoid his chastising about not following safety protocols.

It took a few minutes to load the range ammo into the range magazines. I removed the backup magazines on my belt and left them at my workstation, replacing them with the range magazines. I placed the additional rounds into my jacket pocket. I put on some protective eye gear and hearing protection.

I grabbed a target and stapled it to a target holder. Then I took my supplies and headed to the range. I set up the target and moved to the three-yard line.

I drew and shot three rounds from that distance. Two to the chest and one to the head. I changed magazines and re-holstered.

I stepped back and repeated the drill at the five-yard line.

At the ten- and fifteen-yard lines, I only shot two rounds at the chest before changing magazines and re-holstering.

Back at the twenty-five-yard line, I repeated the same drill.

Due to the cold, my fingers hurt reloading the magazines. When I finished, I took a few minutes and blew into my hands to warm them. The snowfall seemed a little harder.

I decided I'd practice a different drill this time. Draw and move forward to the left in a crouch, three steps with two shots. Scan left and right. Change magazines. Opposite direction next time. I continued that until I was at the target, adding a shot to the head as I got closer and more confident.

I didn't bother looking for where my shots were landing. It would only frustrate me to see if I'd thrown a round off the target.

It just felt good to be outside, shooting.

Reloading was harder this time. My fingers were colder and stiffer.

The sun was disappearing as I moved to shoot with my left hand. I practiced drawing my gun from my holster with my left, holding it upside down, and pulling the trigger with my pinky.

The last handful of times I drew and took a single shot each, working on perfecting my draw in the cold with sore fingers.

When I was out of ammo, I collected my target and went inside.

I stood inside the warmth of the ammo shack and shoved my hands into my pockets. As the heat returned to my fingers, a painful tingling made its presence known.

Sergeant Boone came out. "How was it?"

"Fine."

"Any day's a good day when some shooting is involved, huh?"

I nodded and stamped my feet.

"I know you don't feel like talking," Boone said. "No one does at a time like this. Everyone can respect that, but if you need anything, we're here for you. Any of us. All of us."

He turned and went back to his office without waiting for my response.

20

Kelly Winslow was the office manager for GK Construction in the Spokane Valley, located on North Sullivan Road.

I had first stopped at the address I found on the birthday card envelope from Hamilton Martin's house. It was an apartment building in the Spokane Valley. Kelly wasn't home, so I located the apartment manager, who told me where she worked.

Kelly was in her early forties, with a short haircut and a sweet smile. She wore blue jeans, a cowl neck sweater, and black boots.

She was an attractive woman, marred slightly by a black eye that had faded to a bluish-green over time.

After our introductions, we stepped into the lunchroom to talk in private.

"Do you know Hamilton Martin?"

She sighed. "What has he done now?"

"I'm sorry to break this news to you, but he's dead."

She blinked several times before her mouth opened as she searched for words that she couldn't find.

"He was found murdered last week," I told her.

"Who did it?"

"That's what I'm trying to find out. Do you know anyone who would want to hurt Hamilton?"

She shrugged. "Maybe. He was kind of an asshole."

I pointed to her eye. "Did he do that to you?"

She nodded. "A couple of weeks ago. I broke up with him because of it."

"Did you call the police?"

"No. I sort of deserved it."

"No one deserves it," I said.

She smiled and nodded. "They've told me that before, but I egged him on until he smacked me. I was looking for a reason to break up with him, and he gave it to me. I didn't want the cops called. I just wanted to be out."

"Do you know who might have wanted Hamilton dead?"

"Dead? I don't know anyone who would have wanted to kill Ham, but a lot of the girls around here wanted to kick his ass. Especially after he did this." She pointed at her eye. "But no one wanted him dead—well, at least enough to do something about it."

"So, nobody comes to mind?"

"No, not really. Look, most people liked Ham. He could be charming until he got a couple of beers into himself, and then it was like flipping a switch."

I looked through my notebook. "Did he have a friend named Dennis?"

"If he did, he didn't tell me about him."

"Was he that way? Secretive, I mean?"

"He could be at times. There were certain lines I couldn't cross. Most of them were emotional, and I'd push him, try to get him to grow. A man like that doesn't want to change. He was happy being miserable."

"Did you love him?"

"Oh, I tried, you know, but he didn't love himself. Ham always pushed me away. I don't think he could ever love anyone after Lucinda. It was kinda sad, actually. I would have taken care of that man, but he just pushed away anyone who wanted to love him. He probably got what he deserved."

I watched her for a reaction. When she realized what she said, she smiled with embarrassment. "I probably shouldn't have said that. Huh?"

"Where were you last Sunday? The twenty-sixth?"

She again pointed to her eye. "He did this to me on that Saturday night. We got drunk, and we fought. I told him I didn't want to see him anymore. I spent Sunday night with an ice pack on my face, hoping never to see him again. I guess I got my wish."

"What did you fight about?"

"Hell, it was the same ol', same ol.' He was mean when he drank, and I called him on it. He said he wasn't. Just to prove I was right, I kept poking at him until he smacked me. Then I got to say I told you so, and that I didn't want to see him anymore. He tried to say he was sorry, but I wouldn't let him. I felt justified in getting that reaction, forcing him to raise his hand. I mean, he'd done it before without any real provocation, but this time I controlled when it happened." She paused, thinking. Then she said, "It's funny, though, now that you're here, I'm kind of wishing I hadn't done it."

***

No song greeted me that morning when I awoke, so I left the radio off while I drove. That made three days with no songs playing in my head. There hadn't been any since my emotional meltdown on Sunday when I spent the day in bed. Maybe my subconscious was fighting back now and protecting me. I had let myself start to believe in fairy tales, which caused new and more profound pain, so my subconscious killed the music.

When I parked, I looked at my cell phone. I had missed a call. I'd silenced the ringer while I met with Kelly Winslow. I listened to the voicemail.

"Hi, Dallas. It's Randy. Long time, no talk, right? Anyway, I got your message. I'm working tonight at Miller's Pub. You know, on Monroe? Yeah, well, come by and see me if you got some time. I start at three. If not, give me a call, and we'll set something up. "

***

When I finally left the department for the day, it was dark, even though it was barely 4 p.m. The sun falls early in December.

I hadn't been inside Miller's Pub in years. I'd never been there to drink, only in an official capacity while on patrol. It was a typical dive bar with low lighting and dated furniture. It smelled of stale beer from years of spilled drinks. Several electronic dartboards lined a wall along with two pinball machines, one with an "out of order" sign taped to the front of it.

Two tables were filled with loud revelers cheering the Gonzaga basketball game playing from the sole large screen television. A college football game silently played on the small TV near the bar.

Randy was behind the counter pouring a beer for an older patron slumped at the rail.

The young guy I used to know was in there somewhere, but Randy had gotten much softer around the middle, and his face had gone jowly. His hairline had receded but grown longer in the back. His head looked like a bowling ball with a dead cat wrapped around it. One thing hadn't changed—his big laugh. He let one fly when he saw me and waved.

"Dallas!"

We shook hands. Despite everything I was feeling, I wanted to be happy to see him, but I couldn't muster the enthusiasm. I forced a smile and asked, "How are you doing, Randy?"

"I'm great. Never better. Been working here for almost a year. Can you believe that? How about you?"

"I'm fine."

"Want a beer? It's on me."

"I appreciate it, but I'm not drinking these days."

"Ah. Got you. Fighting the bottle, huh? I understand. Lots of guys go through that."

I had stopped drinking shortly after Bobbie's death. I found myself taking to it easily, and I didn't want to end up a statistic. "Did you talk with Barry?"

"Yeah, yeah. He said you were looking into that girl's murder from back in the day. How can I help?"

"Who was the guy we met down at Dick's, the one who said he was her boyfriend?"

"Who?"

"One night, the three of us were cruising. We were in your Plymouth with your friend, Curtis."

"Ha! I haven't thought about that car in years. Or Curtis, for that matter. He died shortly after high school. Car accident."

"Sorry, man. I didn't know."

Randy shrugged. "The reaper comes for us all sooner or later. I just hope it's later."

I was silent for a moment before continuing. "The four of us stopped by Dick's and met a friend of yours."

Randy laughed and slapped the bar. "When didn't that happen? That's what cruising was all about, right?" The drunk at the end of the bar lifted his head and checked us out.

I smiled, this time for real. Randy liked to be a big man when we were growing up. Things hadn't changed much.

"He had sort of a mullet," I said. "Curly in the back."

Randy snapped his fingers. "Eddie Henning."

"Eddie Henning?"

"Yup. That's him."

"Are you sure?"

"Yeah. He was showing us his new stereo, right?"

"Exactly. Been in contact with him?"

"Haven't seen him in years. Like maybe twenty or more. No, that's not true. I saw him for like two minutes at the fair, maybe three years ago. Just bumped into him and some other dude. Said hello and goodbye. That was it."

"How did he look?"

"Same as the rest of us. Older. He's held it together way better than me, though. Kept all his hair. Lost the mullet, though. Damn, I liked that haircut. Wished I could have kept mine, but the reaper comes for hair follicles, too."

Randy laughed loudly at his joke as he rubbed the bald part of his head. I let him finish laughing, and we spent a few minutes making small talk before I said, "Okay, Randy, I gotta go. I appreciate the help."

"You bet, buddy. Come back in some time when you're off the wagon."

21

I stopped to visit Bobbie on the way to work. It was cold again, near freezing, and light snow was falling. It was another morning without any music to greet me.

I stood at her marker and felt like a fool when I asked, "Are you mad at me?"

The idea of her trying to communicate through the early-morning songs was absurd. Yet, I'd grown oddly comforted by their appearance, and I missed them more than I expected. This was the fourth day of waking without a tune in my head. I was getting agitated.

"I can't get over the idea you're doing this for a reason. You've stopped the music to show me something. Or maybe you can't do it anymore. Is that what happened? Did something bad happen where you're at?"

I shook my head. I was cracking up.

Bobbie couldn't communicate with me. The music in my head was subconscious bullshit, nothing more. By trying to tie it to Bobbie, I was making it worse for myself.

Fighting back the tears, I said, "I'm sorry," before turning and heading to my car.

***

Later in the morning, I ran the name Randy gave me and discovered Eddie Henning wasn't in the system.

Edward Alan Henning, however, was. He had no criminal contacts nor suspicious ones. There were multiple traffic infractions, though, including a driving under the influence back in the early '90s. Other than that, Henning had a clean record.

His address with the Department of Licensing showed him living in the Perry District, a neighborhood that had been revitalized over the past decade. I headed there to interview him.

***

It was shortly after 10 a.m. when I arrived. Like a lot of homes in the neighborhood, it was of Craftsman style, yellow with dark green trim and red accents.

A tall, blond male opened the door after I knocked. He was in tight, long yoga pants with no shirt. He was very trim, and a sheen of sweat glistened on his torso. For a male roughly fifty years old, he was in incredible shape.

"Yes?" he said with an open face, free of suspicion. That changed when he looked over my shoulder and saw my car.

"Eddie Henning?"

"Yes?" Suspicion filled his eyes.

"I'm Detective Nash with the Spokane Police Department. Can I come in and ask you a few questions?"

"Okay," he said, moving out of the way so I could step inside.

He closed the door, and I surveyed the house.

The living room décor could be described as minimalistic. A futon was in front of the window. A small bookcase with a handful of books stood along the east wall. In the middle of the floor was a yoga mat. Soft, gentle music played in the background. Nothing hung on the walls.

In the corner, on a small table, was an essential oil diffuser. The scent it put out was cedarwood. Bobbie had been into essential oils, a concept I repeatedly teased her about. I stared at the diffuser, realizing the one in my house had sat quiet and unused since her death.

"You've got to excuse me. I was doing my morning routine," Henning said, interrupting my thoughts. He picked up a sweatshirt from the floor. He put it on, zipped it up, and sat on the futon. "What's this about?"

"A cold case. Do you know what that is?"

"Yeah. I watch TV." He said it innocently, no sense of snarkiness to it.

I looked around for a television.

"I watch shows on my iPad," Henning said. "A TV takes up too much space, both in a room and in your life. Know what I mean?"

"Mr. Henning," I said, ignoring his question, "I was assigned an unsolved case from 1987, and your name is connected to it."

"My name?" he asked, his face pinching. "What did I do?"

"Did you ever meet a girl named Jennifer Williams?"

"Jennifer Williams?" His face relaxed slightly.

"She was murdered in 1987. I believe you were a senior in high school at that time."

Eddie rubbed his hands together as he spoke. "I knew her. I mean, yeah, I met her. I remember her."

"How did you meet?"

"Hanging out. You know. Through friends."

"Can you be more specific?"

"I don't recall when I met her. Or how. It was downtown, though. It might have been cruising or hanging at the mall. Not the new mall, but the old one. Do you remember? When they had the record store down on Wall Street? And I think Wall Street even went through the center of it, didn't it?"

"I remember."

"So, I just met her, that's all. That's how it was as teenagers. How's my name attached to this?" His left leg nervously jumped as he spoke.

"Were you her boyfriend?"

Eddie laughed. "Her boyfriend? No. We were never close, just acquaintances."

"We have a witness that stated you made comments to the effect you were her boyfriend."

Eddie shook his head. "Detective. I'm gay. There's no way that I had that kind of interest in Jennifer. I never told anyone I was her boyfriend."

I thought about confronting him about his lie right then but decided to wait. I didn't want to give him more information to start building an argument.

I asked him for his personal information—his phone number, where he was employed, the works. When I was done, I gave him my business card.

"If you think of anything that might help in this investigation, please give me a call."

Eddie glanced at the card. "I'll think about it, but I doubt there's anything I can do to help. How did my name get attached to this?"

"Perhaps there was a mistake," I said.

***

I returned to the department and tracked down Glenn. He was hunched over a computer in Crime Analysis, shaking his head and mumbling to himself.

"I hate this."

"What?"

"This!" he yelled and pointed at the screen.

On the monitor was a series of data points and a squiggly line.

"What is it?"

"It's supposed to be the vagrancy calls in Delta Sector for the third quarter between the hours of 8 a.m. and 5 p.m. I've been asked to put together a coherent message for the department to brief the Public Safety Committee. I don't understand what the data is telling me."

"Maybe that's the message."

Glenn smirked. "That will go over well. Sometimes the message is there is no message. Thanks, Buddha."

"Ask one of the nerds for help."

"They don't like being called that," he whispered. Glenn looked around his monitor to see if the analysts had heard me, then he turned to me conspiratorially. "They don't like me being in here. They want to push me out. I think they're poisoning my data to make me look bad. It's a conspiracy of the geeks versus the cool kids. Just like high school."

"Speaking of high school," I said and laid out the Jennifer Williams case. When I finished recounting the Eddie Henning meeting, I said, "He's my guy. I know it."

"You think you cracked a cold case that fast?"

"I don't know. Is that so inconceivable? Can't we hit a home run every now and then? You trust my gut, don't you?"

"Most times, but I'm also there to help you see the things you're missing. I think you're getting over your skis on this."

I nodded halfheartedly. "Maybe."

"No 'maybe' about it. Your head's not fully in the game, Dallas, so listen to your partner."

"You weren't there, man. The guy was nervous, jittery."

"You were a cop, in his house, talking about him being connected to a murder. If someone showed up at my house, in the same situation, asking me the same questions, I gotta say I'd be jittery as fuck as well."

I waved him off. "He also lied, saying he never claimed to be her boyfriend." I tapped my chest. "I remember that moment."

"You're sure?"

"What's that mean?"

Glenn tilted his head. "It was high school, man. That was, like what, thirty years ago?"

"So?"

"So? Really? You remember conversations from way back when?"

"What? You don't?"

"No, I don't, but you do? You remember them as clear as yesterday. Your memory is that crystal clear?"

"Okay, smartass, I don't remember all of them perfectly, but when a kid says he's the boyfriend of a girl who ends up murdered, that sort of sticks with you."

Glenn crossed his arms over his chest. "Again, you're sure it was him?"

"Yeah," I said defiantly. Then there was a moment of self-doubt, a moment of panic. Maybe it wasn't Henning who said that. Maybe it could have been someone else.

"See? You doubt yourself. I can see it in your eyes."

"Wait. No," I said, "I'm definitely sure because my buddy remembered him boasting about it, too."

"You have another witness to his claim?"

"Yeah."

"Then why didn't you pin him down in his house, there and then? You had the goods. You could have cornered him."

Why didn't I?

Glenn let me off answering my doubt when he asked, "And maybe the guy had said she was his girlfriend because she was a beard."

I stared at Glenn, still thinking about why I hadn't jumped at the opportunity to corner Henning.

"Seriously?" he said. "It's a disguise. Gay men claim to be married or have girlfriends—"

"I know what a beard is," I said.

"What I'm trying to point out is, he may not be your guy, no matter how badly you want him to be. You've still got more work to do."

"He's the guy," I said. "I'll find a way to prove it."

"Listen to yourself," Glenn said. "You're all twisted up, just because you think it was serendipity that the case landed in your lap. You're trying to make the case fit your narrative."

"I'm looking at this with clear eyes."

"And I'm telling you that you're not. Take a step back from it, let it breathe, and come back to it later. It's been sitting there for thirty years. A couple more days isn't going to affect anything."

22

I sat on the edge of my bed and stared at the clothes strewn about the room. I hadn't made any further progress on deciding what to do with them.

Staring at her garments for another thirty minutes didn't make sense, so I walked into the living room and sat on the couch. I needed to get a grip and change my attitude on life.

Looking out the front window, I saw a Christmas tree in the neighbor's house. It was lit up with blinking lights. I wanted to smile at the memory of happy times, but I just stared at the tree, mesmerized by the rhythm of colored lights winking on and off.

Bobbie and I loved spending the holiday together. It was a reason for gifts and treats, food, and friends. Christmas was also a wonderful time of year with the snow making everything seem wondrous. It wasn't going to be that this year.

I'm not a religious man. The meaning of Christmas was never anything more than an excuse to get together with family and trade gifts. I haven't prayed since I was in elementary school, and my mother made me. In the worst times of my life, I didn't think once about praying.

But that night, staring at that blinking Christmas tree, I thought about asking God to take care of Bobbie. Maybe if I could just bring myself to get on my knees and beg him to look after her, I could find some peace in my own life.

The more I thought about an all-powerful God protecting my wife, the further my mood soured.

If he could take care of her, then he was probably the reason she was taken from me. At a minimum, he let the accident happen. That's what all-powerful meant, right? That he could affect the outcome of our lives.

Why would he let her die? She never hurt anyone. She did the exact opposite of that. She wanted to help people, always reaching out to help those in need and putting herself second. Why would God let something horrible happen to someone like that?

Across the street, that fucking Christmas tree continued to blink its stupid lights.

I jumped off the couch and closed the curtains with a yank.

23

My desk phone rang. I picked it up after the first ring. "Nash!" I yelled into the phone.

I awoke without another song. That was five days now. Something had happened to Bobbie, I knew it. I mean, something already happened to her, but the loss of the songs had to mean something. It had to, but what if it didn't? I didn't want to think like that anymore.

No matter how much I tried to convince myself the songs had been a trick of my subconscious, the irrational side of me won out.

I was afraid to go to sleep for fear of waking up without a song. When I woke up without the music in my head, I was immediately irritable.

"Dallas?"

"Yeah."

"You okay?"

It was Annie from dispatch.

"Bad night of sleep."

"Sorry to hear that. I was calling to let you know Officer Jarvis is bringing in a woman on a drug charge. He thinks you should talk with her before he books."

"Do you know why?"

"No. I was only asked to alert you that he's on his way in with her."

***

Officer Ken Jarvis had been in the department as long as I had, but he was a patrol lifer. He never wanted to leave the street. He declined opportunities to take advancement tests. He even passed on offers to be in a neighborhood resource officer position. At different points in his career, he'd been on both SWAT and Crowd Control. He took the job more seriously than anyone I knew and loved the brotherhood of officers. To him, the department was truly family.

He stood about 5'10" and was lean and wiry. He walked up to my cubicle and hit my shoulder with the back of his hand.

"Hey, desk jockey, working on your secretarial spread?"

I looked up at his smiling face. A black beanie cap was pulled down to almost his eyebrows, covering what I knew was a bald scalp.

"Heard you brought me a present. What's the scoop?"

"Female suspect in interview room one. She was arrested for shoplifting at The General Store by their loss prevention officer. When he searched her purse following the arrest, he found meth. They called us because it was outside the scope of their limited commission."

"I'm waiting for the punch line. How does this involve me?"

"When I got there, I searched her again and checked her purse. She was in possession of a driver's license and credit card in the name of Hamilton Martin. That's your homicide victim, right?"

Jarvis pulled out a plastic bag from his back pocket and unrolled it with a flick of his wrist. Inside were Hamilton Martin's driver's license and credit card.

I stood and took the bag from him. "Okay, you've got my attention."

"You mean you actually want to do some police work and give the citizens of Spokane some value for their taxes?" He grinned. "You don't want to finish your solitaire game first?"

***

Her left hand was handcuffed to the detention railing that ran the length of the room. Her head lay on her right arm, and she'd fallen asleep. When I entered the room, she didn't move. I closed the door with enough noise to wake her, but not to be a jerk. I didn't want to start the interview off on the wrong foot.

As I sat across from her, she raised her head. Her left eye was blackened, and there was an abrasion on her face that had started to heal. She looked strung out and smelled like she hadn't showered in days. I put the file folder to my right and the yellow pad of paper in front of me. I kept the pen in my hand.

"I'm Detective Nash. This interview is being recorded, both audio and video." I pointed to a camera on the wall, and her eyes followed my pen. "What's your name?"

"Those aren't my drugs."

"I didn't ask about drugs," I said. "I asked for your name."

Her lip curled, and she challenged me with silence, but only for a moment. Then the lip uncurled, and her face softened. "April Scott."

"April, did anyone read you your Miranda warnings when you were brought in here?"

"What's that?"

"Your rights while in custody. You know, they start 'You have the right to remain silent.'"

"Yeah, they read them to me."

"Okay," I said and made a note. "I'm going to reread them just to make sure." I pulled a Miranda Rights Warning card from the file and read them word for word. When I was done, I asked, "Do you understand these rights as I have read them?"

"Yeah."

"Do you agree to waive your rights and talk with me?"

"Yeah, I guess."

"Please sign and date the card where appropriate."

April rattled the cuff on her left hand and watched me expectantly. I stood and unlocked the handcuffs. She rubbed her wrist for a moment. She then picked up the pen and signed the card—with her right hand.

When she was done, she dropped the pen and noticed my look of incredulity. "What?"

"Nothing," I said and tucked the card into the file. "Let's get started. Where do you live?"

"I don't have a home."

"Where do you sleep?"

"Where I can. Couch surf, mostly. Kindness of strangers, that sort of thing."

I jotted her answers on the tablet before continuing. "You mentioned drugs."

"I did? When?"

"When I started this interview, you said the drugs weren't yours."

"Oh. Right."

"What drugs were you talking about?"

"The stuff they found at the store."

"What kind of drugs did they find?" I asked.

She shrugged. "I don't know."

"Do you use meth, April?"

"No."

"You've been arrested before with meth, right?"

"That wasn't mine, either."

"You're jumpy. Your skin is yellowed. Your teeth are damaged. It looks like meth use to me."

She shook her head. "I'm hyperactive."

I studied her for a few seconds. She tried to match my eyes, but hers bounced all over the place. "How did the drugs get in your purse?"

"I don't know. I was at a party. Someone probably hid them in my purse."

"Where was this party?"

"I don't remember."

"When was the party?"

"Last night."

"Who were you with at the party?"

"I was by myself."

"How did you get to this party?"

"I caught a ride."

"With who?"

"I don't remember."

"How did you get the black eye and the scrapes on your face?"

"Someone hit me at the party."

"Who?"

"I don't remember."

"You don't remember, or you don't know them? That's a big distinction."

"I didn't know them."

For a couple of minutes, I wrote on my notepad. The silence of the room worked on April as she fidgeted the entire time.

"Reviewing my notes, I want to make sure I get this correct. An unknown person assaulted you at a party you went to by yourself. Is that correct?"

April nodded. "Uh-huh. Yeah."

"But you can't tell me where this party was?"

"That's right."

"And while you were there, someone slipped drugs into your purse?"

"Yeah. Yeah, that's right."

"To get to this party, you got a ride with someone you can't remember. Obviously, they must have known you to give you a ride to a party. They knew you, right?"

"No, they didn't know me. We just met."

"Where did you meet?"

April bit her lip before answering. "I don't remember."

"Was it a man or a woman?"

"Man. I mean, woman."

I sighed. I didn't feel like playing the game anymore. "What part of anything you just said was the truth?"

"It's all the truth."

"Fine. Let me ask you a different question. Do you know Hamilton Martin?"

Recognition flashed in her eyes before she quickly masked it with indifference. "Who?"

"Hamilton Martin. You've met him before," I said. "I'm absolutely positive about that."

She shrugged. "No clue. Never heard of the guy."

"How'd you know it was a guy?"

Panic flashed in April's eyes. "What?"

"How did you know Hamilton was a guy?"

"It's a guy's name," she said, the panic slowly ebbing away.

"Maybe, maybe not. Who knows in today's world?"

"You ever hear of a woman named Hamilton?" April said.

I let her have that one. "His driver's license and credit card were found in your purse." I pulled a photocopy of Martin's driver's license and credit card from the folder and placed it on the table.

April glanced at it and returned her eyes to me. "Maybe he put them in there at that party. Maybe the drugs are his, too."

"Does that even sound reasonable?"

"Yes." Tears formed in her eyes, and her face transformed into sadness.

"Don't start the tears. I don't believe them."

She wiped her eyes with the back of her free hand, and her look hardened again.

"Let me tell you about Hamilton Martin," I said. "He was sixty-one years old—an electrician. On Tuesday night, he was found murdered in a vacant lot. Somebody stole his truck. Move to today, and here we sit after his driver's license and credit card were found in your purse. There is no way he could have put them into your purse last night when he's been dead for a week."

Her eyes were still wet, but the tears had stopped. "I didn't kill him," she said, her voice defiant. Her voice still shook, but she was trying to force some conviction into it.

"You were found with his driver's license and credit card. I think you were involved. You might even have been the person who killed him."

"I didn't."

"This is a yes or no question. Did you have Hamilton Martin's driver's license in your purse?"

Pause.

"It's a simple question with a simple answer," I insisted. "Did you have his driver's license in your purse?"

"Yes."

"And did you have Hamilton Martin's VISA card in your purse?"

"Yes."

"Did you kill Hamilton Martin?"

"No!"

"Give me a reason to believe you."

"You just have to."

"It doesn't work like that."

"I didn't kill that man."

"But you knew his ID and credit card were in your purse?"

"No."

"You just said they were in your purse. Stick with the truth for a few minutes. Can you do that? You knew the driver's license and credit card were in your purse?"

"Yes."

"You knew the meth was in your purse."

She nodded her head.

"By the nod, I'm assuming that means yes?"

"Yes."

"How did you get the credit card and driver's license?"

"I found them."

"Okay, we're back to lying."

"No, I'm not!"

"One more lie, and I'll end this interview and book you."

"For what?"

"For the meth and the murder. I've got enough now."

"I didn't kill him."

"Then tell me the truth. Show me you can do that."

She sat quietly, looking for a way out. None was coming.

"Did he pick you up?"

"What?"

"Were you working when Martin picked you up?"

"Are you saying I'm a prostitute?"

"I ran your record before walking in here. You've got a history of prostitution and drug possession. It doesn't seem like a stretch to think Martin might have picked you up."

"You're an asshole."

"Yeah," I said and pushed my chair back as I stood.

"Where are you going?" Her voice raised with panic.

"I'm done. All you do is lie. It's making my head hurt. The officer will be in shortly to book you."

My hand was on the doorknob when she said, "My boyfriend did it."

"What's your boyfriend's name?"

"I don't remember. He was a trick."

I studied her face, searching for the truth. Knowing it wasn't there, I said, "We're done."

I opened the door.

"Wait!" she screamed. "I'm sorry."

Officer Jarvis stepped in. "Need help?"

"Hang on for a sec," I said under my breath to Jarvis. To April, I asked, "You were saying?"

"My boyfriend."

"His name?"

"Tony."

"Not good enough."

She lowered her head. "Tony Lawrence."

"Tony Lawrence," I repeated and stepped back to my chair. Jarvis shut the door, presumably to return to the viewing monitor in the neighboring room. I wrote the boyfriend's supposed name on my notepad. "What did Tony do?"

"He killed him."

"Why did he kill Hamilton Martin?"

April was quiet, her eyes bouncing as she thought.

"April, you've got one chance to come clean. Why did your boyfriend kill Hamilton Martin?"

She looked up at me, angry. When she spoke, her words were fast and clipped. "Tony and I were arguing, and he was real mad. We were on the side of the road, and he was hitting and slapping me. Some old guy stopped his truck, got out, and ran over to us. He yelled at Tony to knock it off. Tony had me by the hair and told the old guy to stay out of it."

"Is that really how he said it?"

April sneered. "He told him to 'mind your own fucking business.'"

"What happened next?"

"The old guy grabbed Tony and punched him in the stomach. Told him to leave me alone."

"Did it end there?"

"No. When the guy asked me if I was okay, Tony stood up and stabbed him in the throat with his knife."

"How did Tony stab him?"

"He came up behind him and—" She then mimed an overhead knife attack just like the medical examiner had shown me. A B-movie attack had killed Hamilton Martin, and April Scott just confirmed it.

"What did you do?"

"I told Tony that he shouldn't have done that."

"Uh-huh."

"Tony went through the guy's pockets and took his car keys and wallet. He stole his coat, and then we took off in his truck."

"Why take the coat?"

She paused a moment before answering. "He didn't have one. He was cold."

"Who drove the truck?"

"Tony. He drove. I think he still has it."

"Where does Tony live?"

"In those apartments near where the fight happened. I don't exactly know the address. If I did, I would tell you."

I nodded. "Okay. What color are the apartments?"

"Red with black trim."

For a couple of moments, I finished making notes and stood.

"What's going on?"

"I'm going to make sure you're telling the truth about something."

I stepped out of the interview room and locked the door behind me. I started toward my desk, but Jarvis hollered for me. He was seated at a general use computer provided for patrol officers whenever they used an interview room.

I leaned down to look over his shoulder. Jarvis had run Anthony Lawrence's name through the system and already had the response on the screen. He tapped the monitor with his index finger.

"His address is there on Nevada. That's an apartment building with red and black coloring."

I raised my eyebrows.

"Your girl finally told the truth," Jarvis said.

"Let's go tell her what she won," I said.

Both of us headed back to the interview room. When we stepped inside, I instructed her to stand up, and Jarvis cuffed her hands behind her back.

"What's happening?" April asked.

"You're going to be booked."

"For what?"

"Possession of meth and first-degree robbery, for starters."

"Robbery?"

"You had Hamilton Martin's driver's license and VISA card. You were there when he was killed. I'm not sure if it was you that killed him, but you might have, and you might have stolen the truck. I'm still working on that."

"That's not fair. I told you who did this."

"You were involved, April. You could have reported it. You should have."

Her face turned red. Hatred was evident in her eyes.

"I have just one final question."

"What?"

"Did you feel bad about Hamilton?"

She squinted and said, "He should have known better than to get involved."

***

While Officer Jarvis booked April Scott into jail for Possession of a Controlled Substance and First-Degree Robbery, I completed the arrest report. I also reviewed Anthony Lawrence's criminal record.

He was thirty-four years old, with fourteen prior convictions. Assault. Theft. Malicious Mischief. A DOL search revealed a suspended driver's license. He had an outstanding warrant for failing to appear in court on a Driving with a Suspended License charge. Tony Lawrence was a real winner.

***

It took me fifteen minutes to run over to the apartments listed as his last known address. I asked for a backup officer to meet me there. They were several minutes out, and I decided I didn't want to wait just to find out he wasn't home. I knocked repeatedly, but no one came to the door.

I stopped by the manager's office and knocked on that door as well. No one bothered answering there either.

I canceled the officer responding for backup and cleared the scene.

When I returned to the department, I contacted the patrol lieutenant and passed along the information on Anthony "Tony" Lawrence. I could have done it with a digital blast and have all the teams read it at their briefings, but I still believed in doing it the old-fashioned way. That was the way I learned it coming up through the department, and I preferred it. A face-to-face with the team leader was still my favorite way to pass along important information. Ask them to push it down to the sergeants and the team.

I don't know if it was more efficient, but it always made me feel better.

24

I stood at her grave, my hands in my pockets. It was a cold morning, barely over fifteen degrees. My beanie cap was pulled down over my ears.

I'd been there for ten minutes, but I hadn't said anything yet.

An older woman in a long wool coat stood at a nearby grave, maybe twenty feet away. I could hear her mumbling.

I'd already flicked away the new snow from Bobbie's marker, and I was now studying it. My jaw flexed as I thought.

There were so many things I wanted to say, but all of them made me sound weak, and I was tired of sounding that way.

Even though I was emotionally and physically exhausted, it took me hours to get to sleep last night. Before that, I'd tried to pack up her clothes, but the more I looked at them, the angrier I got. I kicked a pile of them away from me, sending them showering across the room. I knew I was losing it.

I went to sleep in the living room but had to close the curtains so I wouldn't see that blinking Christmas tree across the street. Suddenly, I hated those neighbors.

The woman a few graves away murmured some more. Now she was crying. Could she just shut up? Why was she so irritating this morning?

Sleep was elusive, and when I awoke, I immediately knew the one thing I feared the most. I hadn't gotten a song that morning. If the morning songs were really my subconscious at work, I wouldn't be applying so much importance to them, right? I would know it was some sort of lark. Therefore, they had to be from her. They had to be important. It was that simple.

I wanted to say my piece, but I could feel the anger boiling inside me. This wasn't how I wanted to talk to her, to the love of my life.

If Bobbie knew I loved her, why was she treating me this way?

My body shook for a moment, but not from the cold.

Why was she holding the songs back? Did something happen to her? Or did I do something to offend her? That had to be it. She was mad at me for something. She would do this occasionally, but at least I could talk to her then, figure out why she was upset. Now, all I could do was stare at her headstone—that cold, stupid piece of granite. It stared back at me in a mocking silence.

"Send me a fucking song!"

I stood there for a moment with my fists clenched and my jaw flexing. I was waiting for an answer that would never come.

"Damn it," I yelled and opened my hands. I ran my gloved hands over my face.

When I realized the nearby mumbling had stopped, I looked at the woman. She was staring at me, eyes wide and mouth agape. Her hand clutched her coat around her throat.

"What are you looking at?" I hollered.

I turned and walked back to my car.

25

"I tried boxing your clothes up again," I said. "It didn't go well."

She didn't answer. I took that as a good sign after my meltdown yesterday. I still wanted to talk with her, though, as it made me feel connected.

"Your clothes are spread around the room, kind of the way we used to fold the laundry. I cleaned up the pile I kicked yesterday. I'm sorry for doing that. I need to finish the process or at least put them back where they belong. I don't have much motivation to do it either way. In the end, it doesn't matter, does it? The only one the mess would bother is you."

There wasn't any new snow that day, but the cold was still bitter. It was mid-morning, and the temperature hadn't made it past twenty degrees.

I stared at her headstone, listening to the silence. Somewhere in the distance, a dog barked, and a car honked its horn.

"This morning, I woke up with that heavy guitar intro to 'Outshined' in my head. Do you remember that grunge song from Soundgarden? The one about looking

California, but feeling Minnesota? Yeah, you hated it because it's such an angry song. Bad energy, you used to say. I'm not sure why that's the song I got after so many days of silence, but I'll take it. Hell, I'd take a New Kids on the Block song, to be honest."

I shoved my hands deeper into my pockets. The cold was biting, and I hadn't prepared for it. I was so happy after waking up with a song in my head that I dressed quickly and ran out the door to see Bobbie.

"It was nice to add something to the list again. Have I told you about the list? I started keeping it a couple of weeks ago. I got freaked out when I went this many days without a song, just seeing the list every morning and not putting something new on it. It didn't help out my mental state. I'll tell you that."

I stamped my feet to generate some warmth.

"Are you sending these songs to me? I mean, that's sort of stupid to ask, and I wouldn't believe in that stuff normally, but it feels like you're doing it. I know that sounds crazy. I'm not crazy, right? I mean, I'm standing here talking with you, and that must look crazy, but there's a difference between looking crazy and being crazy. Yeah, I know, I yelled at you yesterday, and that had to look crazy to that poor woman."

I looked across the cemetery and its line of stones, then back to her.

"You know, I almost cried this morning when I woke to that song. That's the weird part, right? I've never believed in any of this afterlife stuff before, and suddenly I'm holding onto it like it's a life preserver. Well, you get it, right? What's it all mean? Maybe I'm willing to believe now."

I glanced around to see if anyone could hear my rambling. The cell phone in my pocket vibrated, taking me away from her.

26

When I arrived at the department, Anthony Lawrence was seated in interview room three. He was handcuffed to the railing, just like April Scott had been. I watched him on the video monitor as the arresting officer, Lee Sheets, gave me the rundown on how he located him.

"It wasn't hard," Sheets said. "I simply watched his apartment while I did my paperwork. I parked in the lot of the apartment complex. It was blatant. I wasn't even hiding. He came wandering up without a care in the world. When I approached him, though, he bolted. I caught him before he could get out of the parking lot."

Lee was a tall, skinny officer whose passion was competing in marathons. Any suspect running from him had no way of knowing they'd lost the race before they even started.

"Did he say why he ran?"

"He knew he had a warrant. He didn't even try to fight."

"Does he know why he's in the interview room?"

Sheets shook his head. "I told him I needed to grab some paperwork before I booked him. He told me to take my time."

I leaned closer to the monitor. "For a guy sought in connection to a murder investigation, he seems rather calm, doesn't he?"

"That's what I was thinking."

***

I could smell the funk as soon as I entered the small room. It was times like this I wished for better ventilation in the tiny interview rooms.

Anthony Lawrence wore a beaten leather jacket with the right pocket torn and dangling. His blue jeans were old and dirty, and his combat boots were scuffed and unlaced, the tongue folded over on itself. His long, greasy hair was pulled back into a ponytail, but a lot of it had escaped in his run from Officer Sheets, and it now drooped in front of his face.

His eyes followed me as I sat and opened my folder.

"I'm Detective Nash. This interview is being videotaped." I pointed to the camera on the far wall. "Both audio and video."

"Interview?"

"Were your Miranda rights read when they arrested you?"

"Wait. What's going on?"

I pulled out a Miranda card and recited the warnings. He stared blankly at me while I spoke. "Do you understand these rights as I've just read them?"

"Yeah, I've heard them before."

"Will you sign the card—"

"I'm not signing shit. Tell me what's going on."

I tucked the card into my file. His rights were read on video, but he hadn't waived them. I had to be careful about how I approached this questioning.

I leaned back and crossed my arms, studying his face for a moment before saying, "We've arrested your girlfriend."

"Who?"

That wasn't the reaction I was wanted. "April Scott," I said.

"Scotty?" He laughed. "That bitch ain't my girlfriend. She's a drunken hook-up at best."

Now, that was precisely the opposite of the reaction I was hoping for. I leaned forward and picked up my pen. "She tells a different story."

"Of course she does. Bitches always do." He leaned back, not afraid of anything this moment represented. "What's she accusing me of?"

"Why do you think she's accusing you of something?"

"I'm sitting here with you. The only trouble I've got is a failure to appear warrant, and I take full responsibility for it—mea culpa and all that bullshit. Besides, you know as well as I do, you'll book me, and I'll appear before a judge tomorrow morning. I'll be released by noon. Easy-peasy. So if Scotty is accusing me of something, I'm not saying anything further until I know what this is all about."

"Where were you on the night of Sunday, November twenty-sixth?"

"The fuck if I know."

"It's important that you remember."

"Why?"

"We believe you were part of a homicide."

He grinned. "She said I killed someone? Nice."

"You don't seem worried."

"I'm not. I didn't kill no one."

"If you didn't," I said, pulling out the Miranda warning card, "then you've got nothing to worry about. I need to ask you some questions. Mind signing this, so we can make it official?"

Tony moved his lips from side to side as he thought. Finally, he waved the card over to him and mimed a pen. He didn't bother faking me out to unhook his left hand as

April had. Instead, he signed his name on the warning card and slid it back to me, along with the pen.

"Thank you."

"Anything to get me outta here quicker."

"April was found in possession of some of the victim's belongings," I said.

"That's on her, then."

I attempted a ruse. "Your fingerprints were on some of those items."

Tony's smile returned. "No, they weren't. You need to work on your bluff. You play poker? If you do, I wanna play with you."

My heart began to race. He wasn't scared or even slightly concerned.

"She said you stole the victim's truck."

"I didn't take anything connected to any murder. She told me she had a new truck, though. Said some guy just gave it to her."

"Why would a guy give her a truck?"

"Come on, man. When Scotty needs something, she sucks dick. Guys give her things in exchange for that. Some guys let her stay with them. Others give cash or other goods."

"You think a guy gave her a truck for some sex?"

"Man, Scotty's good at what she does. It's amazing what guys will give to get."

"It doesn't bother you that she's a prostitute?"

"Quit trying to push her on me like she's my girlfriend. She's just a girl to roll around with now and then."

"You pay her?"

"Not with money, but, yeah, I pay her. It ain't love. Why do you think it has to be that way?"

"How do you pay her?"

"Will I get in trouble if I say?"

"It depends on what we are talking about."

"I can't say. Self-incrimination and such."

"Are we talking drugs?"

Tony smiled and shrugged at the same time.

I sighed. "I care about murder. I don't care that you gave her drugs in return for her services."

"Yeah, that's what I did. Drugs for services."

"What drug?"

He stared at me, waiting for my further affirmation.

"Again, I don't care that you gave her something. I'm trying to solve a murder. She had a drug in her purse. I'm looking to connect dots."

"I gave her meth."

"Thank you for that honesty. I appreciate it."

Tony nodded. "You're welcome."

"Why did you kill Hamilton Martin? Did she ask you to do it?"

He laughed. "Don't try to pin a murder on me. It isn't going to work." He shook his head at me. "I bet you grin like a Cheshire cat when you have a full house, don't you?"

"Why don't you tell me where you were on the night of the murder?"

"What day was that?"

"Sunday. November twenty-sixth."

He thought about it. "Shit, man. I don't know. I could have been anywhere."

"What did you do with the murder weapon?"

He smacked the table with his free hand. "What murder weapon? You want me to say, 'I don't have a gun' so you can say 'I didn't say anything about a gun?' Like I said, guy, I didn't kill nobody. You're barking up the wrong tree."

"Where do you live?"

"Why?"

"I'd like to search your house."

His face grew serious. "What if I give you consent right now?"

"You'd do that?"

"Yes. If we can deal."

"Deal on what?"

"You'll find some drugs. Not the legal stuff, either. Just possession level. I'm not dealing, I swear. If you're willing to look the other way on that stuff, I'll sign whatever paperwork you want."

"I can't look the other way." His face fell, but I wanted to save myself a lot of paperwork and legwork. "I can offer this, though. Whatever drugs I find, if it's possession level, I will impound, put on property, and destroy. I can't leave it there, but I won't charge you with anything. I want to find a murderer, not a drug dealer or a drug user. Deal?"

His confident smile returned. "You got a deal, Detective." He looked up at the camera. "You've got this recorded. We've got a legally binding verbal agreement."

I left the interview room for a moment but soon returned with a Consent to Search card. Tony filled it in, put his address on it, and signed his name. He slid the card back to me. His signature was big and loopy, full of self-assurance.

"There are drugs in a coffee can, under the sink. There's also some weed tucked into the side pocket of the recliner, but that shit's legal now, so that's a freebie, right? If not, it's cool. I can always get more. The officer took my keys when they arrested me," he said as I started toward the door. His face brightened now that he'd removed all risk of being caught for the drugs. "Should we shake on our deal?" he said, extending his free hand.

"We're going to hold you here until I get back."

"In that case, can I get a cup of coffee while I wait?"

***

I met Officer Pauleen Sherman at the Pinewood Terrance Apartments. They were an older set of apartments about half a mile from where Hamilton Martin's body was found.

"We gotta stop meeting like this," she said, with no hint of humor.

I showed her the Consent to Search card signed by Tony Lawrence.

"Looks fine. What do you need me to do?"

"Be my partner and witness. When we get done, I need you to write a report about what we did and found. If it's nothing, so be it."

"Let's hope it's nothing."

I stared at her.

"So, what are we looking for?"

"A red ski coat with gray shoulders and a knife. Potentially, there will be blood on it. The blade will be roughly an inch wide. Look for any clothing with blood on it. There's also supposed to be a coffee can under the sink with drugs in it. I'll take care of it and put it on property."

"It's the least you could do," Sherman said.

I thought about saying something about her attitude and, by the look on her face, she was itching for me to do just that. Instead, I shut my mouth and opened the front door.

We entered the apartment. I was surprised by how tidy the place was, despite the stench. It reeked of body odor and other, unidentifiable funk, but it looked like Tony tried to keep a clean apartment.

"Better than most places I see," Sherman said as she stepped past me.

After we cleared the apartment, I opened a window for some fresh air, and we searched the kitchen. I quickly found the coffee can and packages of meth. The quantity was on the borderline of possession and distribution, but I didn't want to push that argument. Tony and I had a deal, and he'd kept his end of the bargain. In the side pocket of the recliner, I found a small bag of marijuana. I lifted it, examined the small amount inside, then shoved it back into the pocket.

We searched the rest of the apartment but didn't find anything else. Tony knew he had nothing to fear from us searching.

I stood in the middle of the apartment with my hands on my hips. "Damn."

***

Barry called while I was at the property room, logging the meth for destruction.

"Want to grab a beer?"

"Tonight?" I said.

Barry laughed. "No, it's Sunday. I'm talking another night. I promised you that I'd reach out and make plans."

I almost said no but caught myself. "Can we do it tomorrow night?"

"Sounds good."

"Can I pick the place?" I asked.

27

Terrance and Cheryl Williams lived on West Point Road with a view overlooking the Spokane River. I set the appointment with them to let them know we were taking a fresh look at their daughter's case.

It was shortly after noon when Terrance met me at the door. He was in his early seventies, fully bald, and slightly overweight. He stood almost 6'2" with a softening midsection. He smiled, even though the concern was evident in his eyes.

"Come in, Detective. Get out of the cold."

"Thank you, Mr. Williams. I appreciate the time."

"Please, call me Terry. Cheryl will be with us shortly. She's in the kitchen."

We sat in the living room, which had older, well-maintained furnishings. Jennifer's high school picture was on the fireplace mantel next to a burning candle.

"On the phone, you said there was something you wanted to talk to us about. Something about Jennifer's case?"

Cheryl Williams walked into the room. Also, in her early seventies, she had short, well-styled hair. She wore pressed pants and a light-colored sweater. They were still a professional couple, even in retirement.

"This is more of a courtesy visit than anything. I've been asked to take a look at your daughter's file. As you know, we never closed it."

Terry's smile faded as he nodded. "Yes, we know." Cheryl slid her hand into Terry's.

"Occasionally," I explained, "we will open old files to get a fresh set of eyes on them. Sometimes new leads pop up. Sometimes, technology will change, leading us to a new piece of evidence."

"Is there new evidence?" Cheryl asked, leaning in with hope.

"No, ma'am. I'm sorry. There's not."

Terry said, "Why did you come and tell us this, Detective? Why not go about your business and, if you found something, then let us know?"

"That's a fair question, and another detective may have done just that. However, Spokane's a small town. If I were to start asking questions of someone and you were to find out somehow, wouldn't you want to know why I was asking those questions? You wouldn't want to be surprised by it, would you? Especially if the media somehow found out we were investigating again. I've got nothing against them, but it would make for a story. I thought you would want to be out in front instead of reacting to it."

They looked at each other before nodding in agreement.

"Can I ask you some questions?"

"Sure," Terry said. Cheryl nodded.

"When did you move to this house?"

"Oh, about a year after Jennifer…" Terry trailed off, then began again. "We just couldn't stand living in that house on the hill anymore—too many memories of her. Everything hurt so bad. Even the good memories."

Cheryl put her hand on Terry's arm as he spoke.

"It was tough to do, but I believe it was the right choice for our marriage."

"Losing Jennifer was stressful on us," Cheryl said. "I don't know if you can imagine that."

"I can," I said.

"We've been here since then. We have no interest in moving elsewhere. I was in the insurance industry for almost forty years. I sold my book of business about five years ago and retired. Not long after, Cheryl retired as a grade school teacher."

"Thirty years was a long time," Cheryl said.

"After Jennifer's death, did you suspect anyone?"

Both shook their heads.

"What about her boyfriend?"

"Johnny?"

"Yes, ma'am. Johnny McCoy."

"No. He was such a sweet kid. Always so nice to us. He and Jennifer always seemed so good together. He still stops by and sees us occasionally. Even sends us a Christmas card every year. He's done well for himself and his family."

"Did Jennifer ever mention another possible boyfriend?"

Terry's brow furrowed. "Another boyfriend?"

"Yes, sir. We have witnesses who say another male was claiming to be Jennifer's boyfriend at the time."

"She was only dating Johnny," Cheryl said, confusion clear in her voice.

"Do we know this person?" Terry asked.

"Have you ever heard the name Eddie Henning?"

"Eddie Henning," Terry said. "Eddie Henning. No, can't say I have."

"We never heard of this kid before. Was he interviewed after...?" Cheryl asked.

"No, ma'am. This is new information."

Terry leaned forward. "Do you think this Eddie Henning had something to do with it?"

I shrugged. "I'm looking into him. It's an interesting lead. If I find out something, I'll let you know."

"Detective, please don't let him get away with it any longer," Cheryl said.

"I'm sorry if I gave the impression it's a certainty he was involved. At this point, it's only a lead."

"You look like a nice man," Cheryl said. "I know you'll get him."

"Eddie Henning," Terry muttered. "Never heard of him."

28

As I drove back to the station, the song I awoke to that morning ran through my mind. I skipped visiting Bobbie that morning because I was upset over the song.

Skid Row's "I Remember You" was a sappy ballad I never dug when we were in high school. Bobbie loved it. She was really into pop music, and whenever the bands I liked came out with something even close to a ballad, she jumped on it.

We danced to it, walked to it, and even made love to it while we were in college. She really dug that song.

After a time, she stopped listening to it, moving on to newer pop music.

When I woke up to the lyrics in my head this morning, it felt like she was talking directly to me. I fell out of bed to my hands and knees and cried.

The song had to be from her. I was convinced now.

I didn't think I needed to see her headstone for her to know how I felt.

The police radio crackled, pulling me from my reflection. "*Adam two twenty-six, code six!*"

An officer calling a code six meant backup was requested and to step up the response.

The dispatcher immediately jumped on the radio and announced, "*Code six at Boone and A, Adam two twenty-six. Code six.*"

Two units jumped on immediately and stated they were headed toward Adam-226.

I grabbed my microphone and keyed it. "Ida-25, five blocks away."

The dispatcher acknowledged my transmission. I pulled a U-turn, mashed the accelerator, and heard the engine whine in protest.

"Put me out with him," I said.

As I pulled up, Officer Lee Sheets had a white male pressed up against the back of a car. The suspect was fighting to get free, but Sheets was doing his best to control him. He moved to get a neck restraint in place, but the suspect wriggled free, and the fight was on again. The suspect obviously had some martial arts training and was using everything he had to escape.

I applied the brakes, turned the wheel, and jammed the car into Park. Within seconds, I was out of the car and running toward Sheets. Along with Sheets, I grabbed the suspect and pushed him harder into the car.

The guy screamed, "Police brutality!"

Sheets looked at me and rolled his eyes. He then concentrated on the suspect's wrists and got a pair of handcuffs around them.

He grabbed his shoulder microphone and said, "Adam two twenty-six, code four. One in custody."

"Police brutality," the suspect yelled again.

Sheets walked him back to his car and placed him in the back seat. The suspect turned to Sheets and started to yell something. Sheets slammed the door before he could get it out.

"What was that all about?" I asked.

"I pulled him over for running a stop sign. Once I got to him, he started freaking out. Yelling and screaming. As soon as I called for a backup, he got out of his car. He wouldn't follow my commands and was getting more and more belligerent. Dude's whacked out."

"You okay?"

Sheets nodded. "Just another day, right?"

"You need any more help?"

"From a desk jockey?" Sheets said with a wink. "Besides, I'm already going to take a ration of shit for calling code six with this guy. Get out of here before you make me look worse."

I patted him on the shoulder before getting into my car and continuing towards the station.

29

We met at the Lantern, a small bar in the Perry District, where the seating capacity was roughly twenty people.

The Perry District had enjoyed a period of gentrification over the past decade. Before that, it was an area of town abandoned by retailers and young families. It had been taken over by the poor and, unfortunately, a criminal element. Slowly, businesses started to cluster around Perry Street, bringing a modern menu of bars, eateries, and retailers, including salons, yoga studios, and the occasional hemp clothing store. The Lantern had been one of the earlier entrants to the rebirth of the neighborhood.

"I've never been here before," Barry said.

We grabbed a table for two in the corner.

Eddie Henning was behind the bar pouring a beer. He saw us sit but didn't recognize me. I was in blue jeans, a puffy blue winter jacket, and my Seattle Mariners baseball hat.

When Henning came over, he greeted us with, "Good evening, gentlemen. What can I get you?"

Barry concentrated on the beer menu while I made eye contact with Henning.

"I'll have the red ale."

When Henning recognized me, his eyes widened before turning to Barry. "And you?"

"Make that two," he said, dropping the menu on the table.

Henning stepped behind the bar and started the beers, stealing glances at us while he worked.

"Feeling any better since getting back to work?"

I looked at my friend and smiled. He was trying to reconnect. "The distraction is welcome, but it doesn't make the hurt any less."

"I went through that after we found out about Ella's death. Work was what I poured myself into so I could deal with my feelings."

Henning brought the two beers to our table and placed them quickly. He left without a word.

A young couple at the bar finished paying their tab. When they stood to put on their coats, I said, "Why don't we move to the bar?"

"Okay, I guess."

I grabbed my beer and sat on the middle seat. Barry took the place that put him against the wall.

Henning watched with displeasure as we traded seats. He finished a drink order and delivered it to a table. He made small talk with the other patrons for a few minutes.

"Do you remember that case I told you I was working?"

"The one from high school?"

"Yeah. The kid who bragged to us…"

"About being the boyfriend? Yeah, I remember."

"He's the bartender."

Barry looked over my shoulder at Henning while he chatted with some other patrons. "Shut up."

"Truth," I said.

"Is that why you picked this place?"

I put my hand around my beer but didn't drink from it.

Barry shook his head and faced his beer. He muttered, "This was supposed to be our time."

Henning came back to the bar and grabbed a rag. He wiped down the counter and surveyed the establishment, ignoring us.

Barry and I sat quietly, watching Henning. Finally, Henning made eye contact with me and asked, "To what do I owe this visit, Detective?"

"Just wanted a beer with a friend."

"In my bar?"

"Yeah," I said and pushed my untasted beer away.

"A couple of days after we've met?"

"What can I say?"

"That's kind of a coincidence, don't you think?"

I smiled. "You got me. It's not a coincidence. I hoped you'd be working, but I do believe in coincidences. I've seen it numerous times in my line of work. You can call it luck, or you can call it divine intervention. Name it whatever you want, but sometimes, things happen that make us scratch our heads. When it's in our favor, though, we must realize our good fortune and say thank you to the man upstairs."

As soon as the words came out of my mouth, I realized how hypocritical I sounded after getting mad at God and a blinking Christmas tree.

Henning glanced between Barry and me. "And what is the real coincidence in this circumstance?"

"You and I met in high school."

"I doubt that."

"Truth."

"Prove it."

"Ever cruise Riverside?"

Eddie's suspicions remained. "Yeah."

"You used to drive a white Datsun B210, right? Had it tricked out with a new stereo for a while. Pioneer, I think."

"It was definitely a Pioneer," Barry said. Henning glanced at Barry, who lowered his eyes to his beer, taking a sip.

"My friend," I said, bringing Henning's attention back to me, "and I occasionally cruised with his brother, who you were friends with. Randy McKenzie."

"Randy McKenzie?" Recognition flashed in his eyes.

"My brother," Barry said and took another sip of beer, refusing to look up now.

"One night, we ran into you at Dick's Hamburgers. Randy introduced us to you. We all hung out and checked out your new stereo. Remember?"

Henning wiped his mouth as he watched me.

"You had that crazy mullet back then. Wavy in the back, short in the front. Remember that?"

"I remember it. Yeesh," Barry said. Another sip, no eye contact.

Henning studied me carefully now.

"Do you remember what you told us that night about a girl sitting on one of the tables? She was pretty, a real looker. Do you remember her?"

Henning shook his head slowly.

"You said you were dating her. That you were her boyfriend."

"I don't remember that. I would never have said that."

"I do. So does he."

"You definitely said it. I heard it." Barry took another sip and then a second. No eye contact, and he fought back a nervous smile.

Henning looked around for someone to serve a drink. There were plenty of people to help, but he was rooted to the floor.

"Here's the problem, Eddie," I said, pulling his attention to me. He leaned in, but his eyes continued to dart around the bar. "You just lied about what you said." Henning's eyes now locked onto me. "Why would you do that after all these years? I mean, why would it matter? Unless you might have killed the girl."

"I didn't," he said, his voice raised.

A group of five that had come into the bar made a stink to get their drinks. Henning turned to help them, paused for a second as if he was afraid to walk away from our conversation, then hurried away toward the noisy group.

I glanced at Barry, who held his glass in front of his face.

"That was cool," he said with a smile.

I put a twenty on the bar, tucking it under my full beer.

"Let's go someplace else. I got what I wanted."

30

"I figured you'd be back."

The jailers had escorted April Scott into an interview room prior to my arrival. She was in an orange jumpsuit. She crossed her arms across her chest and leaned back in her chair. She was doing her best jailhouse tough-girl act, but I was feeling pretty good that morning, so I let it ride. I woke to Supertramp's "The Logical Song" looping in my head. I'm not sure if it had any special meaning, but the song was about questioning the meaning of life. I was certainly doing that most mornings now.

"Did you catch Tony?"

"Yes and no," I said, taking a seat and pulling my notes from a manila folder.

April leaned forward. "What's that mean?"

"It means we caught him, but he had some interesting things to say."

She squinted. "He's blaming me for this, isn't he?"

"No, he didn't blame you."

"What did he say then?"

"He said he has no idea what you're talking about."

"Detective, I swear, I didn't have anything to do with it."

"I've got no proof otherwise."

"Search his apartment. You'll find that knife. And that jacket. I'm sure of it."

"He let me search his apartment. There was nothing in there."

Her mouth dropped.

"Although he admitted to trading you meth for sex."

"That's a lie," she said quickly. "Those were his drugs. I was just holding for him."

"He also claimed you were bragging about having a new truck."

She flicked her free hand in my direction. "I never said no such thing."

"So far, he told me the truth right out of the gate, and everything has remained the truth. You, on the other hand, have lied to me nonstop. You want to change your tune?"

"Tony killed that guy, I swear. He told me to shut up, or he would hurt me. That's my story, and I'm sticking to it."

"Not much of what you say makes sense."

April stopped talking and crossed her arms.

"I want to go back to the beginning, to the night it all happened."

"No."

"I want to clarify some things, April. If you're innocent, it seems like you'd want me to do that."

She remained silent, her breathing audible.

"Is that silence an agreement for me to continue my questions?"

"No, my attorney told me not to say anything to you."

"Who's your attorney?"

She smirked. "The best money can buy. You'll find out soon enough."

"Really? And who's paying for that? The state?"

"No."

"Your mom and dad?"

"My mom ran out on me when I was a kid."

"So your dad is paying for your attorney? What's his name?"

"Daddy," she said.

"Right." I closed my folder and stood.

When I neared the door, she said, "Detective?"

I turned around.

"You really didn't find the knife and coat?"

"No."

Confusion washed over her face, and she bowed her head.

"Why were you so sure they would be in his apartment?"

She turned her body away from me. The interview was over. I turned and left her to her thoughts.

31

As soon as I returned to my desk, my phone rang. I answered it on the second ring. "Nash."

"This is Ackerman. My office. Now."

The call ended.

***

"Who the hell is Edward Henning, and why are you harassing him?"

"Excuse me?" I said, standing before Captain Ackerman's desk. I hadn't been invited to sit.

"I received a call from Councilwoman Carter. She said she was at the Lantern last night while you and a friend were there in an official capacity. Tell me this was unofficial. She said you were drinking."

"It was."

"It was, what?"

"It was, sir?"

The captain shook his head. "No, Nash. Was it unofficial?"

"Sort of."

"Sort of?"

"Maybe."

"What the hell does that mean?" He ran his hand through his silver hair.

"I met a friend for a beer, although I didn't drink. The bartender there is a suspect in the cold case you gave me."

"The Williams girl? Well, when you were done with your impromptu interview, the bartender was visibly upset. He happens to be a close, personal friend of the councilwoman.”

“What does that matter? Maybe my questioning worked?”

“Damn it, Nash, you realize some of our job is political, don’t you?” He rubbed his forehead while he thought. “Bring me up to speed on this situation.”

I laid out the Jennifer Williams case, my connection to it, and Henning’s background. I told him about my conversations with Barry and Randy, as well as the initial interview with Henning.

“I was unofficial before I went to the bar. I was quasi-official at that bar, I guess.”

“At this point, you’ve got no evidence, right?”

“No.”

“Why would you do that?”

“I wanted to catch him off guard.”

“Aren’t there better ways?”

“Yes, but—”

“No. No excuses. You’re a good detective, Dallas. Is your head in the game right now? Are you thinking things through like you should? The way you played that was like a chess player thinking one move ahead. You’ll only win when you compete against a player doing the same thing. You’re better than this.”

I nodded, accepting some of what he was saying and realizing the tongue lashing would go quicker if I didn’t fight it.

“You can’t harass him at his place of business. You just told me the guy has no criminal record. You might be wrong about this.”

“I realize that.”

“You can’t arrest him on your gut instinct.”

"I know that, too."

"Why not bring him down to the station? Interview him here?"

"That's my plan."

"That's great, but why didn't you do that last night instead?"

"I wanted to catch him off guard. He's been sitting on this for thirty years, thinking he's gotten away with it."

"You don't know for sure he did it!" Ackerman said, his voice rising in volume. "Right?"

I shook my head.

"Then bring him in and interview him." Ackerman's face flushed as he spoke. "Do it right this time. You're a senior detective. Act that way."

"Yes, sir."

The captain leaned back in his chair and sighed. He ran his fingers through his hair one more time before saying, "Now, I've got to call the councilwoman back. I'll apologize for how we conducted business in that establishment, but I'll stand my ground that you're still going to investigate this case. We're not going to be pushed around by political connections. Understand? I'll say it with more politeness than that, but you get that I'm going to have to eat a fair amount of shit to calm this down, right?"

"Yes, sir."

"Well, then, no more screw-ups. You're better than this, Dallas."

***

In the hallway, Detectives Johnson and Parker snickered when I walked out. They had eavesdropped on the ass-chewing Ackerman gave me.

"No more screw-ups, Dallas," Johnson whispered mockingly.

"Better get your head in the game, big hitter," Parker said, mocking Ackerman's favorite term of affection. "Or we're going to have a come to Jesus meeting."

"You guys are assholes," I said and walked past them.

"Geez, the guy's wife dies, and he can't take a joke anymore."

I spun around and walked back to Parker. "What did you say?"

Johnson lifted his hands and stepped back. "Hey, man, he—"

"What did you say, Andy?"

"Dude, I'm sorry—"

I punched him. Hard. He fell into the wall, lost his footing, and dropped to his ass.

Johnson yelled, "Hey!" and shoved me back from his partner.

Blood pounded in my ears, and I struggled to keep my calm. "Don't you ever say another word to me!" I yelled.

Captain Ackerman ran out of his office. "What the hell is going on out here?" Several patrol officers hurried up the hall to see what the commotion was.

Johnson turned to the captain. "Just a misunderstanding, and then Parker slipped. Right, Dallas?"

My eyes never left Parker. "A misunderstanding, Captain. I think it's been straightened out."

Johnson helped Parker to his feet.

"Has it been straightened out?" Ackerman asked.

Parker nodded, rubbing his jaw.

Ackerman looked at us. "In my day, officers were smart enough to take care of misunderstandings in the parking lot or the gym, not in the goddamn hallway. Understand?"

The three of us nodded, getting the message.

Ackerman grabbed my arm and pulled me into him. He put his mouth next to my ear and whispered. "This is what I'm talking about. A chess player who thinks one move ahead."

I yanked my arm free and left the building with no particular place to go.

32

The silence in my car broke with the radio call, "*Adam one eleven. I've got a rolling stolen southbound on Nevada, passing Rockwell.*"

"*Adam one eleven, go ahead,*" dispatch responded.

The officer read the license plate and then announced, "*This is the truck we've been searching for, the one related to the northside homicide.*"

My heart rate quickened, and I turned up the radio.

The dispatcher said, "*Confirmed stolen. Toyota Tundra. Vehicle is registered to Hamilton Martin. Note to call Ida twenty-five when located.*"

I keyed my microphone and said, "Ida-25, I'm in the field."

I'd been aimlessly driving around to cool off after the fight with Parker. I was southbound on Division Street when I activated my emergency lights. I spun the car around and raced northbound.

"*Adam one eleven, we're approaching Walton. I haven't activated my lights yet. Waiting for a couple more units to get in the area.*"

"*Baker two seventeen, on the way,*" another officer called.

"*Baker two fifteen, a couple blocks.*"

"*Adam one fifteen, eastbound at Garland.*"

"*Restricting the channel for Adam one eleven's stop,*" the dispatcher announced to stop all the chatter coming in from the other units.

I pulled my car around a slow-moving minivan and accelerated. The engine roared in disagreement, but the resulting output was fantastic.

"Adam one eleven, he's seen me. He's running. Speeds are fifty miles per hour."

I activated my siren along with my lights.

"Adam one eleven, he ran the intersection at Empire."

A city bus slowly pulled to the side, and I yanked the steering wheel to get around them quickly. The back end of my car fishtailed on the slippery roads, and I eased off on the speed.

"Adam one eleven, he's still southbound on Nevada, speeds back up to fifty."

"Advise traffic conditions," dispatch asked.

I imagined the patrol lieutenant was monitoring the pursuit and had called into police dispatch immediately, a way of virtually standing over the dispatcher's shoulder, in the event he needed to terminate the pursuit for public safety reasons.

"Adam one eleven, road conditions are mixed, light traffic. Vehicle is now westbound on Bridgeport."

I turned onto Bridgeport, fishtailing, and struggling for control. It had been years since I'd driven fast in weather conditions like this. I was several blocks from them, and they were now headed my way.

"Adam one eleven, he's braking. He's going to bail."

I could now see the Tundra racing toward me with three patrol cars behind it, their emergency lights whirring.

The Tundra suddenly slid sideways in the street. The driver's door and passenger door both opened, and two men ran in opposite directions.

I struggled to stop my car, the tires failing to bite into the icy road. When I finally slid to a stop, I jumped out, chasing the driver. A young patrol officer was immediately beside me. His car had stopped behind mine. I hadn't noticed him behind me during the pursuit.

We chased the driver along a cleared sidewalk that gave way to an un-shoveled mess in front of a brown house. The driver turned and high-stepped through the snow in the yard. By now, the patrol officer had passed me and was gaining on the driver. He caught the driver as he attempted to climb a wooden fence. The officer grabbed him by the seat of his pants and yanked him down into the snow. When the driver landed, the struggle was on. The suspect threw punches and fought to get back to his feet. A blow bounced off my shoulder, and I ducked one thrown at my head.

I reached for one of his arms. He jerked it back and punched me in the ribs. I lost my footing and fell in the snow. The officer jumped on his back and drove him to the ground. I scrambled to pile on the suspect, using our combined weight to keep him on the ground.

Each of us yanked an arm free from underneath his body. I repositioned myself to place my knee on the back of the suspect's neck, driving his face farther into the snow.

He yelled into the crunchy white mess, but neither the young patrol officer nor I cared. We didn't let him up until we had him cuffed behind his back. Only then did I remove my knee so he could breathe clean air.

The officer keyed his shoulder microphone. "Baker two seventeen, the driver's in custody."

A millisecond later, a voice over Baker-217's shoulder mic announced, *"Adam one eleven, passenger in custody."*

"Two in custody," dispatch said. *"Unrestricting the channel."*

We stood, leaving the driver on the ground.

I extended my hand. "Dallas Nash."

"Craig Esposito," he said with a smile.

"You're grinning," I said.

"Why wouldn't I? We just caught a bad guy."

Together, we lifted the driver to his feet and started the walk back toward the truck.

Esposito looked me up and down as we walked. "Nice loafers, Detective."

I glanced down at my light brown shoes, which were now entirely soaked through by the snow. So were my pants. "I hadn't planned on a foot pursuit today."

Esposito's grin grew wider. "Where's the fun in that?"

"Put him in your car and then meet me at the truck."

The officer said, "Will do," and headed towards his car, leading the handcuffed driver by his elbow.

I continued to the truck and met with Adam-111, Ken Jarvis.

"This is the truck you were looking for, right?" Jarvis asked.

An Oakland Raiders emblem was in the back window behind the driver's seat.

"Don't let anyone touch the truck without gloves on. Tow it directly to Property."

"You're welcome," Jarvis said, with exaggerated sarcasm. "Glad we could be of service."

"I apologize," I said. "Thank you, Ken."

Jarvis smirked. "You detective types sure get high and mighty when you start wearing chinos."

"They're slacks," I said.

"Whatever. You're a cake eater now, Nash. Don't forget that way back when you used to be one of us."

"Yeah, yeah. Don't hate me because I can write complete sentences."

Jarvis crossed his eyes and jutted his teeth over his bottom lip. "Me patrol. Me arrest 'em for detective. He so smart."

I punched Jarvis in the arm. "And don't forget it."

His laugh was interrupted when Esposito walked up. "What's the plan, Detective?"

"Take both these guys to the station and park them in separate rooms. I'll be there shortly."

"Where are you headed?" Jarvis asked.

I looked down at my slacks and shoes. I hadn't felt the effect of the cold yet, but I'm sure it would come soon. "I need a change of clothes. Even my underwear is drenched," I said.

"You should plan for winter," Jarvis said. "It's obvious you've been riding a chair for too long."

I smiled, feeling the adrenaline still coursing through my system. It was good to be on the street again.

33

Danny Brunson squinted to affect what he must have considered was his best intimidating look. His lip curled in the left corner, revealing a missing tooth. His arms were folded over his chest.

Bouncing his head to the left and right with each word, he said in a slow drawl, "I ain't telling you shit."

"Okay," I said and left the room.

"Wait," he called as the door slammed, leaving him alone to stew in the locked room.

***

"We just found the truck," Irvin Gibson said.

"You *found* the truck?" I asked. "What's that mean?

"It means exactly that. We found it. The keys were on the front seat, and the doors were unlocked. Who does that? They were just asking for trouble. It was almost an invitation for us to take it for a ride."

I had moved over to interview room two to question Gibson, who was the opposite of his friend Danny Brunson. He wasn't trying to play the situation hard. He was twenty-three years old and black. His jeans and button-down shirt looked of quality. They were nicer looking than the stuff I wore.

"Where did you find the truck?"

"Wal-Mart."

"Which Wal-Mart?"

"The one up north."

"There are two up north. Which one?"

"The one near the Home Depot."

"Where exactly at Wal-Mart?"

"On the side. Near the garden section."

"It's winter. There is no garden section."

Gibson lifted his hands and smirked. "C'mon, man, don't play stupid. You know what I mean. When they have the garden section, that's where it is. That's where the truck was at."

"And it was sitting there?"

"Yeah. Just like it was waiting for us," Gibson said. "Keys on the front seat and everything."

"What did you do when you found the keys?"

He shrugged. "What do you think we did?"

"I need you to tell me."

"We got in and went for a ride."

"Whose idea was it?"

He smiled. "His, of course. I didn't want to go, but you know how it is."

I shook my head. "No, I don't. I've never stolen a car."

"I didn't want to get left behind, so I got in the truck with him."

"You knew it was stolen, though."

"It was stolen before we took it?"

I nodded.

"Ain't that something? Does it still make it a crime if we took it from someone who wasn't supposed to have it?"

I nodded again.

"Damn. I was hoping two negatives made a positive, you know, like it does in math?"

I showed him a picture of Hamilton Martin. "Ever seen this man?"

Gibson shook his head.

"The truck belongs to him."

"He'll probably be happy now."

"Why do you say that?"

"Because he'll get his truck back. We didn't damage it. We were just having some fun. We didn't mean any harm."

"Your buddy has stolen cars before."

"Yeah, I know."

"And you've broken into houses."

"Out of necessity. A man needs to eat."

"Did you kill this man?" I asked, my finger on Hamilton Martin's photograph.

"What?" His eyes flew wide. "Are you serious?"

I watched him, letting the accusation sink in.

"Hell no! I didn't kill nobody."

"I didn't figure so."

***

"Want to talk now?"

"I still ain't saying shit," Danny Brunson said, his lip curl growing larger. He leaned back in his chair, the front legs off the floor.

"Fine," I said and stood. "Your friend said everything I needed. We're good to go. I'm going to book you for Possession of Stolen Property. I think I might let Irvin go."

Danny dropped his chair forward. "Wait. What?"

"He talked. That earns him love in my book."

"What if I talk? What will you do for me?"

"That depends."

"On what?"

"On what you want."

***

"You got them both to talk?" Glenn asked, leaning over my shoulder as he read my report. We were at my cubicle.

"Not at first," I said.

"How then?"

I turned to face my partner. "The passenger wanted to talk. He was easy. He knew he wasn't in much hot water, and he was looking out for himself. The driver wouldn't talk until I told him I wasn't going to book his friend."

"The driver talked, thinking he wouldn't get booked?"

"Oh, no, he *knew* he was getting booked. He just wanted to make sure his friend would get booked with him."

"You wouldn't have actually let the passenger go, right?"

I shook my head. "Not a chance."

Glenn tilted his head. "The driver talked so he would get his friend in trouble? Isn't there supposed to be honor among thieves?"

"Have you ever seen that yet?"

"Good point. Do you think they murdered your victim?"

"No, I don't. Here's the thing. The truck was sitting in the parking lot, unlocked, with keys on the front seat, just waiting for someone to realize they could take it."

"You're saying someone wanted that truck re-stolen?"

"It looks that way."

34

After Judge Coughlin signed the search warrant, I drove to the Property warehouse. Corporal Mark Tripp was standing by as I pulled into the parking lot. His camera bag was on the hood of his patrol car.

"So, we're searching the truck?" Tripp asked. "Need fingerprints as well?"

"Yes," I said.

Tripp's smile was wry. "I hate printing vehicles. Everyone in the world touches them. Random people in parking lots, just standing around and talking, will put their hands on a car. Little kids do the same thing. You name it."

"I understand."

The corporal looked up at the gray sky. "But with the weather we've had, who knows? Might not be much for me to get."

We signed in with the desk and headed toward the vehicle section. There were a variety of vehicles stored in the warehouse. Some of them were mangled, brought to Property as part of vehicular homicide investigations. There were also nice, clean, high-end cars that stood proudly in the warehouse. I guessed those were from drug-related arrests and would soon be seized by the department and either sold or put into rotation with the drug task force, the Special Investigations Unit, or the Criminal Task Force.

The Tundra was in the far end, nearest the roll-up door. The last vehicle brought in.

Both of us put on latex gloves before starting the search.

Corporal Tripp slowly and methodically took photos of the vehicle from every angle before opening the door and taking a picture of the interior. Once that was done, we both searched through the inside of the truck. It took only a few minutes to discover there was nothing of evidentiary value.

Tripp pulled out his fingerprint kit and opened it on the concrete floor.

"There's nothing more for you to do, Dallas. You can take off. I'll call you when I'm done."

"All right. Don't forget the rearview mirror."

"Duh."

35

That night, we met for dinner.

It was the first time we talked since the funeral, and even then, it was just a hug and her saying she was sorry.

Carmen Cady picked at her salad, her fork moving the greens and other vegetables back and forth on her plate.

My salad remained untouched.

We were at Twigs in Spokane Valley, the halfway point between her house and mine. It was a convenient place to meet. She'd invited me to dinner, and I accepted, thinking it would help close some of that hole in my heart. It didn't.

After we ordered, we didn't say much. We occasionally smiled at each other, the type of smile that means *I'm hurting, and I don't want to be here.*

When she sipped her wine, her eyes flicked to my glass of water. She quickly put down her drink and looked away, guilty that she was imbibing while I was abstaining.

The waiter came by to check on us. He noticed my untouched salad. "Is everything okay, sir?"

"It's fine."

"Would you like something else?"

"No, it's fine."

His eyes went to Carmen for a moment before he slowly walked away.

"Maybe we shouldn't have done this," she said.

I shrugged.

"I miss her."

"Me too."

"If there's anything I can do."

Silence overtook our meal again, and I lowered my head. I thought about "The Logical Song" and its questioning of the meaning of life.

What if there really was no meaning to it?

What if Bobbie's death meant she really was gone forever?

That meant the songs I'd been hearing were some protective device my brain had cooked up for me to deal with the pain of losing her. I was, therefore, deluding myself into believing she still existed.

She was dead.

I would soon be dead.

In the end, nothing mattered.

I lifted my napkin from my lap and folded it. "I'm sorry. I think I'm going to head home."

"Okay," she whispered, not looking up or bothering to convince me to stay.

I stopped by the check-in station and paid for both of our meals.

"Was everything okay?" the hostess asked, visibly concerned by the look on my face.

"Not feeling well," I muttered and signed the check.

WEDNESDAY
DECEMBER 13th

36

"You know what song I heard this morning? 'Vogue.' Why'd I wake up to that? I mean, I always hated that song. In fact, I don't know a single Madonna song I do like. You know that. She was one of your favorites."

Bobbie's headstone didn't respond.

"You were crazy about that song when we were in college, remember? I kept telling you it was stupid, but you'd make me go out on the dance floor with you. I could never say no to you. You'd do that silly dance with your hands." I shook my head, thinking about some of the dances we attended while in school. Bobbie was a great dancer. I looked like Frankenstein trying to keep the beat.

No snow was falling, but it was frigid. I wrapped my long coat around me, but it did little to keep the chill off. It didn't matter. I was feeling a little happier, thinking about dancing with Bobbie.

***

Later in the morning, Captain Ackerman stormed into the bullpen and tossed a report on my desk. His face was red, and his voice boomed through the department when he said, "I thought I said, 'No more screw-ups.'"

"I don't know what this is."

"Read it, figure out what happened, and give me an update. I'm glad you're back, Dallas, but if this is the new normal from you, we're going to have a real problem."

When he hurried out, heads popped out from cubicles like prairie dogs. Everyone wanted to know what I'd just stepped in.

***

The report stated that Edward A. Henning was the victim of an assault.

The suspect in the assault was Terrance Williams.

Crap.

I looked around, expecting everyone to be watching me as I read the report. No one was. I turned back to the incident report.

Williams had shown up at Henning's house. When Henning opened the door, Williams identified himself. Henning stepped outside on the small front porch, putting him too close to Williams. He should have closed the door and ended the conversation. It went bad from there.

A neighbor witnessed the altercation and called the police, who arrived within a couple of minutes. Henning was hesitant to press charges, but the officers made the arrest based upon witness statements.

Terry Williams was cited for Fourth Degree Assault and released.

***

"Why'd you do it?"

"What do you mean?"

"Why'd you assault Eddie Henning?"

Terry Williams looked at me like I was speaking a foreign language. He had abrasions on his cheek, and his knuckles were roughed up, indications of the fight. "Detective, you said he killed my daughter."

"No, I didn't. I never said that."

"Yes, you did," Cheryl chimed in.

I stepped away from them. We were standing in their living room. "I never said such a thing. I told you both there was another potential suspect. I asked if you knew him."

"We know the code words," Cheryl said, her voice low and conspiratorial.

"Code words?"

"You said he was a suspect," Cheryl said.

"You said he interested you," Terry said. "We know what that means now."

I rubbed my face, trying not to say anything that would further get me into trouble. I turned and saw the picture of Jennifer Williams next to the burning candle. "Did he say anything when you assaulted him?"

Terry's eyes flashed with anger. "Nope. He curled up like a punk."

He was a couple of decades older than Henning. His beating him up didn't make sense. "Henning didn't fight back?"

"Not once."

"And you kept hitting him?"

"Oh, yeah. After what he did to my daughter? He's damn lucky I didn't kill him."

I stared up at the popcorn ceiling.

"Did you know he's queer?" Terry asked with his hands on his hips.

"You mean gay?"

"Those sickos can do anything," Terry said, stabbing his finger at me. "I know he's the one."

"I'm still investigating this case, and you've made it worse."

"Don't tell me I'm making it worse. You people haven't been able to find who killed my daughter for more than a quarter of a century. If I need to beat it out of some Nancy to get the truth, then I'll do it."

I stood. "No more. Both of you need to stay out of this."

"If you did your job, we wouldn't be getting involved, now would we? What did he say when you interviewed him?"

"He said he didn't know her."

"And you believed him? You were the one who said he was a lead!"

"Stay away from him," I said.

I turned and left the house, hurrying down the walk. I didn't see a spot of ice and slipped, sprawling to the ground, half on the sidewalk, half in the snow-covered yard.

Terry muttered, "Serves you right, you bastard," before he slammed the door behind me.

37

Instead of lunch, I went to the department's gym on the second floor. I thought a few miles on the treadmill might, hopefully, clear my mind.

Using a hand towel, I covered the treadmill's screen so I couldn't see my time or distance.

I would typically listen to music while running, but since either Bobbie or my subconscious provided me with morning musical selections, I figured I didn't want to interfere by giving them other options. Therefore, I ran to the rhythm of my feet slapping on the rubber ribbon and my breathing—inhale for two steps, exhale for three. The pattern became hypnotic, and I fell into a trance as I stared at a nail in the wall several feet away.

I focused intently on that small piece of metal until nothing else existed except my breathing. I lost track of time and started to feel free.

"Nash?"

I turned my head, stumbled, and clutched the rails to avoid flinging myself off the rear of the treadmill. I regained my stride and continued running. The front desk officer stood next to the treadmill, his uniform crisp and unaffected by the weather.

"Yeah?"

"I was sent to get you."

"For what?"

***

"It looks like he overdosed. Been dead for some time. Maybe a couple of days," Officer Lee Sheets said.

The body was splayed out over the recliner as if he was kicked back and relaxing before he died.

When did I talk with him? I ran the days back in my head. Sunday. We talked Sunday.

Detectives Parker and Johnson came out from the back room. Their laughter stopped when they saw me.

"What are you doing here?" Parker asked.

"I was asked to come by."

"Why? This is our case," Johnson said.

Sheets spoke up. "I called Nash. I brought him this guy for questioning on Sunday."

I nodded.

"We told you he wasn't needed," Parker said, his face reddening.

"I made the call, Detective," Sheets said, stepping up to Parker until they were nose to nose, although Sheets was looking down his at Parker. "If you don't like it, talk to my supervisor. Or better yet, let's handle it in the parking lot."

I put my hand on Sheets's shoulder and gently pulled him back. "Why wouldn't you want me called?" I asked Parker and Johnson.

"We were trying to save you the work," Johnson said. "Us being friends and all."

Parker leaned over the body. "You really talked with this mook?"

"Yes. I interviewed him on Sunday about a homicide."

Parker stood upright and looked at his partner. Then he turned to me with a smile. "Okay, Sherlock," he said. "You want this case? It's yours now. We've got better things to do."

Johnson patted me on the back as he passed by me. "He'll get over it."

Sheets and I watched the two leave. "They're a couple of prima donnas," Sheets said.

"They're good detectives," I said, trying to be positive about the state of our division.

Sheets smiled. "Don't shovel that company bullshit at me. Do you wonder why so many guys want to stay patrol? You just saw it walk out the door. Too many guys turn into that when they leave the street. It's like *Invasion of the Body Snatchers* or something."

I turned back to the body in the recliner.

Anthony Lawrence wore a red ski jacket with gray shoulders. There was blood on the coat. "This was the jacket the victim wore in the video surveillance footage. However, Lawrence didn't have the jacket when I interviewed him, and it wasn't in this apartment when I searched it."

I straddled Lawrence, careful not to touch the body. I reached into the first pocket and pulled out a folded note.

I quickly read it, refolded the note, and handed it to Sheets. "Bag it."

In the second pocket, I found what I was looking for. When I stepped back, I showed it to Sheets. "I'll bet this is the murder weapon from that homicide, and when I unfold it, there will be blood on the blade." I unfolded the knife. No blood. It was spotless. "I don't understand."

"What did the note say?"

"He was sorry for murdering a stranger and pinning it on his girlfriend."

"It's nice of him to wrap it up for you. Christmas still being two weeks away and all."

"It was nice, wasn't it?"

I studied Anthony Lawrence and knew everything I saw was a lie.

38

He opened the door slightly, revealing bruising on his face and abrasions on the right side of his face. His eyes told the truth: he was afraid. "Are you here to finish the job?"

I chose my words carefully. "It's unfortunate Mr. Williams came to your house and assaulted you, Eddie."

"How did he know where I lived?"

"I don't know."

"How did he even know who I was?"

"I told him."

His shoulders slumped. "Why would you do that?"

"Because you are a person of interest in the murder of Jennifer Williams. Someone our department has never looked at before. I figured they had a right to know."

"But I didn't do it."

"You haven't given me a reason to believe you."

"I told you the truth."

"Eddie, you haven't told the truth."

He shook his head. "I want this to stop. I want it to go away."

"It's not going away, Eddie. I believe you did it, and I'm going to stay after you until I can prove it."

Henning stared at me. "What?"

"I'm going to keep working this case. I'm not going to put it away. I'm going to keep poking away at it until I retire, which is still a long time away. I'm not going to rest until I prove you killed her."

"Why are you doing this?"

"Because you did it, Eddie. I'm starting to feel it in my gut. And I'm going to prove it. I'm going to make your life miserable. And I'll bet you've carried the weight with you every day."

Tears filled Henning's eyes.

"Eddie, she wasn't raped. We know that. We just need to know why it happened."

"I'm gay."

"I know. You told me, and I believe you."

He shook his head. He pushed open the door and walked into his house. I stepped inside, closing the door behind me. Henning turned to face me. "Back then, I did my best to hide it. It wasn't okay like it is now. No one knew."

I nodded.

"Except Jennifer. Somehow, she read me right away. From the moment I met her, she knew. Guys were starting to suspect I wasn't like them because I never had a girlfriend. Some guys in school even started to tease me as Hollywood. Hollywood Henning, they called me. I fucking hated that nickname. Most people thought it was because of how I dressed or because I was in the drama club, but I figured it was because they were sensing who I was.

"I met Jennifer at the mall, and we hit it off. She said she always wanted a gay friend, just like the cool girls in California. We both wanted out of Spokane so badly. We wanted to be different people. She wanted to be famous. I wanted to be myself.

"We came up with a plan. If she would help me establish an alibi for who I was, I'd help her get to California after high school. We'd go together."

"Why did you need an alibi?"

"Do you remember high school? The eighties might have been a turning point for a lot of things, but for a gay kid in Spokane, it was miserable."

"Eddie, it's time you owned up to that moment."

"Detective, I didn't do it. I swear." Exasperation was evident on his face. "She was nice to me. I was trying to hide it from everyone, but she knew. She said she'd tell some of the guys we made it, let the word get around. I thought she was the nicest person for that."

"She told people you had sex?"

"I don't know if she ever did. She said she was going to, but I don't think so. We thought it would be cool, like those high school movies from when we were kids, where the cool girl is always helping the dopey guy. That was her, the cool girl. She wanted to help me. But then she was killed, and it never happened."

"What about her boyfriend? Do you think he would have gotten mad about it?"

"No. She said he was nice, even if he was a sort of dumb jock. Besides, they were breaking up, so she didn't think it would matter."

"Why didn't you tell me this before?"

"Because it's stupid and embarrassing, and I'm not sure anything ever happened with it."

"That's not good enough. You could have told me. This isn't big enough to keep it a secret."

He stared at me.

"This is what I'm talking about, Eddie. You're holding out on me, and it makes me not want to believe you."

He took a step away, then stopped and turned back. "Listen, I did something back then, the day she died. If I admit to it as my alibi, I'm guaranteed to get into trouble."

"What did you do?"

Henning stared at me, considering his options. I gave him none.

"You either tell me the truth, Eddie, or I continue to make you suspect number one for this. The press will find out. Everyone will find out. You need to own up to whatever it is you're holding back."

Henning walked over to his futon and dropped onto it. "That time you're asking about, the day of her death, I went to Seattle with an older friend. He was in college out at Eastern. My parents had no idea what we were doing."

"What *were* you doing?"

"We were going to a party."

"That's all? That could be an alibi." If what Henning was saying was true, he couldn't have killed Jennifer Williams. I felt the case slipping away, but if it was true, why hadn't he told me sooner? Why had he kept it a secret? He was hiding something, and whatever it was, it had to be as bad as Jennifer's murder for him to keep his mouth shut.

Henning stared at me.

"Who was your friend? The one you went to the party with."

"Kerry Hopkins."

"How did you find out about this party?"

"Kerry found it on the Arpanet, remember that?"

I shook my head.

"It was the precursor of the internet. Kerry was taking a computer course at the college and got access to it. He found a group of like-minded students, and soon we were headed to a party."

"Like-minded?"

"Gay, Detective. Closeted, mostly. We were still trying to figure out who we were in a part of the country that wasn't very receptive to it."

"What happened at this party?"

"Mostly what you'd expect. A lot of shy computer types who wanted to talk with others who were experiencing the same feelings. It was okay. Not as cool as I'd hoped. There was a professor there who watched it all. His name was Saul. That's all I remember. Not sure if I ever heard his last name. He came over and chatted me up. It was clear he took a special interest in me. I was flattered by the attention. The drinking didn't help. I thought I was sophisticated, but I was stupid. The wine put me in a situation I've tried to forget for years."

Henning stared down at his hands.

I waited several moments before asking, "What happened there?"

He nodded, not looking up. "Saul asked if I wanted to go for a walk. I agreed, of course. He was older and handsome. A professor talking to me seemed like a big deal then." Henning shook his head as he continued, "We walked through the forest behind the house where the party was. It was a lovely night. I remember a lot of stars were out. Is that strange to still remember that?"

"No."

"We stopped talking, and I knew things were going to get intimate. *Intimate*. Hardly. He pressed me against a tree and became aggressive. He grabbed me hard. It hurt how he held me. He reeked of alcohol. I didn't realize how drunk he was until that moment. I had a sudden moment of clarity and was scared. I told him to stop, but he wouldn't. He dragged me to the ground and continued his… Well, you get it."

Henning looked up and made eye contact then.

"Yeah, I get it," I said.

"I reached out and found a rock about the size of a softball," Henning said. He opened his hand and stared at the palm. "If I close my eyes and think about it enough, I can still feel the weight of it in my hand. I hit him in the head with it." Henning touched the side of his head, above his ear. "It stunned him, but he was still looking at me, so I hit him again. When he fell on me, I hit him once more."

We stared at each other for a couple of moments.

"I might have been able to stop after the first one," Henning said. "I don't know. I mean, I was scared. That's why I hit him again, you know? The third time, well, there was no excuse for that one. Maybe there was, I don't know."

"Yeah," I said, not wanting to say more and interrupt his confession.

Henning looked around his house, wiped his face with his hands, and continued. "I ran back to the party, got Kerry, and made him leave for Spokane right away. He wasn't happy about that. He was pissed all the way home. I stayed at Kerry's house until Sunday night." Tears were streaming down his face.

"What happened to the professor?"

"I killed him."

"Are you sure?"

Henning shrugged. "I think so. I don't know. I mean, I had to, right?"

I studied Eddie. "Did anyone ever come and talk to you?"

He shook his head.

"If you killed him," I said, "someone would have talked with you."

“Detective, it’s been thirty years, and you’re still looking for Jennifer’s murderer. Couldn’t it be the same for me?”

39

After meeting with Henning, I stopped by the department. It was after five, so the detectives' office was quiet. I was going to need some help in tracking down Henning's story. Therefore, it would have to wait until tomorrow.

I thought about going home and making something for dinner. I decided instead to grab a burger, but when I arrived at Red Robin, the loud nature of the restaurant turned me off. Eating with a roomful of screaming kids wasn't appealing.

I got back in my car and sat there for several minutes. I thought about calling my brother, but that seemed like it would turn into a lot of questions about how I was doing. It would be the same thing to call my parents. They had similar questions, but they didn't respect my boundaries like my brother did.

For a moment, I considered having a beer. I didn't drink the night I went out with Barry. Maybe I could run over and have a beer with Randy. I toyed with that idea for a couple of minutes but finally decided I wasn't in a mental position where I wanted to start drinking again.

After a bit, I started my car and drove to the Nevada Quick-E-Mart. Marvin was behind the counter. He recognized me and lifted his chin in a silent greeting. The fluorescent lights were bright, and some unrecognizable hip-hop played through the store's stereo system.

I walked over to the rolling cooker. There were several hot dogs on the machine, sweating over the heat of the grill. I couldn't remember the last time I had a hot dog.

Pointing at the dogs, I asked, "These any good?"

Marvin's face pinched. "Honestly?"

I shrugged. "Gimme two," I said.

"Really?"

"I'm living dangerously tonight."

"Yeah, you are."

I sat in the parking lot of the convenience store and ate them as the snow began to fall again.

It was better than eating alone at home.

THURSDAY
DECEMBER 14th

40

Lieutenant George Brand was waiting for me when I entered the detectives' office. As soon as he saw me, he waved me over to his office.

As I headed toward him, I glanced around to see if anyone was watching. No one was, and I'm not sure if I would have cared. I woke with the song "Break My Stride" playing in my head. The chorus confuses a lot of people into thinking the song is about keeping pace in your life, but it's really about a woman who leaves a man because she's holding him back. At the end of the song, the singer decides he doesn't want another woman like her, and he starts saying no one will break his stride now.

The song put me in a foul mood for some reason. I'd been struggling on and off with the idea Bobbie was sending me messages through the songs. This one made me believe she was happier now without me. I knew it wasn't true, but after pining away for her for weeks only to wake up this morning to believe she might be happier where she was didn't make me feel particularly good about myself.

I stepped into Brand's office and closed the door behind me.

Brand was a strange, bookish man with thinning hair and round, wire-rimmed glasses. He was tall and pudgy, most of the weight added since he'd ended up behind a desk. While he was a patrol officer and later a sergeant, he never inspired the highest confidence on the street. However, he did find a niche while working patrol. Guys liked working with him because he wouldn't shy away from a shitty call, nor one that required a lot of paperwork. He did the job and, if there was a paperwork aspect to it, he did it well. He was just never the guy who was going to break up a bar fight alone, nor had he ever been on one of the specialty teams, either Crowd Control or SWAT. Brand fully bloomed when he was assigned as the lieutenant over the administrative department. Everyone believed he had finally found his calling. Until he pissed off the chief somehow, the cause of which was still a mystery to this day.

Brand leaned back in his chair and crossed his arms over his chest. "Did you take over the homicide Parker and Johnson were assigned yesterday?"

I nodded.

"That wasn't cleared with me. You know you have to clear something like that, don't you?"

"Yes, sir."

"We have a rotation for a reason, Nash."

"I understand."

"Do you? I mean, do you understand how it works from an efficiency standpoint?"

"It's a basic concept, so, yeah, I get it."

"You took their call, and you're going to be up on the rotation very quickly. If you don't clear that call, your workload is going to get too heavy. You're putting yourself into a situation where your performance can be affected due to your workload. That's why the rotation exists—fairness and spreading the workload. Due to your actions, however, I'm not rearranging the rotation list to accommodate this change."

"I wasn't expecting it."

"I should think not. Your partner isn't here to help you, Dallas. I don't want you taking on too much, too quick. Understand?"

"I get it."

"Did you take this case because of the altercation in the hallway? I heard about that from the captain."

"I don't know what altercation you're talking about."

Brand shook his head in irritated jerks. "No, don't do that to me, Dallas. Either treat me with respect, or we'll be talking about another subject completely."

"Are you talking about the incident with Parker?"

"Yes, Dallas, that's exactly what I'm talking about. Did you take the case from him because of it?"

"No, I took it because it tied in directly with a homicide I've got. The victim was a witness in my other case."

Brand clicked his teeth together as he thought. "I don't like it," he said finally.

"Like what?"

"The territorial wars going on between you and Parker."

"It's old dogs versus new dogs. That's all. It's been going on for generations around here."

"If it continues, I'll have to cage you both."

"At least you didn't say neuter."

"I was trying not to be vulgar."

41

"I'm sorry to tell you this…" I said.

April Scott leaned on the table. She was full of expectation, almost excitement. We were back in the interview room at the county jail.

"Your boyfriend…"

"Yes?"

"He overdosed. We found him yesterday."

For a moment, it looked like she stifled a smile, then her face constricted in confusion. Maybe it was my mind playing tricks.

"He's dead?"

"Were you expecting other news?"

She shook her head. "Just tell me what happened," she demanded.

"It was suicide."

"You're kidding. This is a trick. You're trying to get me to say something."

"I'm not trying to get you to do anything, April. Tony overdosed."

She turned her head. "How do you know it was suicide?"

"He left a note."

"What did it say?

"He was sorry for killing Hamilton Martin and pinning it on you."

She thought about what I said for several moments before the pinched look on her face relaxed. It was replaced with sadness. "See? I told you I didn't kill that man."

I didn't respond.

"Do you believe me now?"

"You're still going to trial."

"For what?"

"You were part of Hamilton Martin's death. Somebody has to answer for that."

"My lawyer said I've got a good chance of beating this."

"Who's your lawyer?"

"Why do you want to know? And since Tony confessed—"

"I wouldn't call it a confession."

She shrugged. "My attorney will. I just got to wait it out. They got me in a program here. By the time I get out, I'll have my shit under control, and things will be better. You'll see."

"Okay," I said and stood to leave.

"Detective?"

I turned back.

"Did Tony write anything about me?"

"Like what?"

"Like he loved me or something like that?"

"He told me you were a prostitute."

She thought for a moment before saying, "I did it for his drug habit."

"You've got this all figured out, don't you?"

Her eyes were sad when she said, "I'm working on it."

<h1 style="text-align:center">42</h1>

An email alert arrived saying the fingerprint report from the Toyota Tundra was done.

I opened the report and stared at it, dumbfounded.

Except for the fingerprints of the car thieves, the truck was utterly wiped down. There were no other fingerprints anywhere.

A vehicle should have prints some place, usually almost everywhere, from errant shoppers bumping into the car at the grocery store to mechanics checking the oil. Fingerprints should appear somewhere on that vehicle.

Even the most fastidious owner couldn't be that meticulous in keeping his car clean.

Someone had very systematically cleaned that truck. There wasn't a fingerprint or an ounce of incriminating evidence to be found.

***

"I need a favor," I said after walking into the Crime Analysis Unit.

Glenn leaned back in his chair and smiled. "Just tell me it's real police work."

"It's phone and computer time, but it's RPW."

"Perfect," he said. "Lay it on me."

"Call Seattle PD and the surrounding agencies. I'm looking for a report of either an assault or possibly a homicide that occurred on May ninth or tenth, 1987. The victim would be a white male. Mid to late thirties. First name of Saul. Unknown last name. Possibly a professor at a nearby college. Possibly homosexual."

"Homosexual? Does that matter?"

"I don't know. I'm trying to give you what I know about a potential assault or homicide case. Maybe they noted it had to do with his sexuality."

"Okay, okay," he said. When he was done writing, he looked up. "Is this tied to your cold case?"

"For an alibi, my main suspect just admitted to assaulting, possibly killing, a guy on the same day in Seattle. I'm working to rule him out for mine. If I do, I'm back at square one."

Glenn made some notes and then looked up at me. "I'm on it."

"Thanks, partner."

43

I found Kerry Hopkins with a quick internet and DOL search. He had an independent insurance company located on Wellesley Avenue in the shadow of Northtown Mall.

Light snow was falling as I drove north. It was another day of below-freezing weather.

I parked in front of his office and walked in. A young, bookish woman sat behind a computer. She didn't look up when I entered. At the rear of the office, I saw a man in his early fifties leaned over his desk, intently reading something on his computer.

The office smelled slightly of mildew and had older furniture and artwork on the walls. It looked to have been decorated in the '90s at some point and never updated since.

I waited for the woman at the front to acknowledge me. When she didn't, I shrugged and walked back. She never protested.

With a couple of knuckles, I tapped on the door to the office. The gray-haired, heavyset man looked up from his computer. He blinked several times before asking, "Yes?"

"I'm Detective Nash with the Spokane Police Department. Are you Kerry Hopkins?"

The man looked through his window to the woman at the front desk, then me, and then back to her. He shook his head a couple of times. "Damn it," he said and pointed to the chair across from his desk. "Yeah, I'm Kerry."

"I apologize for walking in here unannounced and surprising you."

"It's all right. She's not working out. If I walk up there right now, I'll bet she's on Facebook or Pinterest or one of those social media sites. I spend half my day asking her to do work and the other half telling her to stop wasting time playing with her friends on the internet. I feel like a damn parent."

"Do you know why I'm here, Mr. Hopkins?"

He nodded. "Eddie. He called me. He was crying when I talked with him. I figured someone would be by soon enough to talk about it."

"Can you tell me what happened?"

Kerry stood and walked over to the office door. He swung it gently closed before returning to his chair.

"Eddie and I went to a party over in Tacoma during my freshman year at Eastern. He was a senior in high school at the time. We'd been friends for several years before then. Anyway, I'd found out about a party on one of the bulletin boards..." Kerry smiled. "Bulletin boards. I haven't thought about those in years. Anyway, some guys were getting together to talk coding, and I wanted to go. I told Eddie, and he went with me."

"Eddie told me it was an alternative lifestyle party."

"You mean gay, Detective? Yeah, it was mostly gay, but that was the back story. We already knew that, so big whoop. The real story, what we were all jazzed about, was coding. We didn't give a damn about sleeping with each other. We wanted to talk about computers."

"Eddie made it sound a little different."

"He was a kid. He wanted to meet guys. He didn't care about computers."

"Were you and he...?"

"No. Never. He was like my little brother. I liked the guy. I still do, but I had no interest in him."

"What happened at the party?"

"That I don't know. A lot of us ended up in various groups, talking about whatever coding issues we thought were cool or that were troubling us. Some guys even brought printouts of what they were working on. It was a cool scene, but Eddie was out of his element. He looked uncomfortable from the beginning. These weren't the kinds of guys he was hoping to meet. I think he wanted to meet jocks, and he was meeting nerds. After a while, he disappeared. I figured he went for a walk.

"When he came back, he was pale. Real shaken-like. He said we had to go. I didn't want to leave because we'd driven over for the night. I'd gotten us a hotel room. The plan was to hang at the party and leave in the morning. Now, he was pulling me out and begging for me to go. I could see something was wrong, so I said okay. He wouldn't tell me what the matter was until we were on the road.

"That's when he said he went for a walk with an older guy, some professor type. Supposedly, this guy came on strong, so much so that Eddie thought he was about to get raped. Eddie said he hit this guy with a rock. Said he hit him several times, and he thought he killed him."

"Did you believe him?"

"He was shaking and crying in my car, so, yeah, I believed him."

"What did you do when you got back to Spokane?"

"I dropped him off at his house, and I went home."

"You didn't report this to anyone?"

"No, I didn't. I'm probably in trouble for it now, and I'll own it, but the guy was scared. He was my friend, and that's what you do for friends, right? He thought he killed that man, and it would be his story versus a dead man's. It wouldn't look good."

"You didn't ask anyone about it on the internet?"

"You mean the Arpanet and, no, I didn't. I didn't want to raise any suspicion. I had a friend ask me why I left, so I said I hooked up with a guy. That was all the answer anyone needed."

We chatted a bit more, and I got Kerry's personal information. He was forthcoming and didn't seem to hold anything back.

I was starting to believe Eddie Henning's story.

44

I was bent over my keyboard when Glenn walked up to drop a couple of papers on the side of my desk.

"Saul Polinsky," he said.

I looked up at my partner, who leaned on his crutches. He still held a piece of paper in one hand.

"Polinsky?"

"Professor at Evergreen State College. Assaulted in May of 1987. Found wandering in some woods, bloodied from an attack. Was taken to the hospital for his injuries. While there, he refused to discuss the attack. When pressed, he described his attacker in a variety of ways—black, Hispanic, even wearing a mask. No complaint was ever made; therefore, no arrest was made."

"Huh," I said, picking up the papers from my desk. It was a Tacoma police report. Tacoma was located forty minutes from Seattle. My eyes quickly scanned the report, verifying the information Glenn had just relayed.

"If you want to talk with Polinsky, you can forget it."

I looked up at Glenn.

"He died," Glenn said, handing me the last piece of paper. "Here's his obituary. He didn't die from your suspect's attack, though. He had a heart attack a couple of years ago. Nothing nefarious. How's this figure in your cold case?"

"I think it just cleared the suspect I liked for it."

"This dead professor did?"

I nodded and told Glenn the story of Eddie Henning and Professor Polinsky.

***

When Glenn left, I pulled out the Jennifer Williams file and reviewed it again. Frustrated by the loss of my new lead, the one I thought was going to break the case, I had to go back to basics. I had to look at the case with different eyes, which is what I should have done from the start.

The original detective, Alan Tannehill, had cleared her boyfriend, Jonathan "Johnny" McCoy, based upon the testimony of two of his friends: Lucas Baker and William Gilliland.

Using the internet and department resources, I researched where the three of them were now.

Johnny McCoy owned a landscaping and snow removal company. The company was in Airway Heights, a city west of Spokane. The company's website touted they'd been in business since 1991, shortly after McCoy had graduated from Washington State University. He had a Facebook account that was private, which didn't matter because I didn't want to send him a friend request. I found a Twitter account he used to retweet tasteless jokes and political memes. He had a clean record, aside from one speeding ticket. He had a concealed carry permit.

Lucas Baker had a dental practice on 29th Avenue. His DOL record showed he lived on Brown's Mountain on the South Hill. He was on the board of directors for several nonprofits. His Facebook page wasn't hidden so I could see pictures of his wife and two sons at their lake cabin. His wife ran a blog selling accessories to other fashionista moms. His criminal record was spotless.

I couldn't find William Gilliland through Google, Yahoo, or any of the other search engines. He had a revoked driver's license due to several arrests for drunken driving with a current Failure to Appear warrant for his arrest. Besides a single DUI conviction, there was no other criminal history of note.

***

I dropped into the office of Dr. Baker near the corner of 29th Avenue and Southeast Boulevard. The building was new and of high quality. It was a glass and steel structure that seemed out of place with the other construction in the neighborhood. Its interior construction was also high quality, but, like the building, it was cold and unfeeling.

In the corner, a video game system sat low, with two kids playing quietly. A doting mother hovered near them, watching cartoon-like characters bop up and down on the screen. The kids squealed with delight and laughed as they played. It was a pleasant sound I wouldn't normally expect at a dentist's office.

I approached the front desk, and the young receptionist smiled. The nameplate on the counter read *Tiffany*. Her dark-rimmed glasses highlighted her green eyes. "Are you here for an appointment?"

I pulled the badge from my belt and discreetly held it over the counter, out of sight from the mother and kids. "I'm Detective Nash with the Spokane Police Department," I quietly said. "I'd like to speak with Dr. Baker, please."

Tiffany's eyes widened. "He's in with a patient."

"I'll wait. Please let him know I'm here."

When she hurried into the back, I sat in one of the uncomfortable chairs and watched the kids play their game. The soft music in the room was familiar, and I tried to place it. It took me several minutes before I realized it was a Muzak version of Def Leppard's "Photograph." The first slap of reality that we've crossed an age bracket is when the music of our childhood appears on classic rock stations. The second slap must be when it's converted to elevator music. There's no coming back from that moment.

The door to the back room opened, and a man roughly my age looked out. When he made eye contact with me, he walked over. "I'm Dr. Baker."

"Is there someplace quiet we can talk?"

I followed him to his office. It was smaller than I expected, but representative of his life. His degree from the University of Washington hung prominently on the wall. Pictures of his wife and sons hung around it, but the degree was the center point of everything.

He sat behind the desk and took his glasses off. He grabbed a cleaning cloth and set about rubbing the lenses. "What's this about?"

"Jennifer Williams."

He stared at me for several moments before saying, "And?"

"We're taking a fresh look at her case."

He put his glasses back on. "Why are you doing that?"

"Her murder was never solved. We occasionally revisit unsolved cases to see if we can find something new."

He steepled his fingers together and rested his elbows on the arms of his chair. "How can I help?"

"I'm following up on the alibi you gave Johnny McCoy."

"And?"

"You stated Johnny, William Gilliland—"

"Bill."

"Bill Gilliland and you were camping when Jennifer was murdered."

"Yes, that's right."

"Where were you camping?"

"Farragut State Park."

"Tents and such?"

He nodded. His neck developed several red blotches.

We stared at each other in silence for several moments. Baker didn't avert his eyes. Instead, he watched me with great interest.

I glanced at the photographs on the wall. "You've made a nice life for yourself, Doc. Nice family. Honorable profession."

"I've done all right," he said.

I turned my attention to him. "Do you know what a polygraph is? You might call it a lie detector test."

His eyes crinkled at the edges.

"I'd like to schedule a polygraph for you," I said, studying his reaction. "You'd be willing to take a lie detector test, right?"

Baker slowly un-steepled his hands and placed them on his desk. "Why? Am I suspected of something?"

"I thought it would be a show of good faith."

"Good faith?"

"You alibied a friend. That always seems convenient. Do you know what I mean? I don't see the harm in sitting in the chair for a polygraph, do you?"

The dentist stared at me, not answering.

I stood and said, "I'll set it up, then I'll let you know when you can come down."

He never spoke as I moved to the door. I hesitated there before turning back to him. His brow was creased as if in deep concentration.

"If the test reveals you're lying, I'll charge you with obstructing an investigation."

"Not that I don't trust you to be honorable, but can I bring my lawyer?" he said.

I smiled. At first, the polygraph had been a bluff, just to see how he would react. If he was up for it, I might have passed on it. They aren't without their inherent flaws, which can be exploited by any competent defense attorney. However, now that he was backed into a corner, I was interested to see how the dentist would behave.

"Of course you can bring your lawyer, Dr. Baker. I'll be in touch."

***

I went to the last known address for Bill Gilliland. It was a bungalow in West Central. If Lucas Baker was on one end of the income spectrum, Bill Gilliland was the opposite. West Central was one of the poorest and roughest neighborhoods in Spokane, and this stretch of houses was crying for either gentrification or demolition. I walked up an unshoveled walk and climbed icy stairs before getting to a porch littered with snow-covered trash.

I knocked on the door and waited. Inside, a television blared. A couple of minutes passed before I pounded on the door.

Footsteps hurried to the door, and a teenaged girl appeared. She was in volleyball shorts, the kind that leaves nothing to the imagination, and a sports bra that did its best to hold her in place. Her long blond hair was stringy and unkempt. She was a few years past Lolita, but still trouble for whoever crossed her path. "What?" she said with the arrogance of youth.

"Is Bill Gilliland here?"

"Who?"

"William Gilliland. This is his last known address."

"I don't know who you're talking about," she said.

"Whossit, baby?" a voice called smoothly from a back room. A Hispanic male, easily in his late thirties, sauntered up to her. He wore only sweatpants. Tattoos ran across his muscular torso and down his arms. Ink ran up his neck, a mixture of words and animals. He slid his arm around the girl's waist and pulled her into him. "Whadda you want?" he said, his eyes carefully examining me, from shoes to hair.

"William Gilliland. Goes by Bill. He's supposed to live here."

He pursed his lips before saying, "Nobody here by that name."

"What's your name?" I asked.

"Why you wanna know?"

"Yeah, why do you want to know?" the girl chimed in.

I opened my long coat to reveal my badge and gun. "I'm Detective Nash. I'm trying to locate Gilliland, and you don't seem to want to help. She looks young, by the way."

"I'm eighteen," the girl protested.

The man smiled, revealing a surprisingly white set of teeth. "Listen, I don't want trouble, Officer. She's legal, and your man ain't here."

"Mind if I search the house?"

His smile faded. "I do mind."

A siren wailed in the distance.

"Why can't I take a quick walk-through to make sure Gilliland isn't here?"

"I don't like cops. No offense, Officer."

I shrugged. "None taken. What's your name?"

He pursed his lips again and looked around, stalling. The wailing siren faded into the distance.

"We can play the name game for a bit," I said. "Or I can walk out of here and call the various units that you don't want me to contact. I'll end up finding out who you are and whether you're on probation or parole. Which one is it? I'm going to go with parole, am I right?"

He ran his tongue along his teeth as he stared at me.

"One call to your parole officer…"

"Antonio Garcia."

"And your name?" I said to the girl.

"I don't have to say shit."

Antonio squeezed her waist and pulled her into him with a yank. She winced in pain. "Bitch, don't play around now," he whispered.

"Melissa," she said like a scolded child. "Melissa Ballard."

"Antonio, if you don't want me to search your apartment because there's stuff there that violates your conditions of parole, I get it. I don't care about you. No offense."

"None taken," he said with a nod and a smile.

"And I care less about her."

"Hey," the girl said. Antonio squeezed her again to stop another protest. She whimpered from the moment of pain.

"What I care about is Gilliland. He's crucial in a murder investigation."

"Officer, there is no one of that name here. Never has been. And, honestly, I don't know anyone named Gilligan."

"Gilliland."

"Yeah, that's what I said. Gilligan."

We stared at each other for a moment until I nodded. "Fair enough. Have a nice day."

He nodded back. "Sorry for the trouble." He quietly closed the door as I left the porch.

***

I arrived at the office of Greenway Landscaping in Airway Heights, located just off Highway 2. It was an older building with a large, gated area behind it. Various trucks with snowplows were parked in the lot. There were also a dozen or so trailers used for hauling lawn equipment that sat empty, waiting for another change in the weather to return them to their usefulness.

A bell chimed when I opened the front door and walked into the office. The elderly receptionist sitting behind the gunmetal gray desk looked away from her computer to me. "Yes?"

"Johnny McCoy, please?"

"One moment." She lifted the receiver for the phone, and a door behind her opened.

A man in his early fifties stuck his head out and looked directly at me. "Come on in," he said with a wave and then disappeared back into his office.

"McCoy?" I asked the receptionist.

She looked confused at what had just occurred.

Johnny McCoy's office was simple. There was 1970s wood paneling on the walls. A map of the county covered one wall. Photos of his family covered the other wall. There was a picture of McCoy and two teenaged girls at SeaWorld petting a dolphin.

"Nice photo with the dolphins," I said.

"Last summer," he said.

Johnny McCoy looked like he was desperately hanging on to his youth. He was tan, far too bronzed for the dead of winter, and his modern haircut was spiked up in the front with gel. He was buff from hours spent pushing weights somewhere. He might have owned a landscaping/snow plowing company, but he sure didn't look that way.

He dropped into the chair behind his desk and watched me as I sat across from him.

I pointed to the picture on the wall. "Where do your girls go to school?"

"Ferris."

"Twins?"

He nodded. "This is their senior year. They're off to college next."

"Have they picked a school?"

"One is going to Southern California. The other, University of Arizona."

"Must be expensive."

"It's okay. They've both been extended scholarships for volleyball. They're good girls. But you didn't come to talk about my girls."

"You haven't asked who I am," I said. "I'm assuming Lucas Baker called you before I got here."

He nodded and opened his hands in an apologetic gesture.

"You're aware the department is looking into the case regarding Jennifer Williams?"

Another nod.

"Tell me what happened that night."

"Seriously?"

"What?" I asked.

"I've told this story I don't know how many times. It's got to be in a file somewhere."

"Tell it again."

McCoy sighed. "You know, I hate talking about this. Hell, I hate thinking about it, to be honest. She was a great girl."

"Well, we never caught who did it. That's why you need to tell the story again. I'm new to the case. Pretend I've never heard about what happened."

McCoy considered what I said, then nodded. "The three of us went camping at Farragut State Park. The guys went up there on Friday after school. I joined them Saturday afternoon after seeing Jennifer that morning. The three of us came home late Sunday night."

"Why did you go late? Why not go up on Friday?"

"I was working. Back then, I worked at Burger King. I had a shift on Friday that I couldn't pawn off on anyone. It's not like today when kids just won't show up for a week and then walk back in like nothing's wrong. The work ethic was different back then."

"When did you learn of Jennifer's murder?"

"Monday morning at school. The detective who pulled me out of class to interview me was the one who broke the news."

"Her family said you were very supportive following her death."

"Mr. and Mrs. Williams are good people. I like them a lot. They've always been nice. I check in on them occasionally."

"Did Jennifer ever tell you about the possibility of another boyfriend?"

He frowned. "No."

I watched him for a moment.

"It was a long time ago, but wouldn't you have been mad about her seeing someone else?"

His face was impassive. "She wasn't, Detective. And if she was, what difference does it make now? She's dead. I've got a family. Life has moved on."

"After all these years, do you have any idea who might have wanted to hurt Jennifer?"

"I racked my brain on that question for a lot of years. Nothing ever made sense. Finally, I had to give up and move on."

"Rumor is you guys were breaking up."

Something passed over his face so fast I almost didn't catch it. His expression returned to its impassive state. "That's not true. We weren't breaking up."

"Are you sure? You looked upset for a moment when I asked."

"Because it wasn't true. I don't like her memory being tarnished. She was a great girl, Detective. She didn't deserve what happened to her."

"Ever hear of a polygraph?"

"You mean a lie detector? Yeah, sure."

"When I asked Lucas if he would take the polygraph to verify the accuracy of his testimony, he asked if he could bring his lawyer with him. Why do you think he responded that way?"

McCoy smiled easily. "Detective, the guy is balling his receptionist. Have you seen her? Who can blame him? Tiffany's a little pop tart. If I had a shot at her, I would probably risk it, too. Lucas is afraid he'd be caught and get in trouble with his wife, who is a ballbuster in the truest sense of the word."

"What about you? Would you take the test?"

"I'm not balling my receptionist," McCoy said with a relaxed smile. "I've got nothing to be afraid of."

"So, you'll take the test?"

"I didn't have anything to do with Jennifer's murder, Detective. She was my girlfriend. I would have hoped her murderer would have been found by now. If my taking the test will help you get one step closer, then let's do it."

I stood and put away my notebook. "Thank you for your time."

45

I worked late until almost seven.

After everyone left, the office took on a peaceful level of quiet. Occasionally, I would hear someone walk down the hallway, but they never stepped into the Major Crimes office.

To be honest, I wasn't working. I had quit working long before five. The last count of Solitaire games I had played was twelve. That didn't mean I stopped playing. It just meant I stopped counting.

When I admitted I didn't want to go home, I knew it was time to do precisely that.

On the way home, I grabbed a hamburger from Carl's Jr. and ate it while I drove, preferring to do that instead of eating alone at my dining room table.

I drove by my neighbor's house, the one with the Christmas tree and its stupid blinking lights.

Inside my house, I slowly walked up to my bedroom. For a moment, I considered the clothes piled around the room, and the boxes now stacked in the corner. Maybe I should work on them some, make some headway, and finally decide what to do with all her stuff.

Instead, I undressed and went to bed.

It wasn't even 8:30 p.m.

46

I awoke with a start, reached over, and turned on the light next to my bed. I grabbed the notebook that was always on the nightstand to write down the lyrics in my head. Through bleary eyes, I stared at them as if they had some meaning.

The clock said it was 3:04 a.m.

I turned off the light and closed my eyes. The lyrics didn't go away. They just kept looping around. The more they did, the more important they felt. The clock now said it was 3:12 a.m. I turned on the light and watched the clock tick by for a few minutes before I made a decision.

I rolled out of bed, wrapped a blanket around myself, and hurried to my computer. I typed the string of lyrics into my computer and Google produced the song "Sign Your Name" by Terence Trent D'Arby. I read the lyrics, thinking to myself there must be something important here.

Was Bobbie telling me something?

Or was my subconscious just moving random bits of old data around?

Maybe I really was losing my mind.

A quick change of sites and I was on YouTube. It took a few attempts to find it, but I finally got the official video. The song was fine, and the video didn't seem to reveal anything. I remember seeing it when I was younger. I still felt unsatisfied, though. Something kept telling me I was missing something important.

I then read the biography of D'Arby on Wikipedia, learning he had legally changed his name to Sanada Maitreya in 2001. It didn't answer the question lurking inside.

I researched the song itself. It was released in December 1987, hit as high as number 4 on the charts, and its B-Side was "Greasy Chicken."

None of that answered the question: *Why did this song feel so important?*

I wandered around my cold house, wondering what I was missing. Finally, I forced myself back to bed after 4 a.m.

Sleep remained elusive for some time.

＊

When I awoke shortly after 7 a.m., I got dressed and went to Bobbie's grave.

It was still dark, but there were lights in the cemetery. After clearing away the new snow from her headstone, I stood there with my hands in my pockets, my coat collar turned up, and my shoulders hunched.

"I woke up with another song this morning," I said. "This one feels different from the others. Like it's important or something. You sent this one, didn't you? I mean, you really sent this one for a specific reason."

I looked around, searching for anyone listening to me. I felt crazy.

"Are you sending me messages? If you are, then I don't understand. Especially this one. Help me understand."

Cars drove by the cemetery, their engines humming loudly through the morning silence.

"What am I supposed to do with this? Am I supposed to sign something? Did I forget to sign something? Did you sign something that I'm supposed to find?"

I looked up in the darkness, hoping for an answer. Another car entered the cemetery. I watched it as it weaved its way through the graveyard to another section and stopped, its taillights glowing red in the morning darkness. A woman got out and walked to a grave and stood silently.

"Maybe you are the one doing this to me, sending me these songs. I'm willing to believe. I don't know. Maybe it's my head doing this. Maybe I'm messing with myself."

I crouched and touched the marble that bore her name.

"I miss you so much."

Tears formed in my eyes, and I fought them back. I stood and shoved my hands deep into my coat pockets, pulling the coat tight around my neck.

"What are these songs supposed to mean? Cheers one day. 'Gimme Shelter' another. 'The Green Manalishi.' I don't understand what you're trying to tell me."

I turned and headed back toward my car. I stopped, spun around, and ran back to her headstone.

"Was someone else supposed to sign something? That's it, right? It has to do with someone else."

47

"I've got the proof Tony Lawrence was murdered."

Glenn Higgins leaned on his crutches. "Okay, I'll bite."

We were standing at Glenn's temporary desk inside the Crime Analysis office.

"When Lawrence was brought in for an interview following the death of Hamilton Martin, he was wearing an old leather jacket. He let us search his house, but we didn't find the coat the victim wore the night of his death or the murder weapon."

"Okay. So?"

"Fast forward three days, and Lawrence is found dead in his apartment from an apparent overdose. Martin's coat and the murder weapon were suddenly in Lawrence's possession. In fact, it was so obvious that he was wearing the coat. There was no way we were going to miss that evidence. The knife was also in the pocket of the jacket."

"There's a reason there was a television show called *America's Dumbest Criminals*," Glenn said. "They do dumb things. Your guy thought he got away with it and decided to parade around in the coat. He gets high to celebrate, but he's not very good at controlling himself, and he overdoses."

"That's what they want us to think."

Glenn's eyes slanted. "Who is they?"

"I don't know that part yet, but April Scott is definitely part of them."

"She's in jail, right?"

"Yes."

"How can she be part of the plan? How do you know this is murder?"

"I don't know, but April wanted me to search Lawrence's apartment, right? When I told her I did and didn't find anything, she was disappointed. No, that's not right. She wasn't disappointed. She was surprised. I think she thought those items would have been in the apartment before I got there to search. Somebody must have planted them for her."

"That's conjecture."

"I agree, totally, but here's the smoking gun," I said. I pulled out the Consent to Search card Tony Lawrence had signed and placed it on my desk. His signature was big and loopy. Then I laid a copy of his suicide note on the desk next to the card. The name on the note was small and tight. It appeared there was no effort to mimic Lawrence's signature. It was clearly a fraud.

"Even the printing on the card doesn't look anything similar," I said, pointing at different letters.

"I agree they don't look alike, but that doesn't mean it was murder."

I smacked the desk. "Yes, it does."

"The guy was a drug user at best and a drug addict at worst. He overdosed. He could have been smashed out of his mind when he wrote that note."

"You don't believe me."

Glenn reached out and put his hand on my shoulder. "It's not whether I believe you or not. It's what we can prove. Do I believe you're on the right track? Yes. Can it be proved in a court of law? Who knows?"

"I'll prove it," I said.

***

"April Scott," I told the deputy behind the counter.

He typed her name into the system. "She's had only one visitor, her attorney. Wanda Acosta. Almost a dozen times."

"Her attorney is Acosta? How the hell can she afford Wanda?"

The deputy shrugged.

"What about calls?"

"We monitor calls, but she only talks with her attorney. You know the rules on monitoring those."

"Shit. So, her father, he's never called or shown up?"

"As I said, Wanda is it."

"Anything else?"

"I want to talk with her."

I waited for thirty minutes while the jail staff brought April to a secure interview room. She walked in, wearing the orange jumpsuit customary for the prisoners. Her face was free of make-up, and her hair was clean but disheveled. She dropped onto the chair across from me and crossed her arms.

"Afternoon, Detective."

"You set up Tony Lawrence," I said.

She leaned her chair back. "I'm not supposed to talk with you."

"What?"

"My attorney is on the way. She said I'm not to talk with you."

"Right, I heard. Wanda Acosta? Is your father paying for this? You said your mother took off when you were a kid, right? So it's got to be your father. What's his name?"

She stared at me.

"Wanda Acosta is the highest-priced defense attorney in the city. How can you afford her?"

"I've got my ways," she said with a satisfied smirk.

My face warmed. "Who are you screwing to get that kind of legal help?" As soon as I said it, I knew it was wrong.

She shook her head. "Not nice, Detective."

The door opened, and Wanda Acosta stormed in. The air of power with her was unmistakable. She was short and full-figured, with an attractive round face that hid a steel mind and an acid tongue.

She slapped her briefcase on the table, opened it, and pulled a yellow pad of paper and pen from inside. After closing the briefcase, she put it on the floor, sat in the chair next to April, and addressed her client. "How are you doing, sweetie?"

"He asked who I was fucking to afford you."

Acosta whirled to me. "Are you fucking kidding me, Detective?"

"That's not—"

Acosta pointed the end of her pen at me. "If you ever say anything like that in my presence, I will have you before Chief Dillon so fast it will make your head spin."

"That's not what I said."

"It's not? Then what did you say, Detective? Why don't you tell me the exact words?"

And with that, she nailed me.

"Why don't we just end this interview?" I asked.

"Oh, yeah, the interview is done, but you still need to tell me the exact words you said to my client." Acosta's pen hovered over her notepad.

The room seemed smaller and warmer. Both women watched me for different reasons. April to get even. Acosta for leverage.

For a moment, I thought about not saying anything, just getting up and walking out. Instead, I knew I needed to own up to my mistake. I said, "I asked who she was screwing to afford you."

"That's the same fucking thing!" Acosta said, tossing her pen on the table.

April Scott smiled. She'd gotten her pound of flesh.

Acosta stood, opened her briefcase, and tossed the yellow pad back inside. "If you ever want to speak to my client again, you will schedule a time to do so with me present, that is convenient for both my client and me. Do you understand?"

I stared at her.

"Do you understand, Detective?" she repeated.

I nodded.

"Secondly, I'm going to talk with the chief. We're on the board of the Spokane Club, and we have a lunch meeting scheduled. Tomorrow. I'm going to give you a head start. You can fall on your sword, or I can impale you with it. Your choice."

I stood and motioned to the guard outside the interview room. He opened the door. "All done?" he asked.

From behind me, Acosta said, "Oh, he's done. He just doesn't know it yet."

***

"You asked her who she was screwing?"

I nodded.

Chief Liam Dillon shoved his hands into his pockets and lowered his head. He closed his eyes while he thought. He had remained standing behind his desk after telling us to sit and explain why we were there.

Captain Ackerman sat next to me, clearly uncomfortable at being in this position while the chief decided my future. When I'd returned from the jail interview room, I immediately reported to Ackerman's office and told him what happened. I should have reported it to Lieutenant Brand, but he would have kicked it up to the captain, anyway. I just skipped the middleman. Once the red drained from Ackerman's face, we walked to Dillon's office. Ackerman knew that we had to get in front of him before Wanda Acosta ambushed him in a public forum.

Chief Dillon was a stocky man who spent many of his younger years weightlifting. Now that he was in his late fifties, he still found time for the gym, but he had the body of a part-time lifter who didn't follow a strict diet anymore. He might have gotten soft around the middle, but there was hard muscle built upon his frame. His bald head had been shaved for years. He had the look of an angry street fighter, much of it purposely perpetrated to deal with the city's administration. However, he was incredibly bright and well-thought-of by the line-level troops.

The clock on the wall ticked away as the chief continued to think. Finally, he looked up and turned to me.

"I'm trying to remember the show. I think it was *M*A*S*H* where it occurred."

"*M*A*S*H?*" Ackerman said.

"Yeah, I'm pretty sure it was that one. Do you know the show?"

We both nodded.

"Remember the characters Hawkeye and Hunnicutt?"

Again, Ackerman and I nodded.

"There was an episode where Hawkeye spent the entire episode worried Hunnicutt was going to get even with him for a practical joke. In the end, that was the revenge."

Ackerman and I looked at each other, confused at what the chief was saying.

"Hawkeye was so wound up and worried sick because he believed Hunnicutt was waiting to spring a practical joke on him from around every corner. Therefore, he couldn't relax. Hawkeye was always waiting for something to jump out and get him, but it never did. The longer it didn't happen, the worse it got for Hawkeye. He tortured himself. That was Hunnicutt's revenge. There never was a practical joke, yet that was the practical joke. Get it?"

We both stared at him.

Dillon shook his head when we weren't getting what he was saying. "Acosta wants you to punish yourself, Nash. The fear of the unknown will eat you up. As cops, we need to deal with the problem and move on, right?"

"Yes, sir."

"If Acosta approaches me, I'll tell her you came to me and I reprimanded you. I will handle her. She's got a terrible reputation, but she's a fantastic lady. That reputation is needed in her line of work."

The chief finally sat at his desk and studied me. "I heard about your fight with Parker. First that and now this. Did you come back too soon after your wife's death, Dallas?"

"I'm fine, sir. The work is helpful."

Dillon turned his attention to Ackerman.

The captain put his hand on my back. "He's doing well. Work is solid, as always."

"Maybe you should talk with Stephen."

"The department shrink?" I said, protest in my voice.

"I could order it."

I closed my mouth.

"How about Gabe?"

"The chaplain?"

Dillon smiled. "Yeah, the chaplain. If you sit down with Gabe or Stephen on Monday, I'll make this go away. Deal?"

"I'll talk with Gabe."

Dillon looked at the captain. "What do you think?"

I stared straight ahead, not making eye contact with either of them.

"He's solid," Ackerman said. "A sit down with Gabe does everybody good."

The chief studied me in silence for a few moments. Finally, he said, "Stay out of trouble, Dallas," and turned his attention to some papers on his desk.

Ackerman and I stood and quickly left.

***

"You look like someone kicked your dog."

I stared at my computer screen. "How do you find someone who has no current record on file with DOL, no recent arrests, and no online presence?"

Glenn dropped heavily into the chair at his desk, his braced leg jutting directly out in front of him. He held on to the crutches. "How's a guy not have an online presence?"

"He doesn't use a computer. If he had one, his digital footprint would appear somewhere, right? And he's not on social media. If he did, he'd be super easy to find. He doesn't own property because a name search would pop him up that way, which it hasn't."

"Do you think it's a conscious decision?"

"What's that mean?"

"Think about what you said. No computer, no social media, and no property. If he's into conspiracy theories, if that's what drives his decisions, he'll be a tough man to find, because every decision he makes will be a conscious one to keep him off the grid."

"Right."

"However, if he's just a guy who doesn't have a computer and property for whatever reason—he's poor, he's a Luddite, whatever—we have to go somewhere he'd jump on the grid to get help."

"What's a Luddite?"

"Someone who hates technology."

"So, where would someone like that end up on the grid?"

"When's the last time you've been to the public library?"

"It's been years."

Glenn smiled. "Do you know you can borrow movies from the library?"

I shook my head.

"You can also borrow books on CD, music CDs, comic books, and magazines. You can even borrow e-books now. It's crazy."

"You go to the library?"

"My parents raised me to appreciate the library. What can I say? I dig it."

"I didn't know that."

"You wouldn't. It's not like I brag about my library card. Anyway, I've got a friend there who might do me a solid."

Glenn turned to his phone and picked up the receiver. After he dialed, he was soon cooing softly into the phone.

To avoid eavesdropping on him, I turned my attention back to my computer. I tried to concentrate, but I wasn't successful.

I couldn't hear what he was saying, but whoever he was talking with was very familiar to him. The cooing and laughter continued for several minutes until he snapped his fingers. I turned his way.

He mimed writing something in the air. I quickly handed him a pad of paper and a pen. Glenn took them and turned away from me. He chuckled again, and the cooing started over.

I ignored him and went back to my computer. An email had come in from Lieutenant Brand that detectives were expected to dress in a professional manner consistent with department policy. It was wordy and policy heavy. I hit the delete button before I made it through the second paragraph. I wasn't sure how many detectives would make it further than I did, but I doubted it would be many.

When Glenn hung up the phone, I leaned back in my chair and studied him. "Who was that you were dripping honey for?"

"That is none of your beeswax, and you're welcome." He tossed the pen and paper to me.

"What's this?"

"William Gilliland's address. Courtesy of a friendly neighborhood librarian."

"How friendly?" I asked, glancing up at my partner.

Glenn stood with his crutches. "It's not like I brag about my library card."

As he hobbled down the hall, I looked at the written address. It was in East Central. It was almost 5 p.m., and I was ready to call it quits after the run-in with Wanda Acosta and a counseling session with the chief.

Unless McCoy and Baker told him, William Gilliland wouldn't know I was looking for him.

If they had talked with him, he knew I was going to ask about a polygraph, so he'd be prepared for it. Regardless, it was likely he wasn't going anywhere, and I wanted to put the week behind me.

48

I woke up with a portion of a song playing in my head.

It was Bob Seger's "Turn the Page." It was a simple refrain that kept looping, but I knew the song. It's about life as a musician and the trials of being on the road. The song talked about how Seger would roll into one town, deal with whatever adversity was there, and then move on again.

After the experience with "Sign Your Name," I believed there had to be some significant relevance for "Turn the Page." Maybe it wasn't Bobbie sending me messages, but someone was. I wasn't going to mess around with the importance of the songs.

I was showered and dressed, went to the kitchen to start a pot of coffee and made some toast. With breakfast in hand, I situated myself in front of the computer and researched the song.

The lyrics were as I remembered them, and nothing jumped out at me as substantial. I even checked out Metallica's version of the song. For a cover, it was respectable, but it didn't give me anything further to go on.

I leaned back in my chair and folded my arms over my chest.

***

It was snowing again, a heavy, wet blanket dropping across the region. Driving an hour towards Farragut State Park made absolutely no sense. Except it felt right once I decided to do it. It felt even better when I got in my truck and started driving eastbound on I-90. I just wanted to get out of the house.

I passed on seeing Bobbie that morning due to the weather. I would stop by and see her on the way home. The weather demanded I get a jump on driving.

Farragut State Park was in northern Idaho, at the tip of Lake Pend Oreille, on the edge of the Coeur d'Alene National Forest. Due to the deepness of the lake, the US Navy had established a training center for several years at Farragut during World War II. Before it was decommissioned and turned into a state park, almost 300,000 sailors went through basic training there.

Usually, the drive was an hour from Spokane. Due to the limited visibility caused by snow and the slickness on the roads, it was almost double that now. Once I hit US 95, northbound in Idaho, traffic slowed to a crawl.

I'd camped at Farragut a few times with Bobbie. They were never long trips, just a few days here and there when we'd throw a tent up and escape from society. The lake was beautiful, and we'd hike for a bit in the forest. Our goal was just to get away from people as much as work.

I thought about Johnny McCoy and his buddies, Lucas Baker and William Gilliland. They didn't have cell phones when they went camping. Baker and Gilliland had gone to the state park ahead of McCoy, and he arrived later. No one thought it was odd for the time.

Why would they?

Things were different back then, but was the limit of communication seen as more than a hindrance? Or was it just accepted? Did everyone consider the separation of friends as seemingly normal? Did everyone accept that upon McCoy's arrival at the state park, he would spend time searching for his friends? Or did they have a particular spot where they always went?

Maybe the friends had a system where they would leave a note for him at the ranger station. I made a mental note to ask them about it the next time I interviewed them.

When I finally arrived at the entrance to the park, there were a variety of vehicles in the parking lot. Several people unloaded cross-country skis, and some carried snowshoes in their hands. I pulled up to the ranger's window.

An older woman with a kindly smile greeted me.

I showed her my badge. "I just want to get out for a moment, then turn around and head back home."

"You go ahead, hon," she said.

I pulled into the parking lot and climbed out of my truck. The falling snow was big, fluffy flakes, but I tried to imagine a summer scene. I closed my eyes and imagined the sun peeking through the thick trees, the smell of pine, and the dusty roads.

Is this where the three friends spent a carefree weekend before they learned the horrible truth of Jennifer's death?

Or is this where they conspired to hide the truth that one of them killed her?

Maybe they all did, I thought. Perhaps they all had a hand in killing her.

Crazier things have happened.

I opened my eyes. My shoulders were covered with snow. I brushed them off and got back in my truck. I waved at the ranger as I drove out of the park.

***

The snow continued to fall in heavy waves on the drive home.

My feeling of confidence slowly disappeared and was replaced with dread. Several cars had slid off the road in various places, their hazard lights blinking in the gray darkness of a winter afternoon.

I gripped the steering wheel too hard and had to force myself to relax consciously. A tight grip on the wheel would not allow me to react quickly in the event something happened.

The typically one-hour drive to Farragut, which had grown to two hours on the way there, would easily surpass that on the way home due to a collision on the freeway somewhere up ahead. Our entire column of traffic was at a standstill.

I checked my gas gauge and was at a quarter of a tank.

Somewhere behind me, a car honked its horn, then another. Soon, a chorus of horns blasted together. I didn't join in. It wouldn't help anyone and would only serve to agitate all drivers involved. After a couple of minutes, the horns stopped.

Soon sirens were heard in the distance, and state and county patrol cars passed us on the shoulders of the freeway. An ambulance, its lights and sirens blaring, followed in the wake of the patrol cars.

Congestion eased over time as state patrol officers directed traffic around an ugly multiple-car pile-up across three lanes of traffic. I imagined somewhere behind us, they would begin diverting traffic off the freeway, so they could begin the long and slow process of documenting the collision and removing the vehicles from the roadway.

The snow continued to fall for the rest of the afternoon, long after I made it home and into the safety of my house. I started a pot of coffee and stood at the front window to watch the falling snow in the glow of the streetlights.

That stupid Christmas tree was blinking again.

It was then I realized I hadn't stopped to see Bobbie.

49

"It's nice to see you, Dallas," Chaplain Gabriel Greene said, escorting me into his office and shutting the door.

"I'm only here because the chief made it mandatory."

His smile slowly faded.

"I'm sorry, Father. You didn't deserve that."

He shook his head and waved his hand, trying to dispel his disappointment. "It's all right, Dallas. I understand. Grab a seat. Want a coffee? I just got this Keurig and, I'll admit, it's a bit of a guilty pleasure having it in my office."

A self-contained coffeemaker sat on the counter behind Gabe's desk.

"I've got French roast, Columbian roast, Dunkin' Donuts blend, hot chocolate—"

"I'll do that. The hot chocolate."

Gabe turned to face me. "I didn't figure you for cocoa."

"I'm feeling out of sorts this morning."

Gabe nodded once, pulled a hot chocolate pod from the rotating dispenser, and clicked it into place within the Keurig coffee machine. A press of a button and it began brewing immediately.

"The coffee culture has changed so much over the past twenty years, hasn't it? Specialty coffees, drive-through stands, these machines. You can go into a convenience store now and get a blended Starbucks drink from the same cooler that sells Pepsi."

I nodded and politely let Gabe continue with his small talk.

I'd stopped by to see Bobbie in the morning. After missing her on Saturday, I was snowed in on Sunday. Eleven inches fell on Saturday, and then the temperature rose enough Sunday for freezing rain to follow. The roads were an absolute mess, so I did the safe thing and stayed hunkered down.

The groundskeepers did an admirable job of keeping pathways clear, but it took me a while to find her headstone. When I did, I cleared the frozen snow away from it. I stood in the snowy mess, up past my ankles, and apologized for not seeing her over the weekend. I'd brought a pair of combat boots to wear while visiting her and changed out of them when I got back to my car.

When the hot chocolate was done, Gabe pulled my cup from the machine and handed it to me. He then pulled a pod out for himself, clicked it into the coffeemaker, and started the process again.

He leaned back against the counter and crossed his arms. "Dallas, while you're here, please be truthful with me. We've known each other for a long time. You know who I am, and I know who you are. I'm not here to judge. I'd like to help."

I sighed. "Gabe, you know I think highly of you and what you do, but I don't want to be here."

"That's obvious."

I sipped my hot chocolate. "It's nothing personal. It's just that you'll want to talk about her, and I don't."

"We don't have to do that. We can talk about anything you want to. It doesn't even have to be about you. We can talk about football if you want."

"You'd be okay with that?"

"Why not? You're just supposed to talk with me."

"The chief, even Ackerman, thinks my problems are coming from not dealing with my feelings surrounding her. I'm sure they'll be on your back if we don't have some sort of conversation about this."

Gabe opened his hands in a *what are you going to do?* Gesture before crossing his arms again.

"She's gone, Gabe. I know that. It's not the first time someone close to me has died."

"It's the first time your wife has died, though."

We fell silent as I thought about that. Gabe turned and pulled his coffee cup from the Keurig machine, then sat across from me. He didn't say anything. Instead, he just sipped his coffee. Eventually, I listened to Gabe's breathing, knowing he would outlast me in remaining quiet.

"I'm getting it under control," I said.

"What are you getting under control?"

"My feelings."

"And what are those feelings, exactly?"

"Sadness."

"Of course, we all experience that. What else?"

"Loneliness, I guess."

"To be expected. Anything else?"

"I don't know."

"Are you sure?"

I sipped from my cup and thought about his question. "If I had to give it a name, I'd say I'm angry."

"About what?"

"About it all. It makes absolutely no sense, right? A fucking deer? She dies because of a deer? If she hadn't gone to her friend's house that night, none of this would have happened."

"How do you know?"

"What?"

Gabe lifted his cup to his mouth but hesitated. He lowered the cup to ask, "How do you know none of it would have happened?"

I raised my hand to stop him. "If you're going to tell me God has a plan for us all, I'm going to get up and leave."

"I wasn't going to tell you that. But if it wasn't a deer, how do you know she wouldn't have been hit by a drunk driver later during that drive home? Or the next day? Or that something else wouldn't have happened? Every day is full of risks, and we move through it all with the happy expectation of surviving."

I stared at him.

"Sometimes, things happen in life for no reason."

"That's an odd thing for a man of God to say."

"Dallas, things don't always make sense. They make sense to God, but to us down here on the ground, there may never be rhyme or reason. We try to apply platitudes like God's will or divine plan to make us feel better, to make us feel like we're smart, and have some bit of control by putting it into God's hands. But who knows, really? In the end, we're dealing with what we see and with our faith, and we must shoehorn the two together."

He suddenly looked weary.

"You okay, Gabe?"

His smile returned, but it wasn't as pure as before. "I'm doing fine, Dallas. This is about you."

I looked at the pictures of the various officers and their families on the walls. A lot of them had young children in the photos. I sipped my hot chocolate and studied their faces.

"We never had kids," I said.

"Did you want to?"

I nodded.

"Why didn't you?"

"We couldn't. We were… When we found out, we put that behind us. It was something we moved past. I think about it now and then, though, what it might have been like to have had a child. It would have been a part of her that would have lived on. That I could have held on to."

My eyes continued to scan the photos while Gabe remained quiet.

"Do you ever wake up to a song in your head?"

He sucked his lips in as he thought and then shook his head. "No, I don't think I have."

"Huh," I said.

"I'm taking it that you do, though. What kind of songs do you wake up to, Dallas?"

"All sorts. Hard rock. Pop songs. Some stuff I haven't listened to in years. Those are the ones that surprise me. I even woke up to the theme song from *Cheers* once."

"The TV show?"

"Yeah, the one about going where—"

"—everybody knows your name?" He smiled. "What do you think it means?"

"Means?" I said. "I don't know if it means anything."

"You must think it's significant because you brought it up here. Did you wake up with a song today?"

"'Lady Strange.'"

Gabe crinkled his nose. "What is that?"

"It's a Def Leppard song. It's old."

"It's not old," Gabe said, "if I've never heard of it."

I stared into my mug for a few seconds. "The songs, they started after she died."

"Do you think she's trying to communicate with you?"

I looked up at Gabe. His eyes were serious, not judging me. "I don't know. Maybe. I mean, I don't normally believe in that stuff. Do you? I wouldn't take you as the type."

"Life is mysterious, Dallas. I don't have all the answers. Sometimes I wish I did, but then life would be very boring with no mystery. Who would want to live that way?"

"You think it could be her sending some sort of code from the afterlife?"

Gabe shrugged. "I'd say probably not. I'm not a psychologist, but more than likely, it's your psyche trying to deal with what's happened and helping you in some way. If the worst it's doing is playing a song for you every morning, then I'd say no harm, no foul, right?"

"I guess," I said, his words causing a wave of sadness to run through me.

"But you're worried about the songs, though. Maybe you think you're going crazy?"

"You're not supposed to say *crazy* to the crazy, Father."

"You're not crazy, Dallas. You're sad. It's life. It happens."

We sat quietly, sipping our drinks. When I finished, I put my cup down on the edge of his desk. "What are you going to tell the chief?"

"That you came by, and we talked. You've held up your end of the bargain."

"Nothing else?"
"I'll keep our conversation in the vault."
I stuck out my hand, and he took it.
"Anytime you want to come back, Dallas."
"Thanks, Gabe. For everything."

50

William Gilliland lived in the basement of an East Central house that had been converted to an apartment. It had a side entrance with several stairs down to its front door. I held on to a makeshift railing to descend the icy concrete stairs.

I knocked on the door and waited. I wanted to back up and get out of the fatal funnel, the area at the opening of a structure that is the most dangerous to stand in, but the stairs were incredibly slick. I pressed up against one of the concrete walls that lined the stairs, limiting my exposure to the door's opening.

The curtains over the door's window parted slightly, and a bearded face appeared. The eyes landed on me.

"Bill?" I asked.

He nodded but continued to stare.

"Can we talk?"

The curtains slowly closed, but the door didn't open. I grabbed the railing and scrambled up and out of the stairwell, waiting for gunfire to ring out. In an instant, my Glock was in my hand, waiting to return fire.

A moment later, the door opened, and Bill's head peered out. He looked up at me, confused. "What are you doing up there?"

"Where did you go?" I said, pulling the gun back from view.

"I had to put some clothes on," he said, turning back into his apartment.

I followed him into the apartment. The smell of body odor and cigarettes was overwhelming. On the big-screen television, a pornographic scene with two women was paused.

"You caught me on my day off," Bill said, dropping onto a ratty couch. He wore a pair of loose shorts and a dirty T-shirt. The T-shirt had the logo *Redtube* printed across the chest. In front of the sofa was a coffee table with a bong, an ashtray full of cigarettes, a roll of toilet paper, and a bottle of AstroGlide on it.

"Go ahead and look around," Bill said.

"Do you know why I'm here?"

Bill lit a cigarette and tossed the lighter on the coffee table. "I figure you're with the property management company or you're looking to buy the place. I'm not late with my rent, so if you're with the management company, it's an inspection."

I opened my jacket, revealing the badge and gun.

His eyes widened. "Oh, shit," he said and leaned forward. He grabbed for the bong and then yanked his hand away from it like it was hot. "That's not mine," he said. "There's weed around here, too. That's not mine, either."

"It's legal now," I said.

He thought for a moment before nervously laughing. "Shit. Old memories, I guess." He took a drag on his cigarette and leaned back on the couch. He put his dirty bare feet on the coffee table.

"Come on, man," I said.

"Huh?"

"You're popping out."

He realized his embarrassment then and leaned forward again, hiding himself with his hands and tucking his testicles back into his shorts.

"Do me a favor, turn off the TV."

Bill laughed. "I gotcha. That stuff distracts me, too. Quality goods and such. You can sit down if you want."

I looked around the small, dirty apartment and immediately knew I would never willingly sit anywhere. I was already counting the moments until I could get back to my car.

Bill sucked on the cigarette a final time before crushing it out. "What are you after, Officer?"

"I'm here about Jennifer Williams."

The slightly goofy smile on Bill's face vanished.

"Have Lucas Baker or Johnny McCoy called you recently?"

He sniffed with disdain. "Johnny wouldn't call me. I haven't talked with him in years."

"How come?"

"You could say we grew apart. Lucas calls once in a great while to check-in. He's got a pretty cushy life, so I'm not all that high on his priority list. I get it. We haven't talked in over a year, but he left me a few messages over the weekend. Crazy coincidence, you asking about them and him leaving me a message, don't you think?"

"Yeah, crazy. Did you call him back?"

Bill waved his hand dismissively. "Nah. When he calls, we usually only talk for a minute about nothing important, so it's not a big deal if I call him back or not. I'll get to it when I get to it. I've had more important things to do."

"Why didn't he stop by?"

"Huh?"

"Why didn't Lucas stop by?"

Bill thought about it for a moment. "He hasn't been to this place yet. I just moved here a few months ago. He doesn't know I live here."

He reached for another cigarette. I thought about asking him not to smoke, but he was bothered as to why I was there. I wanted him to remain as calm as possible for as long as possible.

"Do you remember Jennifer Williams?"

He hesitated for a moment, then lit up without looking at me. "Yeah. She was cool."

"You and Lucas gave an alibi to Johnny. He was the last one to see her alive and then he went camping with you. Is that true?"

Bill nodded. He absently touched a *High Times* magazine on the couch.

"According to all statements, Johnny got out to your campsite shortly after two p.m. and then followed you and Lucas home on Sunday afternoon. Is that right?"

Bill inhaled, exhaled, and then nodded, not making eye contact.

"You're lying."

Bill chewed on his lower lip, his eyes sliding over to me. "No, I'm not."

"I think you are."

He flicked his cigarette, steeled his resolve, and said, "That's the truth."

"Do you watch TV, Bill? Have you seen the lie detector test they have people take?"

He swallowed like he was choking down a mouthful of vitamins. He stuck the cigarette in his mouth and inhaled.

"Do you think you're smart enough to fool one?"

He thought about it before answering, "No."

"I'm going to ask you to take one about the alibi you gave."

"But why?"

"Because I know you're lying."

"If you know, then why do I have to do it?"

"So, I can prove it to everyone and then arrest you for that lie."

His eyes flashed up to me. "What?"

"It's called making false and misleading statements. I believe you helped someone get away with murder for thirty years. Or maybe you were the one who killed her."

The cigarette in his hand vibrated due to his shaking. "I didn't kill her," he said.

"Who did?"

"I don't know."

"You have a suspicion, though."

"No."

"Yes, you do."

He sucked on his cigarette again.

"You have an active warrant, Bill. Do you know that?"

His eyes softened, and he shook his head. "What for?"

"FTA. Failure to Appear. You had a court appearance for malicious mischief last year. Did you forget?"

"Shit," he said, his face falling with disappointment. "I did?"

"Yeah, you did. Should we go to the department and continue talking?"

"Do I have a choice?"

"You do."

He crushed his cigarette. "What do I have to do?"

***

"I've got him," I said, dropping into the chair at my cubicle.

Glenn sat nearby with his leg extended out. "Who?"

"Johnny McCoy."

"The boyfriend in your cold case?"

I nodded. "I found the guys who alibied him. When I confronted one of them about the alibi he gave thirty years ago, he caved. Spilled the beans."

"He said McCoy did it?"

"Well, not fully. I think he's holding out on me still, but he admitted McCoy wasn't there when he said he was. Bill Gilliland did say he and his buddy covered for McCoy. Now that I've got his admission that he lied about the alibi, I'm going to work him some more. As I said, I think he's holding something back, for whatever reason. Maybe he's still got some loyalty, who knows? Regardless, I've got enough to get McCoy."

Glenn leaned back and stared up at the ceiling. "Why would he cave?"

"What?"

He looked at me now. "I mean, this Gilliland has kept the secret for thirty years, right? Why change now?"

"If I was to play armchair psychologist—"

"That's what I'm asking you to do. Doesn't it seem too easy? You walk in, and he just coughs it up. He could have done that at any point in the last thirty years."

"But, he didn't."

"That's right. He didn't. He didn't do it when the original investigator came by. Why?"

"They were tight then."

"Tight?"

"In high school, they were still friends. Doing things together all the time. Now Gilliland lives a separate life from the other two."

"That's enough for him to drop a dime after thirty years?"

I shrugged. "Maybe it was jealousy. He carried an emotional burden, and it's probably eaten him up all these years and held him back from what he could have become. It hasn't bothered his friends or slowed their success, which probably also bothers him. No one has come knocking on his door all these years to push him on the matter. Devlin probably could have broken it years ago if he bothered to interview Gilliland. He never did. I pushed him on the right day, and he finally got to admit McCoy wasn't at the lake with him and Baker. You should have seen the guy. It was like a weight lifted off his shoulders. He actually cried while he wrote his admission. I sort of felt sorry for him."

"He cried?"

"Yeah."

Glenn stared at me. I thought about my interaction with Bill Gilliland, from the first contact to the paused porn movie on the television. I smiled for a brief second when I remembered his involuntary reaction to the bong sitting on the table in front of him. The smile faded, and I closed my eyes.

"What?" Glenn asked, sensing my mood change.

"He was high."

"Stoned?"

"Yeah. The guy was baked and watching porn when I interrupted him."

"So? The admission is slightly tainted. Big deal. That's for the attorneys to argue over."

"Shit."

"You at least know the truth now, and that's something."

I nodded.

Glenn fiddled with his leg brace and left me with my thoughts for a minute. The admission was fine, and I knew it. It's just that I hadn't thought it through before presenting it to Glenn. He had to help me see the information had come too easily for a reason. I should have known that already. My work had been better before Bobbie's death. I could see it now.

"What's your next step?" Glenn asked.

Doubt crept in as I thought about a plan. Finally, I said, "Either I confront McCoy directly or go back and have one more conversation with the other friend, the dentist. Give him a chance to make good."

"If it were me, I'd work on painting your boy into the corner. Ducks in a row, so to speak. Which means get the dentist to verify Gilliland's story. You do that, and then you own McCoy. But, remind me, didn't the dentist want to talk with his lawyer?"

"He said he wanted to bring his lawyer to a polygraph."

Glenn smiled. "That's a totally different thing."

***

"You should probably speak to my lawyer," Dr. Lucas Baker said.

I stared at Baker. I had just told him about Bill Gilliland's admission.

"You don't want to talk with me?"

He leaned back in his chair and crossed his arms. His face was flat, but the red blotches had reappeared on his neck. "I'm not going to let you twist the words of some stoned-out loser into getting me to take back my statement. What I said happened, happened. Nothing is going to change that."

"Gilliland said—"

"If you want to talk about Bill or anything related to Jennifer, I'd like you to go through my attorney."

"Really?"

"Yes, really. I don't like the tone this conversation has taken. I see that you're trying to turn friends against each—"

"Friends? You just called him a stoned-out loser."

"—friends against each other without regard to the long-term implications to them. I've got a successful practice here, and I'm not about to let you screw that up by tromping around like a, like a—"

"Detective?"

"Like a prowling bear through a campsite." His glasses had slipped slightly down his nose as his voice had risen.

I stood and moved to his office door. "Call your lawyer and then come down to the station. If you're not there by tomorrow noon, I'll have an officer pick you up for questioning. Do you understand?"

"We'll be there." With a single finger, he pushed his eyeglasses back into position.

"If you call Johnny, I'll also charge you with obstructing. Do you understand?"

"You can't do that," he said. "I know my rights."

I closed the door on the way out of the office and stopped by the front desk. A young father sat with his son in front of the video game in the corner. No one else was in the lobby. Soft Muzak played through the speakers.

The attractive receptionist with dark hair and dark-rimmed glasses didn't notice me at first. When she finally looked up, her green eyes focused on me, and she smiled. "Yes?"

"Can I ask you a personal question?" I quietly asked.

She glanced left and right before leaning in with a conspiratorial smile.

"Are you and Dr. Baker…?"

She sat upright and blushed. She quickly glanced around for something to do.

"That's all I needed to know," I said and left the dental office.

***

I drove immediately to Greenway Landscaping. The elderly receptionist smiled when I walked in. "Looking for Mr. McCoy?"

"Yes, ma'am."

"He left about an hour ago."

That was before I met with Lucas Baker. "Did he say where he was going?"

"He said he had an appointment, and he'd be back. Should I let him know you stopped by?"

"It's okay. I'll catch him later."

51

It was snowing when I left the house with the beginning lyrics to "Baker Street" playing in my head, the song I woke to that morning. I loved that song growing up. It's one of those times when you realize a song has no repeating chorus and the title is mentioned only once. It's a wonderful tune I've always enjoyed mumbling along with any time it comes on the radio.

Until this morning.

Was Bobbie sending me another message, or was my brain just processing bits and pieces of random information and picked up something on Lucas Baker? Did it then transform that mental flotsam and jetsam into a song I knew to continue this silly charade of otherworldly communication?

I stopped by Bobbie's grave and asked her if she sent me the song. I wrapped my coat tightly around me, fighting off the cold. I waited several minutes for Bobbie to answer me, desperately hoping that she would. When I realized what I was doing, I wondered if this was it.

Had I gone over the edge?

Back in my car, I argued with myself about the importance of "Baker Street" during the slippery commute into the department. It hadn't felt as important as "Sign Your Name," and it didn't feel as intimate as "Just Remember I Love You."

When I finally admitted it could be significant, everything relaxed inside me. Once I did that, the lyrics seemed to retreat to the back burner of my subconscious, and I could focus on the day.

***

When I walked into the bullpen in the morning, there was a new name on the board. It was written in red ink.

Gilliland, W.—Homicide—12/19—Burkett/Delaney

"Baker Street" launched again in my head.

Bill Gilliland was dead, and Burkett and Delany had caught the case. I hurried over to Marci Burkett's cubicle, but she was gone. Her partner, Quinn Delaney, wasn't in either.

Shit, I thought, turning around and looking for an answer to a question I was still trying to formulate. Lieutenant Brand wasn't around.

I headed to Captain Ackerman's office.

"Dallas?" he asked as he put down a cup of coffee.

"Have you gotten the initial report on the Gilliland homicide yet?"

"I'm reviewing some of it now. Why?"

"I interviewed him yesterday."

Ackerman glanced down at the report. "Well, that's interesting. Why, exactly?"

"He provided an alibi for Jennifer Williams's boyfriend. The cold case."

"Yeah, I know the cold case," Ackerman said and slid the report across his desk. I picked it up and read it.

Gilliland was shot in the heart. No casing was found. Moderate-sized entry wound. He fell backward and hit his head on the coffee table. Evidence of trauma to the back of his head. We'd have to wait to know more about the size of the round until the medical examiner removed it.

A neighbor called it in when they heard the gunshot. There was no forced entry, and it didn't appear anything was stolen from his apartment. I flipped through the digital photographs, and nothing looked out of place. I had to concur with the early assessment.

"Someone went to his apartment, was invited in, and shot him," I said, tossing the report on the captain's desk.

"Got an idea on who did it?" Ackerman asked.

"I think so," I said, with "Baker Street" playing in my head.

"Fill me in."

***

Johnny McCoy lived in the Blackridge community off Hatch Road. The expensive homes seemed designed to intimidate visitors with their opulence. I'd already tried to contact him at his office but struck out.

"Baker Street" continued to play in my head, but I ignored it. Johnny McCoy was my guy, and I knew it. I couldn't let a morning song distract me from what I knew was the right path of action.

I wound through the neighborhood until I found his house. I parked on the street and walked up the shoveled sidewalks. Officer Pauleen Sherman had parked a couple of houses closer and exited her car as I walked by.

"Did you request me specifically?"

"What?"

"I keep getting tasked to help you," she said. "I'm starting to think it's either a conspiracy or you're specifically requesting my help. Either way, it's suspicious."

I raised my hands in mock surrender. "I didn't request you. I just asked for a backup, that's all."

She put her hands on her hips. "You say it like working with me is a bad thing."

"That's not what I meant."

"Whatever," she said with a shake of her head. "So, what are we doing here?"

"We're going to attempt contact with a homicide suspect."

Sherman's eyes widened, and she pointed to McCoy's house. "That's the house over there?"

"Yeah."

"And we're standing out in the open? What the hell is wrong with you, Nash?"

"Nothing."

Sherman moved behind a tree. "Where's your officer safety?"

"I'm safe."

"No, you're not. Get behind this tree. We should get another unit up here. Restrict the channel for contact. You're not thinking straight."

"I'm going up there and ring the bell."

"You're crazy," Sherman said.

"That's what I've heard."

I hurried up the sidewalk, thinking Sherman would abandon me to stay in her position of safety. She didn't. When we got to the door, she took one side, and I took the other. I knocked loudly. No one answered, so I knocked again. After a few minutes, I pulled a business card from the inside of my coat and shoved it into the door.

"She's working," an elderly man yelled from across the street.

"What's that?" I hollered back.

He held up his hand and slowly made his way down the sidewalk, across the street, then carefully navigated the icy path of his neighbor's home. He looked to be in his late seventies and probably the neighborhood busybody. He held out a gloved hand and smiled. "I'm Gerald Stone. You police officers?"

"Yeah," I said, shaking his hand.

His smile grew wider as he shook Sherman's hand.

When he turned his attention back to me, he said, "If you're looking for Abby, she's volunteering today at the children's center. That woman is a saint."

"I'm looking for her husband."

"Johnny isn't home. He left last night, around eleven. It seemed strange to me he left at that hour. I'm a light sleeper, you know. Weak bladder. Probably something you didn't need to know. Curse of my age, talking too much." He chuckled. "Anyway, they park their cars outside since their garage is full of stuff. If he were home, his truck would be parked in the driveway." Stone pointed to the driveway.

"What time does Johnny normally return home?"

Stone's lips pursed into a disapproving smirk. "Johnny. What kind of name is that for a grown man? Abby deserves better than him." He realized I was still waiting for my answer and said, "Oh, hard to tell with him. His schedule is all over the place."

I pulled out another business card and handed it to him. "If you see his truck, please call me. Any time of day, okay? It's that important."

"Is he in some kind of trouble?" Stone's face brightened.

I tapped the card. "Any time of day."

"Will do," he said with an excited nod.

"What children's center is Abby working at?"

"The one on Eighth. Know what I'm talking about?"

Both Sherman and I nodded.

We thanked Stone for his help and headed back to our cars. As we neared hers, Sherman stopped and looked at me with concern. "I should report this."

"Report what?"

"Your lack of officer safety."

I thought for a moment, then said, "I understand. I appreciated your help."

When I walked off to my car, she called after me, "Does that mean you want me to report it?"

***

The children's center sat on the corner of 8th and Sherman in an older building that had been converted to aid women and children in need of immediate help. I waited at the front counter after announcing myself to the woman behind the bulletproof glass. She said she'd find Abby McCoy and have her come out front to meet me.

Distractedly, I hummed along with "Baker Street" as it played along in my head. When I realized I was doing it, I stopped. I forced myself to think about other things, but my thoughts kept gravitating back to that song.

When she opened the security door, I could see the concern in her tired eyes. She wore a multicolored sweater, black pants, and winter boots. A scarf was wrapped lightly around her neck. Her face was free of make-up.

She approached me with her hands in her pockets. Her eyes settled on me as she approached. After a deep breath, she said, "I'm Abby McCoy."

"Mrs. McCoy," I said, "I'm Detective Nash. Can you tell me where your husband is?"

"What's he done?" she asked. She didn't seem worried or upset. Instead, she looked pissed.

"I'd like to ask him some questions. Can you tell me where he is today? His office said he didn't show up for work."

Abby shrugged. "He came home last night in a blur. Grabbed some clothes, threw them in a gym bag, and hurried out to his truck. He was going to leave without saying anything to the girls or me, so I yelled at him. That's when he came back and hugged me and said he was sorry, that he was in trouble for something he did a long time ago. Then he kissed the girls and left. That was it. No more explanation than that."

"Do you know what trouble that might be?"

"The only old trouble I know of was when he was in high school. He had a girlfriend who was murdered. He said he was talked to by the police, but they cleared him of it. Is this what that is about?"

"He didn't say where he was going?"

She looked tired and mad, but not surprised. Interesting.

"Not a word. I've called his cell phone, but he hasn't answered. I had to force the girls to go to school today.

They were scared by his behavior. Who could blame them? Seeing their father all frantic, running off. I couldn't sleep last night, either."

I pulled a business card from my coat and handed it to her. "If you hear from him, please call me."

"What's this about? Is it about that high school thing? Do we have anything to be afraid of?"

"I don't believe so." I pointed to the card. "But if he calls you…"

She nodded, reading the card.

***

I called Glenn while I drove and asked him to send dispatch an ATL—Attempt to Locate—alert for Johnny McCoy. After that, I asked him to alert the airport police and border patrol. I wasn't sure if he'd try to make a run for it, but the airport was only twenty minutes outside of Spokane, and the Canadian border was three hours away.

I headed over to talk with the dentist. When I arrived at his office, the receptionist, Tiffany, greeted me with something less than a smile.

"Dr. Baker's not here," she said, her eyes full of hatred.

"Where is he?"

"How should I know? He told me to cancel all appointments for the rest of the week. He wouldn't tell me what was going on."

"Listen," I said, leaning in and lowering my voice. "Tell me where he is."

Tiffany looked over both shoulders, making sure no one was within earshot. She turned back to me and said, "If I knew, I still wouldn't tell you, but I have no idea where he is. He's not answering my calls, and he's ignoring my texts. It's starting to piss me off. What's he done? Should I be worried? Should I call his wife to check in on him?"

I turned and left without responding.

"Thanks for freaking me out," she yelled.

***

I drove to a large McMansion in the Greyhawk development on the east end of the South Hill. There was a newer blue BMW in the driveway.

I thought about calling for a backup officer. Maybe I had gotten it wrong and should have been focused on Lucas Baker. It didn't make sense, though.

Where was *his* motive? And he was already at the campsite when Jennifer Williams was murdered. Even Gilliland said so.

I decided a backup officer wasn't needed.

I picked up my microphone and called dispatch. "Ida-25."

"Twenty-five, go ahead."

"Run a plate for me."

I read off the numbers, and a moment later, she told me it was registered to Lucas and Monica Baker and provided the address that I was sitting at. "Baker Street" started again in my head.

"I'm at that house," I said, cutting off the song in my brain.

"Twenty-five, do you need back-up?"

"Not at this time. I'm code four."

I knocked on the door, and a striking woman opened the door. She wore a cream-colored sweater, black leggings, and brown boots with fur trim. She stood almost as tall as me. "Yes?"

"Monica Baker?"

"Yes."

"Is your husband home?"

"No," she said, and worry washed over her face. She fought it back and put a smile forward.

"Is something the matter?" I asked.

She shook her head, holding her smile in place.

I showed her my badge. "Detective Nash with the Spokane Police Department."

Her smile fell, a sense of relief washing over her face. "Thank God. Maybe you can tell me what's going on?"

"Can I come inside?"

She stepped back, and I walked past her. The house was spacious and ornately furnished. Expressionist paintings hung on the wall.

"Why do you want to speak to my husband?"

"Are your children home?"

"They're at school. I'll ask it again, why do you want to speak with my husband?"

"I'm investigating a murder from when he was in high school."

She lifted her hand to her mouth. "A murder?"

"Yes, ma'am. He alibied the suspect. I need to ask him some additional questions. Did he tell you we already spoke?"

She shook her head.

"Do you know where he is?"

Monica walked over to a plush couch and slowly sat, her knees held tightly together, and turned to the side. Her eyes looked into the distance.

"Ma'am? Did something happen?"

"He came home last night in a panic. I asked him what was going on, but he wouldn't tell me. He kept repeating he was in trouble. I've never seen him like that. He yelled at me to stay out of it. At first, I was really upset with him, but then I got scared. He had trouble sleeping and left early in the morning for the gym. Earlier than he normally would. Now that you're here, I'm worried."

"Have you had any contact with him today?"

"I've called his cell phone so many times, but he won't answer. He's not responding to my texts."

"What was he driving?"

"His Audi."

"Does he own a gun?"

Monica grimaced. "Several. I hate the things."

"Do you know if he took one with him?"

"I wouldn't know. He's got a gun safe, but I don't have the code to it. I never wanted to know it."

"Ever hear of Johnny McCoy?"

"Johnny? Of course. He's over here all the time. Why?"

"We're looking for him as well. His family said he left last night."

My cell phone buzzed. It was the number for dispatch. "Excuse me," I said to Monica and stepped away from her to answer the call.

"Dallas? This is Annie."

"Hey."

"You're next up on the rotation, and there's a homicide we need you to respond to."

"What and where?"

"Patrol is out with a shooting victim. The body was discovered sitting in a car in the parking lot of a vacant industrial building."

"Can you text me the address?"

"Sure, but here's the thing. You just checked out at an address registered to Lucas Baker, correct?"

"Yeah," I said. "Why?"

"The car the victim is in—it's an Audi registered to Lucas Baker."

52

Snow fell as the traffic crawled down the steep hill known as Freya Street. I thought about activating my emergency lights to get to the crime scene quicker, but that would have just made things worse. Traffic was already a mess. Trying to get cars to move aside for me would cause additional snarls. Besides, whoever was dead in Baker's car was going to stay dead. My racing to the location in snowy conditions wouldn't make them any more alive.

My gut told me the victim would be Lucas Baker. It was his car, so it seemed natural.

Although maybe I'd been thinking this thing wrong all along. Perhaps it was Johnny McCoy sitting dead in that car. I'd started playing that angle right before walking into Baker's house.

"Baker Street" played again in my head, and it took several tries to force it back out.

Bill Gilliland was dead. He'd let someone into his house, and I doubted that was McCoy. Not after avoiding talking for years and not after Gilliland told me how he felt about that. It was more plausible he let Baker into his home, and Baker killed him.

Or Baker and McCoy went together. Yeah, that would be more likely. Baker got them in the door, and McCoy did the dirty work. If he killed Jennifer Williams thirty years ago, there would still be something inside him willing to kill to keep that secret.

For a fleeting moment, I glanced at the empty passenger seat and wished Glenn was there so we could bounce ideas back and forth.

I passed a NAPA auto parts store, turned left, and pulled into the parking lot of a vacant building. Several patrol cars were there. I parked behind one of them and got out.

Yellow caution tape was already put up, indicating the inner and outer perimeters. An officer stood at the first line of tape with a clipboard. When I reported in, he lifted a transparent plastic sheet and wrote my name on the list, checking me in.

The car was a new black Audi A6. It would have been a sharp ride if it wasn't for the dead guy sitting in the front seat.

Lieutenant Caleb Mitchell stood near the car, looking at the body through the window. When he saw me approaching, Caleb nodded once and said, "I'm getting tired of snow and murder."

"Together or separate?"

Caleb looked up into the gray sky before letting his eyes fall back on me. "Both. I'm tired of them both, but we get paid for one."

"Aren't you working nights?" I asked.

"I was. Now, I'm on days, just like that," he said and snapped his gloved fingers. "It's called the departmental hokey-pokey, Dallas, but it's played with lieutenants, captains, and majors. You put your favorite one in, and you take the least favorite out. Then shake the schedule up. That's what it's all about. Don't you want to play?"

"No," I said, "I've risen as high as I want to go."

I turned to study the body in the car. Its back was pressed against the driver's door.

"We haven't identified the victim yet, but we've run the plates on the car. We're not sure it's the registered owner."

I moved to the passenger side and opened the car door to lean in. There were two shots to the chest with bloodstains around his gray sweatshirt. His glasses now sat cockeyed on his face.

Scanning the floorboards and the seats, I didn't see any cartridges. I closed the door and turned back to Caleb.

"That's Lucas Baker, the registered owner of the car."

"How do you know for sure?"

"He is—was—a witness in a cold case I'm working. I've talked with him a couple of times. Another witness, Bill Gilliland, was murdered yesterday. Burkett caught that case."

His eyebrows shot up. "Sounds like someone is eliminating your witnesses, Dallas. How many more do you have?"

"That's it," I said. "No more witnesses." The forensic truck pulled up near where my car was parked. "Has the coroner been called?"

"Not yet."

"Let's call her, since this shouldn't take long," I said. "Everything is contained within that car. We could get it towed to the evidence room, and the lab geeks could finish anything they need there. Besides, we know the victim and the likely shooter."

I pulled out my phone and called Burkett. The gun used in this murder was likely the same one used to kill Gilliland. Therefore, the bullets would be the same. The call went to voicemail.

"Marci, it's Nash. Hey, see me about your Gilliland homicide. I picked up one that may be related."

When I hung up, Caleb asked, "So the motive was to keep them quiet then?"

I pulled the latex gloves off and shoved them into my pockets. "That's what's bothering me. The friends had already kept quiet for thirty years. At best, we had circumstantial evidence in the case, so why kill them?"

***

I returned to the Greyhawk development and found the blue BMW still parked in the driveway. She opened the door as I carefully walked up the slippery sidewalk.

Monica Baker hugged her body tightly as she watched me. "You're back soon, Detective. Was it his car?"

I stepped onto the low porch. "Yeah."

She pursed her lips to one side. "Well, did you find him?"

"Yeah."

"So, what did he have to say for himself?"

I shook my head. "I'm sorry."

She blinked several times while the realization sank in. Finally, she closed her eyes, and her chin began to quiver. She shook her head multiple times, fighting off whatever thoughts she was having. We remained on the porch for several moments as she fought for composure.

When she opened her eyes, she said through stops and starts, "I suppose you need to ask me some questions."

"Yes, ma'am."

She stepped out of the way and let me in.

53

That morning I woke to Jimi Hendrix's "All Along the Watchtower." I wrote the song on the list I keep on my nightstand. After showering and getting ready for work, the song continued to play, but it was the opening line that continued to bother me, partly because I didn't think I remembered it right. *There has to be some way out of here? There has to be some way to get out of here?* I couldn't make the words fit the rhythm.

Was it from the other side? Was Bobbie trying to tell me she was alive and somehow cognizant?

I put my hand on my dresser as my knees suddenly felt weak.

It was impossible. I knew it. This was simply a good old-fashioned case of mind-fucking, and I was doing it to myself. I was going crazy and letting it happen because I wanted it to happen. It made me feel good. It gave me some sort of weird hope.

I got in my car and drove quicker than I should have. When I parked, I hurried to her grave and stood over it.

"It's not you," I said softly. "It's me. The music in my head, it's me. It's all me." I tapped my head with a finger.

"Those songs aren't from you. I know they aren't. They can't be. You're dead. You're not coming back. It's not possible."

I've got to find a way out of here?

I covered my ears and said, "Please, baby. Stop it. I can't take it."

I'm not sure how long I stood there, but it was must have been several minutes. Tears streamed down my cheeks, and my arms had grown tired from holding my hands over my ears. I slowly lowered my hands and opened my eyes.

Several gravesites away, the same woman I'd yelled at days ago, watched me again. When she saw me notice her, she quickly turned away.

I stood silently in front of Bobbie's marker, hoping she'd talk to me.

After a time, I left her and walked to my car.

***

"You look like dog shit," Marci Burkett said as she walked up to my desk.

I leaned back and stared at her.

"I take that back. You look like dog shit that got stomped on and then scraped off on a curb."

"Thank you for your concern."

"You're welcome. Got your voicemail. So you picked up a homicide yesterday that links to the one we landed? If that's true, and you want, Quinn and I will take it, and you can take our spot in the next rotation."

"Nah. I'll take over for you guys—no need to trade bumps on the rotation list. Your guy was a witness in a cold case I've been working. The guy killed yesterday was witness number two."

Burkett whistled. "Okay, big hitter, if that's how you want to handle it. We'll deliver the file and notes to you in a bit. If you need anything from Quinn or me, let us know."

"It's okay. I've got this."

I turned to my computer, but Marci hung around and continued to watch me for a moment. "Hey, Dallas?"

"Yeah?"

"Sorry for the dog shit comment."

"Don't worry about it."

"But you don't look good today. Is there anything I can do?"

"I'm good. It's just been a tough morning."

She smiled politely and walked away.

***

My phone rang, and I answered it, "Nash."

"Our money is gone."

"Excuse me?"

"It's all gone."

"Who is this?"

"Abby. The wife of that son of a bitch you're looking for. He took our money."

"Why don't you slow down and tell me what happened?"

She took a deep breath before letting it out. Then she did it a second time. "I'm sorry, Detective. I'm so effin' angry right now I could scream. In fact, I already did before calling you."

"Tell me what happened."

"I sat down to pay the bills this morning. I do the bookkeeping for our landscaping business. I opened up the bank account online since I pay all the bills through their checking service. When I opened it up, we were overdrawn. In all the years I've handled the bookkeeping, I've never bounced a check once. Never. Until today. Can you believe that? Yesterday, there was a seventy-five-thousand-dollar withdraw from the operating account."

I scratched the sum on a piece of paper next to the phone.

"I mean, who does that to their family, right? So I jumped over to our personal accounts. He's pulled out all the money from our liquid accounts. That's three different banks."

"How much is that?"

"Over two hundred thousand."

"So, Johnny pulled nearly two hundred seventy-five thousand dollars out from your business and personal accounts. That amount of money gets reported when withdrawn."

"What good does that do me?" she said and then screamed. I held the phone from my ear until she finished. "I'm sorry, Detective."

"It's understandable."

"Do you think he killed his friend?"

"What?"

"Monica Baker called me in hysterics last night. Said her husband was murdered. She said he was acting just like Johnny was. All crazy and secretive, wouldn't tell her where he was going. Then a detective comes to her house and tells her he's dead. Won't tell her much but asks her a lot of questions about Johnny. Was that detective you?"

"Yeah."

"What's he done, Detective? What is my husband involved in?"

"He's a suspect in a homicide. Several now."

"Homicide? You mean murder?" Her voice shook. "My husband murdered someone? He killed Lucas, didn't he? He killed his best friend."

"I don't know that for sure, but that's what I suspect."

"What am I supposed to do? What if he shows back up?"

"Ma'am… Abby… I don't believe you're in any danger. Your husband and Lucas may have been involved in a homicide more than thirty years ago. I think it's just coming to a head now."

The phone was silent for several moments until she said, "What do I do now?"

"Regarding the money, get me an accounting of what was taken, including the account numbers and times of withdrawal. Can you come down to the station for a statement?"

"Definitely."

"As soon as you get that information, call me, and let's get you in so we can get this information. If he has that amount of money, he can be headed anywhere."

54

That night I sat in the living room, staring at the blinking lights of the Christmas tree in my neighbor's window.

It was snowing again, and Christmas was less than a week away.

Outside, a group of carolers were singing "Silent Night" as they walked along the street. I got up, moved to the front door, and turned the outside light off. The singers continued on their way.

I resumed my seat on the couch and watched the winking lights.

55

It had been five days since Lucas Baker's murder and six days since Bill Gilliland's. Johnny McCoy was in the wind. There was no way to know if he would return home to see his kids. However, if there was one reason for a family man to risk everything, I was betting it would happen because of the Christmas holiday.

Suddenly, I was investigating two more murders. Even though I believed I knew who the killer was, the new cases meant follow-up interviews with friends and family, reviewing assisting-officer reports, attending the autopsies, and generally more paperwork.

Patrol and surrounding agencies had been notified of McCoy's disappearance, but he hadn't surfaced. For a man who lived out in the open for thirty years since the murder of Jennifer Williams, he was surprisingly adept at disappearing from the radar screen.

I was parked in my truck, watching his house.

His family's Christmas morning would be different this year. There would be no coming downstairs to find presents under the tree. No mom and dad hugging with smiles as the kids opened their gifts. This year the man of the house would be missing, a suspect in a murder three decades old as well as two deaths less than a week old. Life would never be the same for the women in that abode.

My brother, Dean, and his wife, Arlene, had invited me to spend the day with them, but I told them I had to work. I didn't have to, but I was looking for an excuse to avoid the holiday. Thanksgiving had been bad enough. Today would be unbearable in a family setting, and I didn't want to be around anyone. I wanted to be alone.

As I sat there, a drum riff played in my head. I woke to it that morning. At first, I didn't know what it was from, but it sounded heavy—lots of drums and bass. I mimicked the sound as best I could while I made my morning coffee. As I continued to repeat the rhythm, the song it came from was at the edges of my memory.

I couldn't place it. When my coffee was made, I filled a cup and took it with me to my music collection and pulled CDs, scanned song titles, and put them back. Several times I put discs into the player only to pull them back out and move on to another.

Another cup of coffee was made, and I returned to the CDs. At first, I jumped around with no system. Then I moved through them alphabetically.

When I made it to the Os, I stopped at Ozzy Osbourne. I had several of his albums. Mumbling the rhythm, I pulled out his first album, *Blizzard of Ozz*. I ran my finger through the song titles. No luck. His next album, *Diary of a Madman*, seemed familiar. It had been some time since I listened to it. Was it the album title that caught my attention? Was it speaking to me? I dropped the CD into the player and jumped through each song, listening only to the opening notes. It was the first music in the house since her death.

"Little Dolls" was the fifth song on the album and opened with the heavy drum beat before the crunching guitars entered. It had been at least five years since I heard that song. It was about drug use and the inability to escape it. As soon as I identified the song, I stopped the disc, removed it, and put it back where I found it.

What was the significance of the song? Was Bobbie my drug now? Was the belief in her continuing existence and my inability to escape it the parallel I was searching for?

Why did it matter if there was no significance to the song?

I'd heard Madonna's "Vogue," the theme to *Cheers*, and the Coca-Cola jingle and didn't try to place significance to them. Actually, I got mad that there wasn't. So why did I continue to twist myself up by trying to believe these songs were from her?

Maybe only some of the songs were from her. The rest could just be debris swept up in the wake of my memories, coming through because there was a conduit to her.

It was a convenient explanation. I knew it to be so, but I didn't care. That's what I was going to believe. Some songs were purposeful, and some weren't.

So again, did "Little Dolls" have any significance to my life? I struggled to place its value in my current life.

I was lost in my thoughts and didn't immediately notice when an older white Nissan Maxima pull into the neighborhood. It looked like one of those jobs kids soup up with obnoxious mufflers. The car stopped in front of the McCoy residence. For some time, no one left the vehicle. I got the suspicious feeling the driver was watching the neighborhood to see if anyone was observing the house.

For surveillance, Christmas was the best cover ever; there are new vehicles in every neighborhood that day. I wasn't worried about being made as I was in my truck, and I was far enough back from the McCoy residence it would be tough to make me out.

Eventually, the driver's door opened, and a man exited. Even from a distance, I could see who it was. He crossed the snow-covered street and headed to the front door.

I called dispatch and notified them of where I was and asked that backup officers be sent with sirens silent.

Johnny McCoy opened the door and entered the home.

I exited my vehicle and headed toward the residence. A connected garage stood slightly forward of the house. I stood at the edge of the garage, listening. For a moment, I remembered the older man from across the street and turned toward his house. He stood in his opened doorway, a mug of something in his hand. When he saw me notice him, he waved slightly and shut the door.

From inside the house, I could hear raised voices between a man and a woman. Eventually, the woman yelled, "Get out!"

I removed my gun from its holster. For a second, I thought about leaving it in its holster. I wanted to fight and roll around on the ground with McCoy. I longed to hit and be hit, but he'd shot both his friends. He might be carrying his gun at this moment, and I wasn't about to give him that much leverage just because I was feeling a moment of self-pity and anger. Pauleen Sherman might have been right to question my officer safety, but I wasn't ready to die that morning.

The front door opened and slammed a second later. "Bitch," was muttered from around the corner.

I stepped back farther out of sight and pulled my gun back into my chest so he couldn't reach out for it.

When Johnny McCoy turned to the corner, he saw me standing there with my Glock pointed at his chest. "Shit," he squeaked and turned to run. He lost his footing due to the slippery ground and fell.

"If you run, I'll shoot," I said.

McCoy looked up at me. "You can't do that. You're the cops."

When I shrugged, he said, "No witnesses."

McCoy looked across the street.

"The old man doesn't like you," I said. "He'd support me shooting you."

McCoy turned his face away from me and held his hands out.

Engines roared in the near distance, letting me know patrol officers were headed this way.

"We're going to stay like this for a minute. That way, I don't have to shoot you, and you don't have to die. Christmas doesn't have to get any worse for your kids."

***

Officer Ken Jarvis was the first to arrive and took McCoy into custody. After handcuffing him, he transported him to the interview room.

The second officer on the scene processed the vehicle for towing. An inspection after arrest found a handgun tucked between the driver's seat and the console. We'd finish a more detailed investigation of the vehicle at the evidence warehouse following a search warrant.

Abby McCoy opened the front door before I could knock.

"Did you have to arrest him on Christmas morning?" she asked between clenched teeth. Two high school-aged girls watched us from another room. "My daughters have to watch their father go to jail for Christmas."

Her voice was low so the girls couldn't hear. I leaned forward and out of sight of the girls. "I did my best to make it as quiet as possible. You know as well as I do what he's done."

Abby studied my eyes for a moment, then walked into the house, leaving the front door open. I followed her inside and closed the door. She was with her daughters, saying something that caused them to walk to another portion of the house slowly. She waved for me to follow her to a kitchen table.

She sat and stared into the snow-covered backyard. "So, where are things?"

I sat near her and quietly explained as much as I could about the investigation. When I'd arrived at today, I said, "What happened when he walked in this morning?"

"He said he wanted to see the girls."

"You didn't want him here, though."

"He doesn't deserve anything. As far as I was concerned, he forfeited his right to his family. He's a killer. He took our money. I hope he never sees my girls again."

***

Johnny McCoy's left hand was cuffed to the railing in interview room one. He looked up as I walked in.

"I want a lawyer," he said.

"Okay." I sat across from him, putting my notepad to the side.

"I want a lawyer. I'm not answering any questions until I get one."

"I understand. Want some coffee?"

"No."

We sat in silence for a bit, listening to the hum of the lights.

"What are we doing here?" McCoy asked.

"It's Christmas."

"Yeah, I know. I mean, why are we just sitting here? Why haven't you asked about my attorney or taken me to jail?"

"My wife died last month."

McCoy started to say something but held back.

"Car accident," I said. "This is my first Christmas without her. I spent Thanksgiving that way. That was miserable, but Christmas… I told my brother I had to work today rather than go to his house. Can you believe that? Who wouldn't want to be with family?"

McCoy watched me. I'm sure he was trying to determine if I was telling the truth.

I hadn't intended to tell McCoy about Bobbie. It wasn't my plan to see if I could connect with him by talking about her. When he asked for an attorney, I just didn't want to leave that interview room. I'd found a reason to be at the job, and I tried to hold on to it for as long as I could.

"Truth be told," I said, "if you hadn't shown up, I would have sat on your house for the entire day. Just for the excuse not to celebrate."

McCoy lowered his eyes.

"I visit her grave on most days. It's oddly comforting. Is that weird?"

McCoy shrugged.

"It's okay if you don't want to talk, but I don't want to go home yet. If you want to go over to jail and get processed, I'll do it. We can leave now. You'll get your phone call, but Abby's not taking it. You know that, right?

She's furious, lost, confused. She doesn't know which way is up and the last person she'll want to talk with is you. You're as alone as I am."

McCoy leaned his head back and stared at the ceiling.

"We can just sit here and be quiet for all I care."

He closed his eyes. "Sitting's good."

"About that coffee?"

"Yeah," McCoy said, "I think that sounds good. Thank you."

I left McCoy alone and made a pot of coffee. I returned with two Styrofoam cups and a couple of miniature containers of creamer. "I didn't know if you used them."

"Will today."

I opened both creamer containers for him, and he poured them in. He stuck his finger in the cup and swirled the coffee to blend the mixture. He put his finger in his mouth, before wiping it off on his pants. Then he sipped his coffee. "Appreciate it."

"I used to drink mine black," I said. "She got me drinking it with creamer. Not the flavored stuff she liked. Just regular creamer like this. But she liked the flavored stuff, you know? French vanilla, cinnamon, peppermint, that kind of thing. I can't go anywhere and drink it black now. It always has to have at least some cream in it. After she was gone, I opened the refrigerator and saw the flavored stuff she used sitting in the door. Caramel. I didn't care for that flavor, but it didn't matter. I cried when I saw it. Funny that something like that would set me off. Now, when I go to the grocery store to get some creamer for me, I still buy one for her and put it in the door where hers is supposed to be. Is that stupid?"

He shrugged again.

We sat quietly then for a couple of minutes, just two guys drinking coffee in a police interview room on Christmas morning.

"You're really not going to ask me questions?"

"I said I wouldn't."

"We're going to end up talking about it at some point, anyway, right? I mean, once I get my lawyer."

"It won't be today, being Christmas and all."

"The lawyer would advise me to say nothing, right?"

"I'm not a lawyer. I don't know what they would advise you to say or not to say."

McCoy ran his finger around the rim of his Styrofoam cup.

"I don't care if you answer them today or tomorrow. If you're okay delaying the processing a few minutes, that's all I care about. I don't want to be alone the rest of this day with what's going on inside." I tapped my chest for emphasis.

McCoy thought about it for a moment, then shook his head, obviously fighting his own emotions. We listened to the hum of the fluorescent lights and sipped our coffees. When we were done, he said, "Can I have another cup?"

I got up and refilled the coffee. When I returned, I doctored his coffee for him and brought a stirring straw along this time. He sipped it and smiled sadly. "This is the first Christmas I haven't spent with my girls," he said.

I watched him speak. His lips trembled, and tears formed in the corners of his eyes. "I should have been there for them." He sipped his coffee, the cup shaking in his hand. "I know you're messing with me," he said.

"How am I doing that?"

"Telling me about your wife. You think that's going to make me think about my family? Maybe make me realize I'm not going to have them around anymore."

"I wasn't messing with you, Johnny. My wife is dead, and I don't want to go home. I don't care if you answer a single question today. We will do that another day. For all I care, we could sit here, drink coffee the rest of the afternoon, and talk about music. I'm really into music lately. You?"

He studied my eyes, searching for my truth. When he found it, he said, "I don't want my attorney."

56

I flicked the small button on the wall to activate the camera, and the red light blinked awake.

"What's that?" McCoy asked.

"We're being recorded. If I'm going to ask questions, we need to have an official record of them."

He stared at the light for a bit then turned to me. "Yeah, all right."

After I read him the Miranda warning, he said he understood his rights and agreed to waive them.

I slid my notepad in front of me. "Tell me about Jennifer Williams."

"What do you want to know?"

"In 1987, she was your girlfriend, correct?"

"Yeah."

"Tell me about the day she was found dead."

McCoy stared at his nearly empty coffee cup but didn't answer me.

"Johnny?"

He raised his eyebrows.

"The day she was found?"

He took a deep breath, let it out, took another one, and then said, "I loved her, you know?"

I watched him, not replying. Instead, I waited for him to hopefully say the things he'd been holding back these years.

"She didn't love me the way I loved her, though." McCoy picked up his cup and swallowed the last of his coffee. "Don't get me wrong, she loved me, but not like I loved her, not as much as I loved her. Does that make sense? It's sad to say that out loud finally, I mean, I've thought about it a lot over the years, but never mentioned it to anyone. Young love, you know? Why do we even call it love at that age? I mean, high school is a messed-up world, a messed-up time. Everyone trying to be someone they're not, something they're not.

"Except I knew who I was. I think that's what made me different from most everyone else. I was a guy who played baseball, drank beer, worked at Burger King. Life was simple for me, you know? I realized I was going to WSU because my parents were paying for it, not because I had any particular talent. It wasn't like I was going to play college ball. I wasn't that good. I knew that and was okay with it. I didn't feel bad about it. Not jealous or anything. Like I said, I knew who I was at the time. I mean, I thought I did. At least, I'd like to think so. It's hard to remember who I was back then, even though I try.

"What I do remember very clearly was knowing early on, if I wanted anything in life, then I was going to have to work hard for it. That was a simple fact of life, and I was okay with it. That's how it was with Jennifer. She was way prettier than any girl I thought I could have gotten, and she still agreed to go out with me. Right away, I knew I loved her. Bam! Hit me in the face with how lucky I was. I would have married her as soon as high school was over before college started. I even told her that."

He inhaled slowly and let it out. "She said she never wanted to get married, though. Ever love someone more than they love you, Detective? It's sort of a fucked-up situation to be in, especially when you're in the lesser position."

"Why do you think that? That she loved you less."

"You can just tell, know what I mean? I was always saying, 'I love you' first. She said it back for a while, then it became 'me too,' then it was 'uh-huh,' then there were no answers."

He picked at the edge of his Styrofoam cup while he thought. I remained silent.

"That day, that Saturday, she wanted to talk, away from friends, away from family. Said she had big news but didn't want anyone to know. I suggested a place where I'd sometimes meet a guy to buy weed. How the world's changed, huh? You can walk into a store and buy it out in the open now. Can cops buy weed since it's legal?"

"What was the big news?"

McCoy tore a piece of Styrofoam away from the cup. "She was breaking up with me."

"Was that the first meeting or the second meeting?"

"What?" McCoy said, looking up.

"In the original report, it says you two met, but she returned home and was seen by her parents. I'm guessing there were two meetings."

Sadness crossed his face. "Oh, yeah. I forgot about the first one. We met at Winchell's for a couple of donuts. Remember when we had Winchell's here? She was sad that morning. I tried to cheer her up, told her I loved her, that sort of thing. I told her I'd follow her wherever she wanted to go to college. When I said that to her, though, I think she just got sadder. The more I said I loved her and would be loyal to her, the more withdrawn she became. I knew something was wrong then, but I couldn't put my finger on it."

"That was the first meeting."

"Yeah. She must have gone home, gotten all riled up over what I said because she called me at my house. That's when she wanted to talk away from everyone, do it in private. Her tone freaked me out. She sounded forceful. That wasn't how she normally sounded."

He went silent, so I prompted, "So you met?"

"Yeah. She wanted to break up with me. That's the whole reason to get together that second time, although I didn't know it. She said she had big news, but she was delivering it in this really forceful way, like I had to hear it now, that it was super important. She was setting me up to break up with me."

"Did she tell you why?"

He picked some more at the Styrofoam cup, tearing a piece away from the rim. "She said I wasn't interesting anymore." His voice rose slightly. "She said after school was out, she was going to move to California with some fag friend of hers and start a new life. Said she was going to be an actress, maybe a model. Become famous. It was just ridiculous bullshit she was feeding herself and me."

A large chunk of the cup was torn away by his fingernail.

"Once she started talking, it was like a dam burst, and water came gushing out, except the water was words. Understand what I'm saying? First, she complained about her parents, how they were stifling her, and how she couldn't wait to get away from their small-minded ways. Then she bitched about how much she hated this town, the weather, its people. When I said I liked it here and the weather, she called me stupid. I tried to defend her parents as being nice, and she said I was pathetic. She said I was just a stupid hick boy that she was tired of pretending to love so she could fit in with the small-minded bitches at school." He bit his lower lip to stop it from trembling. "I remember those words pretty clear."

He sat quietly then, staring at his torn cup.

"I don't know why she did it, but she wouldn't stop, even after I stopped talking. She kept poking, getting meaner, taking shots. I was so mad at her. I mean, she had to see it, right? She called me a hick several times. I asked her to stop saying it, but she wouldn't. I don't know why she liked that word so much. She said she was better than this town, said she was going to leave it behind and never come back. It was like she was standing there, pointing her finger at me, laughing as she broke up with me. She wound herself up, crazy like, just hateful to the point where I didn't even know who she was anymore. She looked at me with such anger and said, 'I wish the guys on the team could see you. Crying like a little bitch. At least take this like a man.'"

He blinked several times at the memory he was faced with. He glanced up at the ceiling lights, sighed, then looked down.

I prompted him with, "What happened next?"

"I couldn't understand why she was so mean about it. She could have just broken it off and went on her way, right? Did she have to be cruel? It was cruel what she did, right?"

"It sounds cruel."

"Yeah," he said with a nod. "It was cruel."

He rolled what remained of the Styrofoam cup between his fingers.

"What did you do?"

"I don't remember that so well."

"What do you mean?"

McCoy half shrugged. "I couldn't take any more of her belittling, and I grabbed her. I sort of blacked out. When I woke up, she was in my hands."

"What did you do?" I asked again.

"I don't know how it happened. I loved her. I really did."

"Did you kill her, Johnny?"

"I didn't mean to," he said. "I don't even remember it happening. One moment she was yelling at me, calling me names, then…"

"She was dead? You killed her?"

He nodded.

"Johnny, what did you do?"

"You saw the report, right? Do I have to spell it out?"

"I need to know."

McCoy placed his finger on a torn portion of Styrofoam. He slid it a few centimeters in each direction. "I hit her."

"Then what?"

"She fell back into the building, and I grabbed her."

"Was she conscious?"

"I dunno. I don't think so."

"Then what happened?

McCoy flicked the small piece of Styrofoam. "I choked her."

We sat quietly for a couple of moments until McCoy looked up, his eyes wet. He repeated, "I choked her."

"What did you do next?"

"I ran. What else was I supposed to do? I just left her there and ran." He tapped the table with his fingers. Tears filled his eyes. "I should have owned up to it then, but I was too scared."

"That's when you went to the lake with Bill and Lucas?"

"Yeah."

"Did you ask them to provide an alibi for you?"

He nodded.

"Did you tell them what happened?"

"Yeah."

"Exactly what you told me?"

"Yeah, uh-huh. I think if they had told me to go to the police, I would have done it. I mean, I was messed up about it. More than you can imagine. More than it can seem now."

"They agreed to lie for you. Why?"

McCoy looked at me like I just asked an idiotic question. "They were my friends. That's what you do for friends."

"I don't know if I would do that for my friend."

"Well, they did it for me."

"For thirty years."

He tore another chunk free from the Styrofoam cup.

"Why did you shoot Bill Gilliland?"

McCoy looked up and swallowed. "I didn't want that to happen. I didn't go there for that."

"What did you want? Why did you go there?"

"I wanted to ask him why he told you what he did. Why, after so many years, would he sell me out?"

"Did you go alone?"

"I couldn't. Lucas had to go along. Bill wouldn't have talked with me alone. He blames me for how his life turned out. That's why he turned on me. Can you believe it? The funny thing is, Bill and I were best friends before what happened with Jennifer. After that, we started to pull apart. He changed, too. Got really into drugs. Sort of dropped out. I know lying for me screwed him up over the years, I know that, but he chose to do that back in that park. I didn't ask him for it. Both Lucas and him offered it up."

"You took a gun to your meeting with him. Why?"

"I usually carry one in my truck. Besides, I figured I might have to intimidate him or something."

"You would have to intimidate your friend?"

"He wasn't my friend anymore. I didn't know the guy anymore. And I had a lot on the line."

"What happened?"

"He didn't scare." He closed his eyes and let out a short, disbelieving laugh. "The little son of a bitch didn't scare."

"How did it play out?"

"He said he was happy I was finally going to get caught. That I was finally going to lose everything. Going to lose my family, my house, my business. He laughed at me. I mean, full-on laughed at me. That fucking guy checked out of life for thirty fuckin' years, and he's having a laugh riot at my expense?"

McCoy tapped his chest. His eyes cleared, and he focused on me. "I raised a family in that time, built a business, put a life together. I never meant for that thing to happen with Jennifer. I've carried that guilt with me my whole life. Do you know what that's like? I'm not saying I'm the victim in the situation. I'm only trying to say that I've felt shitty inside for a lot of years. Guilty, you know? But I did my best despite that. Him, though? He used that moment to quit on life, quit on himself. He blamed me for that, always resented me for my success. His jealousy continued to fester until he finally had his opportunity to get me back."

"Until the day I walked into his apartment," I said.

"Until the day you walked into his apartment. That's right."

"Did Lucas know you brought a gun with you?"

"Not at first, no. Not until we were walking to Bill's apartment. I told him to chill out about it. Said I just wanted it to make sure I had my bases covered. Lucas knew Bill was a wild card. You know, Lucas had shit to lose as well. We were both there to protect the lives we'd built. I could lose everything, but Lucas knew he could lose a lot as well. We were there to talk some sense into him. Scare him, if we had to."

"So, why did you shoot him?"

"He wouldn't stop laughing." McCoy ran his fingers through his hair. "I didn't blackout for that one, though. I wish I would have so I wouldn't see it whenever I close my eyes."

"Tell me."

"He was carrying on, saying how much he was going to enjoy me going down, how much he was going to enjoy reading my name in the paper. I pulled the gun out and showed it to him, told him to shut up, that he wasn't going to do anything like that, that he was going to tell the cops he lied, that he made the story up to get even with me.

"He laughed at that, laughed at the gun. He might have been high. Who knows with Bill? Irregardless, he wasn't taking the moment seriously, and I sure as hell was. He kept laughing until he got to the point where he was mocking us. That's when I shot him."

We sat quietly and let the admission hang in the air. Finally, I asked, "What did Lucas do?"

"What did he do? Shit, he freaked out. I mean, I did too. I didn't mean for it to go that far. I only meant to talk with him to make sure he would continue to keep the secret. I didn't want to hurt him, but he was threatening me, threatening to hurt my family. I couldn't tolerate that. I guess I just snapped. Does that make sense?"

"Yeah, I get it. What happened after?"

"We knew that was it. You had Bill's admission, and now he was dead. I was going to have to run. Lucas said he would run with me."

"Why would he run?"

"Because he was a dumbass."

"Huh?"

"He was unhappy with his life."

"Was he worried about the alibi?"

McCoy made a face. "Lucas? Maybe now, but the whole alibi thing was his idea. He didn't want me to go down for Jennifer. He never liked her in the first place. He thought she was a bitch. Called her worse until I told him to knock it off. When he suggested telling everyone I was at the campground earlier than I was, Bill jumped on it right away."

"So Lucas was going to run because he was unhappy? What's that mean?"

"He didn't want to be married and didn't want to have kids. The stupid bastard. He's pushing fifty and suddenly sees his life slipping away. He takes up with that little squeeze in his office, but that doesn't calm him down. It only makes things worse. The guy was a mess on the inside."

"What happened when you two met up to run?"

"What do you think happens when a guy like that truly faces reality? It's fun to roll around with a pop tart and play the game of 'someday, baby,' but do you think he really wants to give up his life? Do you think he wants to give up Monica? She's a ballbuster, but she's a damn fine ballbuster. He's got a huge house on the hill. Drives nice cars. Membership at the country club. He's grown comfortable. Starting over would be hard for the man, and

Lucas wasn't built to do hard. Sitting in that car, facing reality, it all hit him in the face."

"Why did you shoot him?"

McCoy put his free elbow on the table and rested his head in his hand. "I shouldn't have done that."

"He told you he wasn't going to run."

McCoy pushed the torn pieces of Styrofoam around on the table. "I knew it would only be a short time before some cop showed up on his doorstep about Bill's death. Hell, you had gone to his office and told him about Bill's confession. What did he think was going to happen? He said he would get a lawyer and stand his ground. He told me he wouldn't say anything. I knew he'd do his best, but if push came to shove, he'd cave. He was weak."

"But you said the alibi was his idea."

"Thirty years ago, yeah. We were tight then. Like it was us against the world. Today? It's Dr. Lucas Baker, trusted family man and respectable community member with a cute piece of pie on the side, thank you very much. He wanted me to alibi him when he was running around with Tiffany. Probably not the same level of risk, though, huh?"

"Did you feel bad afterward?"

"For killing my best friend? Are you kidding me? Of course, I did. I'm not a monster. I didn't expect to shoot him. I just saw everything slipping away, and I freaked out. I wish I could take it back. All of it. What I did isn't something that's getting wiped from the books."

"Your wife said you cleared out the bank accounts."

McCoy sighed. "Only the liquid cash. There's plenty of money that isn't liquid. I wouldn't have left her and the girls high and dry. I just needed money to run."

"Where were you going?"

He rolled his head around in an exaggerated fashion. "Oh my God, that's the problem, right? I don't know how to do this. Where the hell am I supposed to go? I drove up to the Canadian border and stopped outside the border checks. Have you seen how much security is there now? Well, it's amazing. I imagined someone, maybe even you, had put out some sort of alert for my name. Am I right?"

I nodded slightly.

"Yeah, I thought so," McCoy said. "I couldn't exactly drive through there without expecting some sort of problem, right? They check your ID now, and I figured my name would be on a list somewhere. I turned around and made my way back down. I spent a couple of nights in Podunk towns just to stay off the radar. I planned to visit the girls on Christmas, make it down south, and cross the border into Mexico. I knew I'd deal with the ID issue crossing the border, but from what I've seen on TV, even where that damn wall has been built, you can still get through it or over it fairly easy."

"You're not going to be doing that now."

He flicked another piece of Styrofoam with his finger. "I guess Bill was right. I've finally lost it all. Wherever he is, he's probably laughing his ass off now. You know, a part of me always knew this day was coming. I thought I was paranoid and that I could outsmart it by being careful. In the end, though, I guess everyone gets their due."

TUESDAY
DECEMBER 26th

57

I was completing the report on McCoy's confession when Captain Ackerman walked up to my desk.

"Nice work, Dallas."

"How's that, sir?

He pointed at the scoreboard. Three names had been moved to black: Williams, Gilliland, and Baker. "That's a helluva Christmas present to walk into."

I nodded.

He patted my back and moved on.

I returned my attention to the report, but it was short-lived. Marci Burkett stuck her head around the corner of my cubicle. "Really? I gave you a freakin' softball and the captain's in here glad-handing you like you're some glory boy. This good ol' boy bullshit is something."

"You think I'm part of the good ol' boys' club?"

Marci winked. "Anybody but you, Dallas. You're one of the good guys."

I turned back to my report, and she disappeared behind her cubicle.

The phone rang. Another interruption to my report. I checked the caller ID: Graham Hathaway, prosecuting attorney.

"Nash," I said.

"Dallas, it's Graham."

"I'm hoping for good news."

"April Scott's attorney—"

"—Wanda Acosta, I know."

"Yeah, Wanda. She's asking for a speedy trial."

"Seriously?"

"Yeah. They want this thing to go next week if possible. It's not, but we're looking sometime in January to get this to court."

"What's this mean?"

"They know we don't have much to go on, so Wanda's forcing our hand."

"You're still going through with it, though, right?"

There was silence on the line.

"Graham? You're still going through with it, right?"

"We're still running it, yeah. I've got to tell you, Dallas, this isn't our tightest case. I would have preferred more to go on. Wanda's not even willing to deal on this. She's going to try and suppress the discovery of meth as a product of an illegal search. If she wins that argument, then the search the arresting officer did to find Hamilton Martin's driver's license and credit card will be thrown out. The whole case falls apart then."

"The search the security guard did was fine. We both know it."

"You better hope a judge thinks so. I'll do my best to argue it."

"What's setting you off, Graham?"

"Wanda. She puts me on edge. She's a killer in the courtroom."

"Just remember April worked with a killer outside of the courtroom, even if the evidence is weak."

"All right, Dallas, I get it. We're sticking with the plan. I only wanted to advise you of the speedy trial."

I said I appreciated it and signed off.

58

That night I went up to The Lantern for a beer. Eddie Henning was behind the bar. Even for a Monday, the place was packed. The locals were extinguishing their holiday hangover with the help of some crafted libations.

I grabbed the only free seat behind the counter, the one nearest the wall. His eyes were full of suspicion as he walked over.

"Just a water," I said.

While he poured my water, his eyes flicked to me several times. The two guys next to me complained about spending Christmas with their families. The young couple seated at the table behind me talked loudly about the Facebook posts their friends had uploaded following Christmas. Jealousy was the theme.

When Henning sat my glass in front of me, he said, "There you go, Detective. Will there be anything else?"

The guy next to me turned my direction at the word *detective*.

"When you have a quiet five minutes, come and chat with me. I'll give you an update."

His brow furrowed. "Is it necessary?"

"Not really," I said. "We caught the guy who did it. Thought you might like to hear the story and an apology."

Henning relaxed and nodded, his shoulders dropping visibly, before moving elsewhere in the bar.

TUESDAY
JANUARY 30th

59

Five weeks passed before the start of April Scott's trial. That constitutes a speedy prosecution in our new, modern world.

Graham Hathaway and his team had done all the heavy lifting once it went to his office. I moved on to new cases and, at times, forgot about Hamilton Martin and April Scott.

When the trial finally rolled around, it lasted only three days.

April Scott cleaned up well. She wore business slacks and a jacket. Each day, her hair was clean and done nicely. She even had make-up applied. If I hadn't already met the woman underneath those layers of artificiality, I would have thought her attractive.

There weren't any supporters there for April except a gray-haired man who sat in the back. At first, I wasn't sure he was there for her, but he watched April intently. I asked Graham who he was, but he didn't know. The man hugged April before the start of each day's proceedings.

Graham brought in the evidence they had to work with, the evidence we had collected to charge her with robbery in the first degree and possession of a controlled substance.

When it was my turn to testify, the only thing I could say was the truth, the whole truth, and nothing but the truth. My gut and conjecture were never allowed on the witness stand.

Wanda Acosta brought in the suicide note, and the evidence found at Tony Lawrence's supposed suicide. They brought in April's arrest photos and explained how Tony had assaulted her as part of their relationship. I kept waiting for Acosta to eviscerate me on the stand for our confrontation in the interview room, but she kept it professional. She knew she had what she needed without dragging me through the mud. She'd save that for another day.

When April was on the stand, she explained to everyone how Tony used to beat her. I knew it was a lie, but I couldn't defeat it. She laid everything at Tony's feet.

April held up surprisingly well under cross-examination. I watched the jury and knew from their reactions they felt for her.

Wanda Acosta orchestrated the defense beautifully.

We had lost before the jury ever deliberated.

60

April walked out of the Spokane County Jail, smiling. Wanda Acosta hugged her as she exited the building. I saw them from the windows of the detectives' offices. April was found not guilty of first-degree robbery, but guilty of the possession of a controlled substance. In the follow-up sentencing hearing, the judge gave her time-served along with a mandatory drug program—a slap on the wrist.

Acosta and April hugged once more before heading in opposite directions. Acosta walked back towards the courthouse. April headed slowly towards the parking lot. She looked around expectantly, panic on her face when she realized someone wasn't waiting for her. As she moved out of view, I ran from the detectives' office, down the hallway, slid around the corner, shoved the doors open, and was outside. I jumped down the steps, hoped for a safe landing and caught a break with the weather and slippery sidewalks.

I ran towards the parking lot, hoping to get a glimpse of her before someone picked her up. She walked out of the parking lot and made a turn southbound on Adams Street. A black Lincoln MKZ approached on Mallon Avenue and pulled up next to her. The gray-haired man from the courtroom climbed out and held her tight. Their hug ended, and he kept his hands on her shoulders for several moments. I couldn't see what he was saying before they embraced again. April Scott sobbed as she clung to him.

I leaned against the edge of a nearby building to hide. Finally, they got into the Lincoln, and it pulled slowly away.

As I hurried back to my office, I repeated the license plate number to myself.

***

Back at my desk, I performed a DOL search on the license plate number. It came back to a late-model Lincoln registered to Dennis Keppel, with a home in the Dishman-Mica area of Spokane Valley.

Dennis?

I flipped back through my notes. Could this be the Dennis that Hamilton Martin's neighbor mentioned? If so, why would he be picking up April Scott?

I switched to my internet browser and typed in Keppel's name.

He was a vice president for Sterling Financial Services.

I couldn't find Facebook, Twitter, or any other social media accounts for him. He had a partially completed LinkedIn resume that showed he'd been with Sterling Financial for twenty-six years. Nothing before then. An advanced degree from Whitworth University. There wasn't a picture of him on the account. I continued moving through link after link, hoping to find something, anything.

On the third page of search results, I found Keppel's name attached to a link to the Spokane Valley Gun Club. I clicked it and was redirected to a newsletter from several years prior. Along with the reports of new members and fundraising opportunities was a picture of that year's Thanksgiving Thunder, a holiday skeet shooting event. A group of men was pictured with their names underneath. Standing next to each other, with arms around each other's shoulders, were Dennis Keppel and Hamilton Martin.

61

The house was in the southern portion of the county and sat on fifteen acres. The nearest neighbor wasn't anywhere within shouting distance.

I pulled up in front of the house and called radio to put myself out at the address. Snow covered the acreage, looking like a white blanket between the home and road.

I walked up to the front door and knocked. A man in his mid-sixties appeared as the door opened. He was tall with bony shoulders. His thinning hair was parted to the side. He looked like a man who'd recently lost a lot of weight. He wore a baggy flannel shirt, sagging blue jeans, and boots. Over his shoulder, I saw April Scott seated on the large couch with a fleece blanket wrapped around her.

"Detective Nash, Spokane Police Department," I said and showed him my badge.

"I know who you are, Detective," Dennis Keppel said. "Would you like to come inside?"

The house was exceptionally warm from a wood stove in the corner of the main room. A mounted deer's head hung on one wall. Several wilderness paintings were on the remaining walls. Dark wood adorned every piece of furniture in the house.

April's eyes slanted as she watched me.

"Please sit down," Dennis said, his voice hoarse. "What can I do for you?"

I sat on the edge of a recliner. "How do you figure into this?"

"It's not a secret," Dennis said.

"You're her father."

"Like I said."

Dennis began coughing. It was hard and wet and doubled him up. His face reddened while he hacked. When he was done, he straightened and said, "Sorry, I'm battling a cold."

"Some cold."

Dennis glanced back to April, and she watched him with concern.

"Is your wife home?" I asked.

"My wife, April's biological mother, abandoned us when she was little. We haven't seen her since. April became my sole responsibility then. I never remarried."

April watched her father intently as he waited for me to ask my questions.

"Where were you the night Hamilton Martin was killed?"

"Are you going to accuse me of killing him? If so, you haven't read me my rights."

"That's correct. I haven't."

"Don't say anything, Dad," April said.

Dennis held up his hand. "It's okay, honey. He's trying to make up his mind on some things, right, Detective? Are you recording this?"

I shook my head.

"Anything I say then is between us. You have no proof now. You'll have no proof when you leave."

A burning piece of wood popped in the fireplace.

"Ask your questions, Detective," he said.

"How long were you and Hamilton Martin friends?"

"Almost forty years. We weren't friends in the past handful of years, unfortunately. Life can change a man. I'm sure you already know that, though, what with your line of work and all."

"When did you find out he was frequenting your daughter?"

Dennis glanced at April, and she looked away. "She told me one night when she was mad. I was trying to get her help, but she didn't want it."

"What did you do when you found out?"

"I did what any father would do: I got upset. I didn't believe her at first. I thought she was lying just to get a response from me. How could I believe her? How could Ham do such a thing? He used to play with her when she was a little girl. Could you believe a friend would do something like that? That he was doing *that* with her. I just couldn't believe it."

"Did you confront him about it?"

"Definitely. Yes."

"What did you do?"

"I told him to stay away from her. Stay away from me. That we were no longer friends."

I looked at April, who was watching her father intently. "Did he? Stay away from her, I mean?"

"He said I should mind my own business, and that she was a grown woman. Life has a way of changing a man. Ham would never have said that to me if Lucinda was around. He would never have done it in the first place if Lucinda was here. He loved her. Her death changed him. Made him bitter. Made him mean."

"Did you mind your own business, as he suggested?"

"She's my daughter. Of course not. I was trying to reach her, but she wasn't listening to reason."

"What did you do then?"

"I told her either she broke it off with him or I was done providing a safety net. There would be no running home to me when things got hard. She said she didn't need me to rescue her anymore. She said Hamilton promised to take care of her."

I looked back at April. "Did he?"

She lowered her eyes.

Dennis said, "He paid her for her favors but never took care of her."

April started crying.

"She'd always go back to him when she needed more money, and he'd take advantage of the situation. It was a sick cycle, and I was dragged into it because I loved my daughter. She'd come home for a short time and then leave when she started using again. I knew where she went, but I was mad and refused to go after her. But then I saw them in his truck. It was complete chance. I wasn't looking for them, you know?"

"The night of the murder, you mean?"

He nodded. "They got into an argument while he was driving, and they stopped."

"What was the argument about?" I asked April.

She struggled to control her tears.

Dennis said, "April was going to tell Ham's girlfriend about their arrangement unless he started giving her money regularly. He stopped the truck, kicked her out. Then he got out and slapped her a couple of times, told her never to threaten him again. When he saw me pull up behind, he yelled at her for setting him up. Then he turned on me. He was crazy as hell about the situation. I tried to grab April and get out of there, but Ham hit me. I fell, and he kicked me then. April came to my defense, but he hit her, too."

"Is that when you stabbed him?"

Dennis nodded. "Yes, I stabbed him."

"No," April said, tears running down her face.

"April, honey, please stay out of this."

"I did it," she said, her voice breaking through amid the sobs.

"Detective, she's trying to protect me," Dennis said.

I held up my hands. "Just tell me the truth."

April wiped her eyes with her fingers and took a deep breath. When she had some control of herself, she said, "He saw me walking along Division and picked me up. I'd lost my coat, and I was cold. It had just started snowing, and I was shaking. He let me wear his while I warmed up. Why he was nice, I don't know. Maybe he thought we would… I don't know. I really didn't care. I just wanted him to take care of me. To be nice. I liked it when he was good to me."

Dennis Keppel lowered his head as he listened to his daughter.

April continued. "I put my hands in his coat, and he had a knife in there. He always carried it in his jacket when he drove. He didn't like how it felt in his pants pocket. It was one of those knives with that little nub that flicks out the blade. Do you know what I'm talking about? Yeah? Well, it was familiar to me. I used to play with it when I was with him at his house. So he picked me up and wasn't saying much. I tried to make some small talk, but he wasn't having much of it. He was in his head about something.

"I started getting pissed about that. I mean, the things I'd done for him, well, he always said he would take care of me, but he hadn't given me money in a while. Hadn't let me stay at his house in weeks. He didn't want me anymore since he got that new girlfriend. A real girlfriend, he called her. I was mad. I threatened to tell her. That's when he stopped the truck and dragged me out of it. He was mad. I mean, really mad. Scary mad."

I nodded, understanding now how it came together. Hamilton had recently assaulted his girlfriend, Kelly Winslow, who, in turn, broke up with him. He would still be angry about that. Now, April was threatening to tell Kelly how Hamilton had been visiting her, a prostitute. I would imagine his anger boiled to a level April hadn't expected.

"I didn't know my dad had seen us together or that he was following us, but when Ham saw him, he got even madder. I wouldn't have thought that was even possible. He slapped me so hard and yelled that I was trying to get him in trouble. I was used to him hitting me. He did that when he got mad, and I was okay with it, but he never hit me like that. It scared me how mad he was. When my dad walked up, Ham attacked him. My dad's a strong man, Detective, but Ham was in a dark and violent place. He knew how to fight. My dad didn't. My dad's not a violent man, and Ham was hurting him."

I studied Dennis. He didn't look strong; he looked sick.

The three of us sat there in silence for a moment until I prompted, "That's when you…"

"Yeah."

"He was kicking my dad. He didn't even know I was there when I did it."

"We were scared," Dennis said. "It looked bad. I mean, it looked like a set-up. At least, that's the first thing that went through my mind."

"You didn't know his girlfriend had broken up with him, did you?"

April's eyes widened.

I nodded. "Maybe a week prior. He'd probably still be mad about it. Then you threatened him, and he responded in a way you weren't expecting."

Dennis looked at his daughter and then back at me.

"Why did you take the wallet?" I asked.

"I don't know," Dennis said. "I really didn't know what I was doing. I thought we should make it look like a robbery. I grabbed his wallet. I gave it to April and told her to drive my car and go home. We'd figure out what to do from here. When we got home, she left the coat, wallet, and knife in the truck and vanished."

"I was so freaked out that I had to get high," April said.

"I knew I had a murder weapon and evidence in my garage, along with a stolen truck. I went into cleaning mode. I put the jacket in a garbage bag. I wiped down the knife with bleach. And then I gave the truck the same treatment.

"The next morning, I drove the truck to the Wal-Mart near where Ham was found and left it there, unlocked with keys on the front seat. I was careful not to touch anything on the truck or park near the entrance where there might be a camera."

"You didn't realize April had taken the driver's license and a credit card from the wallet?"

"Not until she was arrested."

"Why did you drag Ham into the middle of the field?"

Dennis looked to April, then back to me. "We didn't."

I put my hands on my knees and studied them. "He didn't die right away then. You took his jacket and wallet. Maybe you thought he was already dead. Maybe you thought he was on his way. Either way, it doesn't matter. He wasn't dead when you left him. The way I figure it, he got to his feet and looked around, seeing the apartments across the field. Maybe he figured that was his only way to get help. If he had turned around and walked into traffic, maybe he could have gotten help quicker. Who knows what the traffic was like at that time? Who knows what a dying man thinks? Regardless, he was in the middle of the field, but you didn't put him there."

The three of us sat in the quiet of the house. Light snow fell outside.

Dennis struggled to contain a cough. The harder he fought it, the worse it became. He finally bent over and hacked. It didn't sound like a cold. His face purpled from the exertion.

"Can't seem to kick this cold," he said.

"How did you find Tony?" I asked.

"I don't know what you're talking about," Dennis said.

I clicked my teeth together as I thought. Dennis was okay sharing information about Hamilton Martin's death because he knew that was in self-defense. April's trial made any future prosecution murky for her. However, the murder of Anthony Lawrence was still unsolved. I doubt he would give me anything now, but I was willing to play it out for a bit to see if I could get anything.

"You probably knew where he lived because you'd picked April up there before. Maybe dropped her off at one time. Am I right?"

Dennis's face remained passive.

"Did you plan on killing Tony?"

Dennis gave nothing away. He was a poker player if I'd ever come across one.

"That's why April wanted me to search his place. And why she was surprised when I didn't find anything. We found him before you could put the evidence in his apartment."

Dennis watched me, and I noticed April's tears had stopped. She only had enough for Hamilton Martin.

"How did April know you were going to put the coat in the apartment? I checked the visitor logs at the jail. The only one who ever came to visit her was Wanda Acosta. You hired Wanda, so you must have sent a message through her, although Wanda couldn't have known what that message was because she's a professional. It would have to be hidden, maybe as simple as a letter in an envelope."

"You've got a theory for everything, Detective. This one seems far-fetched."

"If you could afford Wanda, you could have bailed out April. Why leave her in jail until her trial? Why didn't you visit her?"

His eyes softened, and he looked to his daughter. "Tough love, Detective. If I bailed her out, she would have run to the first dealer she could have found and been on the stuff again. This way, she would at least be dry for a couple of months, getting some sort of counseling." He turned back to me. "I'm hoping she'll continue the program now that she's out."

"How did you get Tony to let you inside his apartment?"

"I don't know what you're talking about."

"I haven't Mirandized you. Nothing is admissible. Why not just tell me?"

"You have your theory. I'm still lost as to who this Tony is."

"You told him you wanted drugs," I guessed.

Dennis shrugged.

"That would seem reasonable," I said. "He would have drugs, and he would think someone at his door would want to buy them, but you hadn't planned on killing him, so something must have gone wrong. How were you going to get into the apartment if he wasn't there? Were you going to kick it in? Maybe you hadn't thought it through. It was done hastily. Your daughter was in jail, and you needed to act. You went and knocked. He opened up, and you showed him a gun. A gun must have been involved, right? You and Ham were both members of the shooting club. That was your contingency plan."

Dennis crossed his arms. His face was impassive.

"You forced him to overdose, then. When he slipped off, you went out to your car and recovered the jacket and knife. Or did you bring them with you? No, they would have been in the car, you wouldn't have carried them up. So you went back to your car to collect them. Then you put the jacket on Tony and put the knife in the pocket. You wrote the note and signed it, not putting much effort into forging the signature. Am I still doing okay?"

Dennis checked his watch, not revealing if I was on the wrong path.

"Then you walked out of his apartment and waited for us to do our job. We found Tony, the jacket, and the murder weapon. It didn't have any blood or fingerprints on it."

"Can you arrest a person on theories alone, or do you need evidence?"

"You said killing Martin looked bad, like a set-up," I said. "At that moment, you could have called the police and stated your case. Instead, you covered it up—like a pro, I will add. You took his coat, wallet, and the murder weapon. You took his truck and then wholly wiped it down. There wasn't a print left on it when you abandoned it in the parking lot. You never went to see April in jail, so you're not on a visitor log. You never called her, meaning you realized you would be recorded had you done so.

"That's a lot of forethought for a vice president from a financial services house. Just who are you, Mr. Keppel? How did you get so much experience with this?"

He carefully wiped the area under his right eye, never averting his gaze from me. The guy was cool under pressure.

I stood and walked to the door. With my hand on the knob, I turned back to him. "Why invite me in? Why tell me about Hamilton Martin?"

Dennis said to his daughter, "April, honey, please wait here." He stood and walked toward me. "Let's step outside."

On the front porch, Dennis pulled the front door closed. He lowered his voice. "I'm dying, Detective. I've got stage four cancer, and I'm not getting treatment. I don't want to go through it. April needs to get clean before I'm gone so she can handle life on her own. If you can build a case about Hamilton Martin's death, you can arrest me, or you can let it be. It's your choice. If you think I was somehow involved in this Tony person's death, which I'm not, then spend your time and effort proving it. At best, I've got a year left, and I need to get my daughter ready."

I studied Dennis for a moment before asking, "Who's your doctor?"

***

I had no evidence linking Dennis to either crime. I only had what he told me in his house about Martin's death. I had nothing tying him to Tony. It was a case of knowing who did it but not being able to prove it. The evidence pointed in the wrong directions.

April had already been tried for a robbery related to the murder and found not guilty. The prosecutor more than likely wouldn't try her for murder now that I knew it went down a different way. I'd need something so damning they couldn't say no, but I couldn't see how it existed.

I would write a report later that detailed my conversation with Dennis and April, father and daughter. It wouldn't change the medical examiner's report on Anthony "Tony" Lawrence. That would still remain a report of an overdose, a possible suicide. We had closed the case on Hamilton Martin's death. Would reopening it and trying to tie it to the woman who had already been found not guilty on the same evidence prove to be a good use of my time, let alone the departments?

I drove slowly away and saw both of them standing in the window, watching my departure.

62

I was in my truck, pulled off on the side of the road, watching the house. No music played in the cab. The lyrics to Journey's "Wheel in the Sky" played in my head. That was the musical greeting I woke to that morning.

I let the lyrics drift around and around in my head. At times, I even softly sang the song to myself after I decided to embrace it.

I didn't visit Bobbie that morning, and I felt slightly guilty. Should I feel guilty? I didn't know what I was supposed to feel anymore. It had been almost three months since she died, and I was still having trouble thinking straight. At that same time, I hadn't made any progress in boxing up her clothes. The room was the same mess I'd left it in weeks ago. I'd just grown accustomed to seeing the garments strewn about now.

I don't know how long I expected to stay out there watching them. I'd given myself four hours. There was nothing planned for the day, and I'd brought a sandwich and thermos of coffee along to keep me company.

April Scott finally left the house by herself after the first hour passed. She got into her father's Lincoln and pulled out onto Dishman-Mica Road. I eased onto the road and followed her. Ten minutes later, she parked at a little strip mall, climbed out of the car, and walked into a Starbucks.

She sat in an overstuffed chair in the corner, a book in one hand, a coffee in the other. I walked up to the counter and ordered a small black coffee. When it came, I walked over to the prep counter and added cream and sugar. With my coffee, I sat in the open chair next to her. April looked up at me, smiled politely without recognition, then returned to her book.

I watched her until she looked back up, this time without the smile.

"Detective?"

"Has your mother ever tried to contact you?"

"What?"

"It's a simple question. Has your mother ever tried to contact you?"

"Why would she? She abandoned me. She took off with some loser and left us behind."

"How old were you when this happened?"

"About six."

"Roughly eighteen years ago? Huh."

"Why are you asking about my mother?"

I sipped my coffee, slowly taking in the coffee shop. "I think it would be hard for a mother to abandon her kid, don't you? Have you ever thought about why she did that?"

"Why do you care?"

"I'm funny that way. I care about random things and will do homework when a subject interests me. Your childhood interests me, April. I love the internet and how much data is available to us now. It took some work, but I found out your mother's name was Audrey Scott and that she changed her name to Keppel when she married Dennis. They were married when you were roughly two years old."

"Yeah? So?"

"So, Dennis Keppel is your *adopted* father."

"What about it?"

"It took a little more work, including some phone calls with some very patient people, but I figured out the identity of your real father."

"I could have told you that. His name was Patrick Hanson."

"Yeah, Patrick Hanson. Do you know his story?"

She shook her head. "I'm not following."

"Did you know he had a prison record?"

She squinted at that news.

"He was released and went missing almost immediately. He had conditions on his release and was supposed to check in with a parole officer. No one ever heard from him."

"So what? He's missing," April said, working the problem out for herself. "Sounds like the loser I've always heard he was."

"Maybe. Don't you want to know how long he's been missing?"

"I don't care."

"Eighteen years, April. He's been missing eighteen years. The same amount of time your mom has been missing."

She closed her book and put it down.

"I searched the DOL records in every state for your mom. There were plenty of Audrey Scotts, but none with her birthday. Could she have changed her name? Sure. But her social security number should have popped up, and her birthday would have been tied to that. It's not like she was trying to escape from the mob, right? She didn't have to get a new face, new name, new life, right?"

"What are you saying?" Her voice was soft and unsure.

"What do you remember from that time?"

"Nothing. It was a long time ago."

"Did your dad act strangely after your mom left?"

Uncomfortable, she looked around the restaurant, seeking an escape, but not moving towards one.

"There's something, isn't there? You're realizing something now, and it doesn't feel quite right. You don't know how to put your finger on it, do you?

"It's nothing."

"How do you know?"

She shook her head. "You're messing with me."

"Why don't you tell me what you think, and I'll weigh in? I promise I'm not screwing with you."

April studied me. She reached for her coffee but pulled back before picking it up. She said, "There's a part of the property in the back that he told me to stay away from when I was little. I always took it as gospel. He said the neighbors were mean and didn't like it if we went back there. He said I would get in trouble. He never went back there either. As I got older, I never had any reason to explore it. I mean, teenagers don't explore the back of their own properties, right? You go explore the rest of the world. Not your own."

"Don't you find that interesting?" I said, and stood. "In light of the things we've just discussed."

"What do you mean?"

"If you decide you want to talk further, you know how to get in touch with me." I put my business card on the table next to her coffee.

***

All I had was suspicion. I couldn't legally get on fifteen acres of land and traipse around looking for a corpse on a hunch.

The suspicion started when I thought about Dennis Keppel and how he stayed in the back of the court proceedings. Then I realized he never went to jail to see his daughter. It doesn't take a rocket scientist to know prison communications are monitored, and Keppel is a smart man. He stayed off the jail's logbooks and sent communications to his daughter through attorney-carried letters.

Those thoughts brought me back to his confession about the night of Hamilton Martin's death. He removed Ham's wallet and jacket and fled with his truck, thereby creating the illusion of a robbery. Keppel then cleaned the truck of all fingerprints, so there was no tracing either him or April.

He somehow got himself into Tony Lawrence's apartment, where he forced a man to overdose and then faked a suicide.

That was a lot of cold, calculating moves.

How did a vice president in a financial planning firm get that much forethought?

Dennis Keppel was indeed dying of lung cancer. Keppel authorized his doctor to talk with me, and I was shown the reports that confirmed it. But the more I thought about it, the less I cared.

I hoped I'd planted enough seeds for April to go looking for something or to ask her father about it. I watched and waited, parked in the same spot I had been in that morning. Light snow was falling, and the temperature was hovering in the mid-twenties. The gray sky hung over the city like a heavy blanket. I couldn't remember the last time I had seen a blue sky. Was it before Bobbie's death? I know it was just the weather, but that thought made me sadder than I had been in some time.

When she got home, she parked the car and went inside. A few minutes later, Dennis Keppel came outside and stood at the side of his Lincoln. He coughed for several minutes. It looked painful. When he was done hacking, he got into his car and drove away.

Twenty minutes after Keppel left, I saw her exit the patio door and walk behind the house. She headed toward the rear of the property. In some time, I lost sight of her. I quietly sat until "Wheel in the Sky" reentered my thoughts, and I softly joined in the chorus.

I jumped when my cell phone vibrated. "Nash," I said after answering.

"I'm not sure what I found," she said.

"What does it look like?"

"One stone. Nothing else around it. Everything cleared away."

"What do you think it is?"

"I'm afraid to say it."

"I'll be right there. I'm not far away."

***

I parked in the driveway and double-timed it to the back of the house, lifting my feet to clear the couple of feet of snow. Part of me worried I was being set up, but it didn't feel like it, so I pushed the concerns away. I hadn't called for backup. I wasn't on the clock. Plus, I was in Spokane Valley, a different jurisdiction. Everything I was doing was wrong. If it was going to go down badly, I didn't need to drag the department into it.

April was in the distance, standing still, her arms wrapped around herself. As I approached, I could see she was staring intently at a large, semi-flat stone. The snow had been cleared away from it. Footsteps came in from the opposite direction. I followed them with my eyes. It looked like they went along the property line, through the trees, disguising themselves.

"Someone has been out here," she said. "They cleared away the snow."

Like I do with Bobbie's headstone.

"I know what this is," she said.

"It might be," I said softly. "We'll have to verify for sure."

"Why would he do it?"

"I don't know."

We stood there silently for several moments.

"All these years," she muttered.

We remained quiet in the falling snow, each dealing with our own thoughts. I'm sure she was thinking of the mother she never knew, dealing with a set of emotions buried under years of regret and anger. I was thinking of how I was going to have to put together a crime scene.

I heard footsteps and huffing and turned to see Dennis Keppel running through the snow toward us. Malice wasn't on his face. It was fear.

When he was close enough, he stopped and opened his mouth to say something, but then doubled over, hacking. He coughed for several moments, fighting both cancer and the fear that had gripped him. After he regained control, he stood upright and extended his hand. "April, please, come over here."

"What is this?" she asked and pointed to the stone.

"Please, honey, come here," he said, now extending both hands to her.

"Tell me what this is," she said, her voice raising in hysterics.

He dropped his arms.

"Is this… is this…?"

Tears filled his eyes.

"How could you do this?"

"You don't understand."

"Tell me!"

He took a step toward her.

"Tell me what you did!" she yelled, spittle flying from her lips.

Dennis looked at me briefly, before focusing back on April. "Honey…"

"Tell me!"

Dennis stood frozen, looking at his daughter, pleading for her to do anything but ask questions.

"Tell me!"

"She ruined our family," he whispered.

"What?"

"She was taking you away." Tears appeared suddenly.

"What do you mean?" April asked, her voice now soft.

Dennis lowered his head.

The three of us stood in the cold, no one making a move.

Finally, Dennis lifted his eyes and said, "He got out of prison and came for her."

"Who?" April asked. "My biological dad?"

"It happened while I was at work. They started up again, just like that. Audrey didn't give any thought to me when he came back. She told me she still loved him and was going to California. With you. She didn't care that it was going to be hard on you. She didn't care that you were my daughter now. She only wanted to be with him."

"How did it happen?" I asked gently.

He didn't look at me. His eyes were solely on April.

"How did it happen?" April asked, repeating my question.

"I asked if I could share custody with you. She told me you weren't my daughter. That I had no right to you because she never wanted to go through the paperwork for adoption. That I wasn't your father."

"I gave up then. I told her she could go, that I wouldn't stop them. I could see how it would play out. I had no legal right to be with you, even though you *were* my daughter, not his. He wasn't good enough for you. He was a loser. He couldn't care for you like I could. They were going to take you away, and I'd never see you again. I asked them to wait for a couple of days so I could spend some extra time with you before they left."

Dennis looked at me then, not able to face April with what he was about to admit. "They agreed, of course. It allowed them more time for themselves. God, I hated them together. When they were supposed to come over to pick up April, I dropped her off with a friend. When I brought her home, I told her mommy had left."

April covered her face at the realization and turned in circles.

"Audrey told her friends she and Patrick were leaving. Her parents were both dead by then. She didn't have any siblings. There was no one to miss her except some friends, and they all knew she was flakey, especially since Patrick had shown back up.

"When a couple of her friends called to ask if I'd heard from her, I said she took off in the night with him and left April and me alone. I told them she said she would send for April when they got settled." He smiled sadly. "Some of them felt sorry for us."

"Sorry?" April said, dropping her hands from her face. *"Sorry?"*

"You may not believe this, honey, but I miss your mom every day. I come out here now and then to check on her and to tell her I still think about her."

"What about him? Is he out here, too?"

"Him? What about him?" Dennis said, anger in his eyes. "He doesn't deserve to be remembered. He ruined our family."

"He was my father."

"He wasn't anything to you."

"He never had a chance," she said.

Dennis lowered his eyes.

***

A county patrol car arrived just as Dennis and I walked to the front of the property. Deputy Edmunds got out and studied us both.

"Detective Nash, Spokane PD," I said. "Take him into custody."

"For what?"

"Murder."

Dennis faced me. "Who's going to take care of my baby now?"

"She either learns how to take care of herself, or she doesn't."

"Didn't you talk with my doctor?"

"I did, but in the end, it doesn't matter. There's no guarantee if I let you go, you wouldn't be hit by a car tomorrow, and she'd still be alone. I need to do what's right, and this is it."

I held his head as I guided him into the back of the patrol car.

63

The gray sky overhead was repressive. It was still cold, but there was no snow forecast for the foreseeable future. The weather was supposed to warm later in the week. The worst part of winter would, hopefully, soon be over.

When I arrived at her grave, I bent over and cleared some snow and debris that had blown in on the headstone. There wasn't much, but by now it was a habit, like lightly touching her face in the morning as she smiled.

I shoved my hands in my pockets and stared at the marble.

A sadness worked its way through my chest, and I frowned. After a while, I simply shrugged.

"It's getting better," I lied.

***

During the day, Captain Ackerman and Lieutenant Brand both dropped by my cubicle to slap my back and congratulate me on fully making it back to the department and into the rotation. Solving two unknown homicides tends to make a guy the flavor of the month.

Marci Burkett stopped by to check on me. Her partner, Quinn Delaney, was in tow. He'd gone through a recent rough patch with a divorce and rumors of financial difficulties. He looked better now and made some nice comments about getting together for a beer if I wanted to talk. I smiled politely at them both, and they walked off as they always did, laughing and joking with each other. There was a lot of speculation in the department that there was a thing between them, but I doubted those two would ever cross that line.

Parker and Johnson circled my cubicle, the young sharks realizing there was no blood in the water for an attack. My closure rate had suddenly jumped, and I was the detective du jour. Parker would never say boo, but Johnson nodded in my direction once, a sort of acknowledgment of a good job.

64

"You couldn't get the father on the murder of the drug dealer, but you nailed him on two murders from almost twenty years ago?"

"Yeah."

My brother leaned back in his chair with his arms crossed over his chest. We were at Borracho's for Taco Tuesday, a plate of tacos between us and each of us with a Negro Modelo. It was the first beer I'd had in months.

"That sounds like a lucky break," Dean said.

"It's called coincidence and, as I was telling someone recently, when it works in your favor, you grab on and thank the Lord or whatever you believe in."

"I believe in tacos," he said.

"At least you believe in something."

He stuffed a taco into his mouth. When he was done chewing, he asked, "What happened to the girl?"

I shrugged. "She's going to need some help. She's been through a lot. Drugs, prostitution, her parents, Hamilton Martin's homicide. I'm still not sure if that was self-defense or not."

Dean sipped his beer. "Are you going back after her?"

"I'm going to let it go and stop worrying about it. I've got to do that soon, or I'm going to develop an ulcer."

"Sounds like a healthy attitude."

"It's a jaded attitude built on the realization my days are getting shorter."

"It's almost spring. Shouldn't they be getting longer?"

"I mean with the department. I don't know how much time I've got left. I'm getting irritated with the guys I work with, and the department isn't the family I want."

"Is this about Bobbie?"

"Everything revolves around her being gone."

We both picked up tacos then and ate quietly. Some current, supposedly popular music played while we ate. Younger patrons, wearing Gonzaga University gear, drifted into the restaurant. They would soon push out the older, after-work crowd, turning Borracho into a nightclub. It was the nightly evolution of the downtown scene. The daily reminder for those of us over forty that our quote best days unquote were behind us, and bedtime was now 10 p.m.

"Still hearing songs every day?"

"Nope," I lied, not bothering to tell him about that morning's song

"You're lying."

I smiled. "I'm sure they'll stop soon enough. Just like there will come a day when I go through most of the day without thinking about her."

Dean smiled. "That may not be for quite some time, Dallas."

"It will eventually happen."

"Maybe, but that's okay. You know that, right?"

"I don't want it to happen."

"Stop arguing, Dallas, it's healthy. It's called healing, and it's a part of moving on. I've watched you your whole life, and I know that's something you're not very good at. You've never gotten over anything."

"I've gotten over plenty."

"Remember that dog we had growing up?"

"Trooper?"

"Yeah, that mutt. You moped around for almost a year after he died."

"He was a great dog."

"Except you really didn't like him until he died, and then you couldn't get over it."

"Are you saying I didn't love Bobbie?"

Dean shook his head. "No, dummy, I'm saying you don't want to get over her because this is how you are. You're going to keep yourself sad about this for as long as you can. Because that's who you are: Dallas Nash, the last of the martyrs."

"Your bedside manner sucks."

"That's what family is for, Dallas. Kicking you when you're down."

I stared at my brother, wondering if he was right. *Was this who I am?*

"Sometimes, you need to stop thinking, Dallas," Dean said. "Eat tacos and drink beer because tomorrow will be here before you know it, and you'll need your strength to battle new monsters and old demons."

65

The house was silent, the only noise being the late-winter rain hitting the roof, a signal that another change of season was right around the corner. Winter wouldn't go quietly, though. More snow was expected to fall over the weekend when the temperature would drop again, but for now, the hope of spring showed its eternal promise.

Upon returning home from dinner with Dean, I wanted to listen to some music. Every song I thought about was either too sad or too happy. The house would remain silent another night.

The beer I'd had with Dean earlier was the first I'd had since shortly after her death. The couple at the restaurant went down quick and easy, so I stopped at the store for a six-pack. I had resolved to come home and finish packing her clothes. I figured some additional beer would help. While standing at the check-out register, I suddenly realized that I didn't want more beer, returned the six-pack to the cooler, and went home.

Now, after staring at her clothes still hanging in the closet and the piles of garments on the floor, I decided on a course of action. I would box everything up and separate them into two groups. I would donate the first group to some agency, maybe a women's shelter, which probably seemed the most appropriate. The second group I would keep. I still couldn't wrap my mind around the fact I wanted to retain some of her clothes, but it was an argument I no longer cared to have with myself. I didn't care if keeping some of her clothes would be seen as weird by others. I wanted to do it because I missed her. If others had a problem with it, screw them.

The work went faster than expected. Initially, the progress was slow, but once I got into a rhythm on deciding where things went, boxes filled quickly. I soon wandered back through the house, wanting to hear some music, the effect of the earlier beers now wearing off.

I rummaged through my music collection, knowing full well I would see the same CDs I saw earlier. It was my music collection, for crying out loud. I couldn't find anything I wanted to hear more than silence.

"Shit!" I yelled in my own house. The single word echoed its foolishness for a moment before reminding me I was alone. That pissed me off, and I followed it up by shouting a string of profanities until I was hoarse and breathless.

When my tantrum ran its course, I walked to the refrigerator for a beer and cursed myself for not getting some. *I'm losing control*, I thought. I slammed the refrigerator door shut and felt a wave of exhaustion descend on me.

I wasn't ready to call it a night, knowing I had promised myself to fight through this to the end. With heavy feet, I walked back to my bedroom and hurriedly finished packing the clothes away, then stacked the boxes.

When all was said and done, there were no clothes to give away. I had decided to keep all of them. Studying the tower of cardboard boxes, I stood there with my hands on my hips.

In the morning, I would carry the boxes into the basement.

In not getting rid of her clothes, I was only putting off the task until another day. I would have to address them sooner or later, but it no longer had to be now.

Was I doing what my brother said? Was I purposefully keeping myself sad so I wouldn't lose her memory?

In the continued silence of being alone, I crawled into bed, hoping to wake in the morning with a new song in my head.

Did You Like the Book?

I love when friends and family recommend a book for me. I'll often give it a read just because the recommendation came from someone I trusted. That's probably how we all are.

If you enjoyed this story, I'd truly appreciate it if you would tell your friends and family or leave a review at where you got the book.

All writers need feedback on their work—not only to help other readers discover them, but so they know they're delivering the goods with their stories.

Thanks for reading and I hope to see you again!

About the Author

Colin Conway is the creator of the 509 Crime Stories, a series of novels set in Eastern Washington with revolving lead characters. They are standalone tales and can be read in any order.

He also created the Cozy Up series which pushes the envelope of the cozy genre. Libby Klein, author of the Poppy McAllister series, says *Cozy Up to Death* is "Not your grandma's cozy."

Colin co-authored the Charlie-316 series. The first novel in the series, *Charlie-316*, is a political/crime thriller that has been described as "riveting and compulsively readable," "the real deal," and "the ultimate ride-along."

He served in the U.S. Army and later was an officer of the Spokane Police Department. He has owned a laundromat, invested in a bar, and run a karate school. Besides writing crime fiction, he is a commercial real estate broker.

Colin lives with his beautiful girlfriend, three wonderful children, and a codependent Vizsla that rules their world.

Find out more about Colin at colinconway.com.